Douglas Banville

JOHN BANVILLE, the author of twenty novels, has been
the recipient of the Man Booker Prize, the James Tait
Black Memorial Prize, the Guardian Fiction Award, the
Franz Kafka Prize, a Lannan Literary Award for Fic-
tion, and the Prince of Asturias Award for Literature.
He lives in Dublin.

ALSO BY JOHN BANVILLE

Nightspawn

Birchwood

Doctor Copernicus

Kepler

The Newton Letter

Mefisto

The Book of Evidence

Ghosts

Athena

The Untouchable

Eclipse

Shroud

Ancient Light

The Sea

The Infinities

The Blue Guitar

Mrs. Osmond

Snow

April in Spain

The Singularities

Additional Praise for *Marlowe*

Named One of *Publishers Weekly*'s
Best Summer Books of the Year

"Somewhere Raymond Chandler is smiling, because this is a beautifully rendered hard-boiled novel that echoes Chandler's melancholy at perfect pitch. The story is great, but what amazed me is how John Banville caught the cumulative effect Chandler's prose had on readers. It's hard to quantify, but it's also what separated the Marlowe novels from the general run of noir (which included some damn fine novelists, like David Goodis and Jim Thompson). The sadness runs deep. I loved this book. It was like having an old friend, one you assumed was dead, walk into the room. Kind of like Terry Lennox, hiding behind those drapes." —Stephen King

"Terrific fun . . . [*Marlowe*] could be passed off as a newly discovered Chandler manuscript found in some dusty La Jolla closet. . . . Any fan of Chandler's work is going to enjoy it."
—*The New York Times Book Review*

"Half the pleasure of this book, at least for a Chandler fan, is to notice [Banville] getting the little things right. . . . Against a dozen other detective novels on my desk, I'll take a Raymond Chandler any day of the week, even when its written by somebody else—assuming that somebody is [John Banville]."
—NPR's *All Things Considered*

"It's vintage L.A., toots: the hot summer, rain on the asphalt, the woman with the lipstick, cigarette ash and alienation, V8 coupes, tough guys, snub-nosed pistols, the ice melting in the bourbon. . . . The results are Chandleresque, sure, but you can see Banville's sense of fun." —*The Washington Post*

"I opened the book hopefully—and I closed it entirely satisfied, even thrilled. . . . It's all there, the Chandler voice: the crisply detailed description and sly similes that set a scene precisely, the world-weary bemusement of the narrator, his gimlet eye for the ladies, and the delicately ominous foreshadowing. . . . It's clear Banville does love Marlowe, and he's reminded me why I love him, too."
—*Tampa Bay Times*

"From its pitch-perfect opening sentences, [John Banville's] channeling of Raymond Chandler is one of the season's best mysteries."
—*San Francisco Chronicle*

"Insightful, thorough—so very smart . . . I found myself turning the pages fast and wishing I still smoked and that I had a higher threshold for whiskey."
—*Pittsburgh Post-Gazette*

"I was impressed by the plotting of [*Marlowe*], its perfect pacing and use of misdirection. . . . Banville nails the spoiled L.A. atmosphere that is Chandler's forte."
—*Salon*

"A tremendously fun and diverting tale . . . The author of a somber but beautifully written series of mysteries set in the same era as Chandler's novels, [Banville] was a savvy choice for the job. His nimble plotting drives [the novel]. . . . Marlowe, however, remains the undisputed star of the show, a hardened, magnetic presence."
—New York *Daily News*, "Page Views"

"All of the essential ingredients are there, afloat in a tumbler of Santa Monica sleaze. . . . But Mr. [Banville] can also make words do things Chandler could only dream of. . . . The fun lies in watching two styles tangle. . . . With an artfulness worthy of the original, Mr. [Banville] has made it new, though he doesn't forget whom he owes."
—*New York Observer*

"What [Banville] captures in Chandler's voice is the weary twist of ambivalence. . . . That baseline of doubt, the whiff of regret and then betrayal, form the essential atmosphere of noir fiction. And [Banville] gets that exactly right."   —*The Oregonian*

"Banville has largely perfected Chandler's much-mimicked, seldom-bettered knack for similes and one-liners. . . . Best of all, though, he conjures the world-weary loneliness of Chandler's creation, a character who, in just seven novels, the world saw far too little of. [Banville] clearly loves writing this and the fun he's having—his affection for Chandler's world—shines through. . . . Entirely irresistible."   —*The Guardian* (London)

"[*Marlowe*] is probably better than an actual Chandler: more coherent, and more consistent, more careful. Banville is simply a more elegant writer. Chandler was a metaphorical rogue trader; Banville is a class act."   —*New Statesman* (London)

"[The fact that] this novel is so enjoyable is a testament to the effectiveness of the formula that Chandler labored so hard to perfect."   —*The Telegraph* (London)

"Seen as a crime novel in its own right, it is a cut above anything else out there."   —*The Irish Times*

"Despite Robert B. Parker's lengthy experience in the PI genre, his sequel to *The Big Sleep*, *Perchance to Dream*, pales in comparison with [Banville's] pitch-perfect re-creation of the character and his time and place. As for the language, [Banville] nails Chandler's creative and memorable similes and metaphors. . . . While the mystery is well-plotted, [Banville] elevates it beyond mere thoughtful homage with a plausible injection of emotion in his wounded lead."   —*Publishers Weekly* (boxed and starred review)

"Banville offers a stylish homage to Raymond Chandler in this tightly written caper. . . . The focus . . . is on style and mood, and the Irishman, perhaps surprisingly, nails both. The homage game is a tricky game to play, but [Banville] makes all the right moves. Great fun for Chandlerians." —*Booklist*

"[Banville] . . . delivers a more complex and satisfying mystery than other authors have done in the past. This latest incarnation of Chandler's sleuth will appeal to fans of Chandler and Marlowe, but newcomers to one of the first great PIs in crime fiction will find much to enjoy here as well." —*Library Journal*

"A treat for fans." —*Kirkus Reviews*

"Banville channeling Chandler is irresistible—a double whammy of a mystery. Hard to think anyone could add to Chandler with profitable results. But Banville most definitely gets it done." —*Richard Ford*

MARLOWE

=== A NOVEL ===

JOHN BANVILLE

A HOLT PAPERBACK

HENRY HOLT AND COMPANY   NEW YORK

Holt Paperbacks
Henry Holt and Company
Publishers since 1866
120 Broadway
New York, New York 10271
www.henryholt.com

A Holt Paperback® and ⒽⒷ® are registered trademarks of
Macmillan Publishing Group, LLC.

The Library of Congress has cataloged the hardcover edition as follows:

Black, Benjamin, 1945–
    The black-eyed blonde : a Philip Marlowe novel / Benjamin Black. — First edition.
        pages   cm
    ISBN 978-0-8050-9814-3 (hardcover)
    ISBN 978-0-8050-9815-0 (e-book)
    1. Marlowe, Philip (Fictitious character)—Fiction.   2. Missing persons—Fiction.
3. Social classes—Fiction.   4. California—Fiction. I. Title.
    PR6052.A57B59 2014
    823'.914—dc23   2013026790

ISBN: 9781250906908 (trade paperback)

Our books may be purchased in bulk for promotional, educational, or business use.
Please contact your local bookseller or the Macmillan Corporate and
Premium Sales Department at (800) 221-7945, extension 5442, or by e-mail
at MacmillanSpecialMarkets@macmillan.com.

Originally published as *The Black-Eyed Blonde* in
hardcover in 2014 by Henry Holt and Company

First Holt Paperbacks Edition 2023

Designed by Kelly S. Too

Printed in the United States of America

1   3   5   7   9   10   8   6   4   2

To Joseph Isaac and Ruby Ellen

MARLOWE

1

It was one of those Tuesday afternoons in summer when you wonder if the earth has stopped revolving. The telephone on my desk had the air of something that knows it's being watched. Cars trickled past in the street below the dusty window of my office, and a few of the good folks of our fair city ambled along the sidewalk, men in hats, mostly, going nowhere. I watched a woman at the corner of Cahuenga and Hollywood, waiting for the light to change. Long legs, a slim cream jacket with high shoulders, navy blue pencil skirt. She wore a hat, too, a skimpy affair that made it seem as if a small bird had alighted on the side of her hair and settled there happily. She looked left and right and left again—she must have been so good when she was a little girl—then crossed the sunlit street, treading gracefully on her own shadow.

So far it had been a lean season. I had done a week playing bodyguard to a guy who had flown in from New York on the clipper. He had a blue jaw and wore a gold wristband and a pinkie ring with a ruby in it as big as a boysenberry. He said he was a businessman and I decided to believe him. He was worried, and

sweated a lot, but nothing happened and I got paid. Then Bernie
Ohls in the Sheriff's office put me in touch with a nice little old
lady whose hophead son had pinched her late husband's rare coin
collection. I had to apply a little muscle to get the goods back, but
nothing serious. There was a coin in there with the head of Alex-
ander the Great on it, and another one showing Cleopatra in profile, with that big nose of hers—what did they all see in her?

The buzzer sounded to announce that the outer door had
opened, and I heard a woman walk across the waiting room and
pause a moment at the door of my office. The sound of high heels
on a wooden floor always gets something going in me. I was about
to call to her to come in, using my special deep-toned, you-can-
trust-me-I'm-a-detective voice, when she came in anyway, without knocking.

She was taller than she had seemed when I saw her from the
window, tall and slender with broad shoulders and trim hips. My
type, in other words. The hat she wore had a veil, a dainty visor of
spotted black silk that stopped at the tip of her nose—and a nice
tip it was, to a very nice nose, aristocratic but not too narrow or
too long, and nothing at all like Cleopatra's jumbo schnozzle. She
wore elbow-length gloves, pale cream to match her jacket, and
fashioned from the hide of some rare creature that had spent its
brief life bounding delicately over Alpine crags. She had a good
smile, friendly, so far as it went, and a little lopsided in an attrac-
tively sardonic way. Her hair was blond and her eyes were black,
black and deep as a mountain lake, the lids exquisitely tapered at
their outer corners. A blonde with black eyes—that's not a combi-
nation you get very often. I tried not to look at her legs. Obviously
the god of Tuesday afternoons had decided I deserved a little lift.

"The name is Cavendish," she said.

I invited her to sit down. If I'd known it was me she was coming to call on, I would have brushed my hair and applied a dab of
bay rum behind my earlobes. But she had to take me as I was. She

didn't seem to disapprove too much of what she was seeing. She sat down in front of my desk on the chair I had pointed her to and took off her gloves finger by finger, studying me with her steady black eyes.

"What can I do for you, Miss Cavendish?" I asked.

"Mrs."

"Sorry—Mrs. Cavendish."

"A friend told me about you."

"Oh, yes? Good things, I hope."

I offered her one of the Camels I keep in a box on my desk for clients, but she opened her patent leather purse and took out a silver case and flipped it open with her thumb. Sobranie Black Russian—what else? When I struck a match and offered it across the desk she leaned forward and bent her head, with dipped lashes, and touched a fingertip briefly to the back of my hand. I admired her pearl-pink nail polish, but didn't say so. She sat back in the chair and crossed her legs under the narrow blue skirt and gave me that coolly appraising look again. She was taking her time in deciding what she should make of me.

"I want you to find someone," she said.

"Right. Who would that be?"

"A man named Peterson—Nico Peterson."

"Friend of yours?"

"He used to be my lover."

If she expected me to swallow my teeth in shock, she was disappointed. "Used to be?" I said.

"Yes. He disappeared, rather mysteriously, without even saying goodbye."

"When was this?"

"Two months ago."

Why had she waited so long before coming to me? I decided not to ask her, or not yet, anyway. It gave me a funny feeling, being looked at by those cool eyes behind the veil's transparent black mesh. It was like being watched through a secret window; watched, and measured.

"You say he disappeared," I said. "You mean out of your life, or altogether?"

"Both, it seems."

I waited for more, but she only leaned back a farther inch or so and smiled again. That smile: it was like something she had set a match to a long time ago and then left to smolder on by itself. She had a lovely upper lip, prominent, like a baby's, soft-looking and a little swollen, as if she had done a lot of kissing recently, and not kissing babies, either. She must have sensed my unease about the veil, and put up a hand now and lifted it away from her face. Without it, the eyes were even more striking, a lustrous shade of seal-black that made something catch in my throat.

"So tell me about him," I said, "your Mr. Peterson."

"Tallish, like you. Dark. Handsome, in a weak sort of way. Wears a silly mustache, Don Ameche–style. Dresses nicely, or used to, when I had a say in the matter."

She had taken a short ebony holder from her purse and was fitting the Black Russian into it. Deft, those fingers; slender, but with strength in them.

"What does he do?" I asked.

She glanced at me with a steely twinkle. "For a living, you mean?" She pondered the question. "He sees people," she said.

This time I leaned back in my chair. "How do you mean?" I asked.

"Just what I say. Practically every time I saw him, he was about to leave urgently. *I gotta see this guy. There's this guy I gotta go see.*" She was a good mimic; I was beginning to get a picture of Mr. Peterson. *He* didn't sound like *her* type.

"A busy fellow, then," I said.

"His busyness had few results, I'm afraid. At any rate, not results that you'd notice, or that I noticed, anyway. If you ask him, he'll tell you he's an agent to the stars. The people he had to see so urgently were usually connected to one of the studios."

It was interesting, the way she kept switching tenses. All the same, I had the impression that he was very much the past, for her, this Peterson bird. So why did she want him found?

"He's in the movie business?" I asked.

"I wouldn't say *in*. Sort of scrabbling at the edges with his fingertips. He had some success with Mandy Rogers."

"Should I know the name?"

"Starlet—ingénue, Nico would say. Think Jean Harlow without the talent."

"Jean Harlow had talent?"

She smiled at that. "Nico is firmly of the belief that all his geese are swans."

I got out my pipe and filled it. It struck me that the tobacco blend I was using had some Cavendish in it. I decided not to share this happy coincidence with her, imagining the jaded smile and the twitch of disdain at the corner of her mouth that would greet it.

"Known him long, your Mr. Peterson?" I asked.

"Not long."

"How long would not long be?"

She shrugged, which involved a fractional lift of her right shoulder. "A year?" She made it a question. "Let me see. It was summer when we met. August, maybe."

"Where was that? That you met, I mean."

"The Cahuilla Club. Do you know it? It's in the Palisades. Polo grounds, swimming pools, lots of bright, shiny people. The kind of place that wouldn't let a shamus like you put his foot inside the electronically controlled gates." That last bit she didn't say, but I heard it all the same.

"Your husband know about him? About you and Peterson?"

"I really can't say."

"Can't, or won't?"

"Can't." She glanced down at the cream gloves where she had draped them across her lap. "Mr. Cavendish and I have—what shall I say? An arrangement."

"Which is?"

"You're being disingenuous, Mr. Marlowe. I'm sure you know very well the kind of arrangement I mean. My husband likes polo ponies and cocktail waitresses, not necessarily in that order."

"And you?"

"I like many things. Music, mainly. Mr. Cavendish has two reactions to music, depending on mood and state of sobriety. Either it makes him sick or it makes him laugh. He does not have a melodious laugh."

I got up from the desk and took my pipe to the window and stood looking out at nothing in particular. In an office across the street, a secretary in a tartan blouse and wearing earphones from a Dictaphone machine was bent over her typewriter, tapping away. I had passed her in the street a few times. Nice little face, shy smile; the kind of girl who lives with her mother and cooks meat loaf for Sunday lunch. This is a lonely town.

"When's the last time you saw Mr. Peterson?" I asked, still watching Miss Remington at her work. There was silence behind me, and I turned. Obviously, Mrs. Cavendish was not prepared to address herself to anyone's back. "Don't mind me," I said. "I stand at this window a lot, contemplating the world and its ways."

I came back and sat down again. I put my pipe in the ashtray and clasped my hands together and propped my chin on a couple of knuckles to show her how attentive I could be. She decided to accept this earnest demonstration of my full and unwavering concentration. She said, "I told you when I saw him last—about a month ago."

"Where was that?"

"At the Cahuilla, as it happens. A Sunday afternoon. My husband was engaged in a particularly strenuous chukker. That's a—"

"A round in polo. Yes, I know."

She leaned forward and dropped a few flakes of cigarette ash beside the bowl of my pipe. A faint waft of her perfume came across the desk. It smelled like Chanel No. 5, but then, to me all perfumes smell like Chanel No. 5, or did up to then.

"Did Mr. Peterson give any indication that he was about to decamp?" I asked.

"Decamp? That's an odd word to use."

"It seemed less dramatic than *disappeared*, which was your word."

She smiled and gave a dry little nod, conceding the point. "He was much as usual," she said. "A little bit more distracted, perhaps, a little nervous, even—though maybe it only seems that way in hindsight." I liked the way she talked; it made me think of the ivy-covered walls of venerable colleges, and trust fund details written out on parchment in a copperplate hand. "He certainly didn't give any strong indication that he was about to"—she smiled again—"decamp."

I thought for a bit, and let her see me thinking. "Tell me," I said, "when did you realize he was gone? I mean, when did you decide he had"—now it was my turn to smile—"disappeared?"

"I telephoned him a number of times and got no answer. Then I called at his house. The milk hadn't been canceled and the newspapers had been piling up on his porch. It wasn't like him to leave things like that. He was careful, in some ways."

"Did you go to the police?"

Her eyes widened. "The police?" she said, and I thought she might laugh. "That wouldn't have done at all. Nico was rather shy of the police, and he would not have thanked me for putting them onto him."

"Shy in what way?" I asked. "Did he have things to hide?"

"Haven't we all, Mr. Marlowe?" Again she dilated those lovely lids.

"Depends."

"On what?"

"On many things."

This was going nowhere, in ever-increasing circles. "Let me ask you, Mrs. Cavendish," I said, "what do *you* think has become of Mr. Peterson?"

Once more she did her infinitesimal shrug. "I don't know what to think. That's why I've come to you."

I nodded—sagely, I hoped—then took up my pipe and did some business with it, tamping the dottle, and so on. A tobacco pipe is a very handy prop, when you want to seem thoughtful and wise. "May I ask," I asked, "why you waited so long before coming to me?"

"Was it a long time? I kept thinking I'd hear from him, that the phone would ring one day and he'd be calling from Mexico or somewhere."

"Why would he be in Mexico?"

"France, then, the Côte d'Azur. Or somewhere more exotic— Moscow, maybe, Shanghai, I don't know. Nico liked to travel. It fed his restlessness." She sat forward a little, showing the faintest trace of impatience. "Will you take the case, Mr. Marlowe?"

"I'll do what I can," I said. "But let's not call it a case, not just yet."

"What are your terms?"

"The usual."

"I can't say I know what the usual is likely to be."

I hadn't really thought she would. "A hundred dollars deposit and twenty-five a day plus expenses while I'm making my inquiries."

"How long will they take, your inquiries?"

"That too depends."

She was silent for a moment, and again her eyes took on that appraising look, making me squirm a little. "You haven't asked me anything about myself," she said.

"I was working my way around to it."

"Well, let me save you some work. My maiden name is Langrishe. Have you heard of Langrishe Fragrances, Inc.?"

"Of course," I said. "The perfume company."

"Dorothea Langrishe is my mother. She was a widow when she came over from Ireland, bringing me with her, and founded the business here in Los Angeles. If you've heard of her, then you know how successful she has been. I work for her—or with her, as she'd prefer to say. The result is that I'm quite rich. I want you to find Nico Peterson for me. He's a poor thing but mine own. I'll pay you whatever you ask."

I considered poking at my pipe again but thought it would seem a little obvious the second time around. Instead I gave her a level look, making my eyes go blank. "As I said, Mrs. Cavendish—a hundred down and twenty-five a day, plus expenses. The way I work, every case is a special case."

She smiled, pursing her lips. "I thought you weren't going to call it a case, as yet."

I decided to let her have that one. I pulled open a drawer and brought out a standard contract and pushed it across the desk to her with the tip of one finger. "Take that with you, read it, and if you agree with the terms, sign it and get it back to me. In the meantime, give me Mr. Peterson's address and phone number. Also anything else you think might be useful to me."

She gazed at the contract for a moment, as if she were deciding whether to take it or throw it in my face. In the end she picked it up, folded it carefully, and put it in her purse. "He has a place in West Hollywood, off Bay City Boulevard," she said. She opened her purse again and took out a small leather-bound notebook and a slim gold pencil. She wrote in the notebook briefly, then tore out

the page and handed it to me. "Napier Street," she said. "Keep a
sharp eye out or you'll miss it. Nico prefers secluded spots."

"On account of being so shy," I said.

She stood up, while I stayed sitting. I smelled her perfume again.
Not Chanel, then, but Langrishe, the name or number of which I
would dedicate myself to finding out. "I'll need a contact for you,
too," I said.

She pointed to the piece of paper in my hand. "I've put my telephone number on there. Call me whenever you need to."

I read her address: 444 Ocean Heights. Had I been alone, I would
have whistled. Only the cream get to live out there, on private
streets right by the waves.

"I don't know your name," I said. "I mean your first name."

For some reason this brought a mild flush to her cheeks, and
she looked down, then quickly up again. "Clare," she said. "Without an *i*. I'm called after our native county, in Ireland." She made
a slight, mock-doleful grimace. "My mother is something of a sen-
timentalist where the old country is concerned."

I put the notebook page into my wallet, rose, and came from
behind the desk. No matter how tall you might be, there are certain women who make you feel shorter than they are. I was looking down on Clare Cavendish, but it felt as if I were looking up.
She offered me her hand, and I shook it. It really is something, the
first touch between two people, no matter how brief.

I saw her to the elevator, where she gave me a last quick smile
and was gone.

Back in my office, I took up my station at the window. Miss Remington was tap-tappeting still, diligent girl that she was. I willed
her to look up and see me, but in vain. What would I have done,
anyway—waved, like an idiot?

I thought about Clare Cavendish. Something didn't add up. As a private eye I'm not completely unknown, but why would a daughter of Dorothea Langrishe of Ocean Heights and who knew how many other swell spots choose me to find her missing man? And why, in the first place, had she got herself involved with Nico Peterson, who, if her description of him was accurate, would turn out to be nothing but a cheap grifter in a sharp suit? Long and convoluted questions, and hard to concentrate on while remembering Clare Cavendish's candid eyes and the amused, knowing light that shone in them.

When I turned, I saw the cigarette holder on the corner of my desk, where she had left it. The ebony was the same glossy blackness as her eyes. She'd forgotten to pay me my retainer, too. It didn't seem to matter.

2

She was right: Napier Street didn't exactly advertise itself, but I saw it in time and swung in off the boulevard. The road was on a slight rise, heading up toward the hills that stood in a smoke-blue haze way off at the far end. I cruised along slowly, counting off the house numbers. Peterson's place looked a bit like a Japanese teahouse, or what I imagined a Japanese teahouse would look like. It consisted of a single story and was built of dark red pine, with a wraparound porch and a shingled roof that rose in four shallow slopes to a point in the middle with a weather vane on it. The windows were narrow and the shades were drawn. Everything about it told me no one had lived here for quite a while, though the newspapers had stopped piling up. I parked the car and climbed three wooden steps to the porch. The walls with the sun on them were giving off an oily smell of creosote. I pressed the bell but it didn't ring inside the house, so I tried the knocker. An empty house has a way of swallowing sounds, like a dry creek sucking down water. I put an eye to the glass panel in the door, trying to see through the lace curtain behind it. I couldn't make out much—just an ordinary living room, with ordinary things in it.

A voice spoke behind me. "He ain't home, brother."

I turned. He was an old guy, in faded blue overalls and a collarless shirt. His head was shaped like a peanut shell, a big skull and big chin with caved-in cheeks in between, and a toothless mouth that hung open a little. On his jaw was a week's silvery stubble, the tips of it glittering in the sunlight. Sort of a Gabby Hayes gone badly to seed. One eye was shut and with the other he was squinting up at me, moving that hanging jaw slowly from side to side like a cow working on a piece of cud.

"I'm looking for Mr. Peterson," I said.

He turned his head aside and spat drily. "And I told you, he ain't home."

I came down the steps. I could see him waver a bit, wondering who I was and how much trouble I might represent. I brought out my cigarettes and offered him one. He took it eagerly and stuck it to his lower lip. I lit a match on my thumbnail and passed him the flame.

A cricket soared out of the dry grass beside us like a clown being shot from the mouth of a cannon. The sun was strong and there was a hot dry breeze blowing, and I was glad of my hat. The old boy was bareheaded but seemed not to notice the heat. He took in a big draw of cigarette smoke, held it, and expelled a few gray wisps.

I tossed the spent match into the grass. "You didn't ought to do that," the old man said. "Start a fire here, the whole of West Hollywood goes up in smoke."

"You know Mr. Peterson?" I asked.

"Sure do." He gestured behind him to a tumbledown shack on the far side of the street. "That's my place there. He used to come over sometimes, pass the time of day, give me a smoke."

"How long's he been gone?"

"Let me see." He thought about it, doing some more squinting. "I guess I last seen him six, seven weeks ago."

"Didn't mention where he was off to, I suppose."

He shrugged. "I didn't even see him go. Just one day I noticed he was gone."

"How?"

He peered up at me and gave his head a shake, as if he had water in his ear. "How what?"

"How did you know he was gone?"

"He wasn't there anymore, is all." He paused. "You a cop?"

"Sort of."

"What's that mean?"

"Private dick."

He chuckled, stirring up the phlegm. "A private dick ain't a sort of cop, except in your dreams, maybe."

I sighed. When they hear you're private, they think they can say anything to you. I guess they can, too. The old man was grinning at me, smug as a hen that's just laid an egg.

I looked up and down the street. Joe's Diner. Kwik Kleen launderers. A body shop where a grease monkey was tinkering in the innards of a very unwell-looking Chevy. I imagined Clare Cavendish stepping out of something low and sporty and wrinkling her nose at all this. "What sort of people did he bring here?" I asked.

"People?"

"Friends. Drinking buddies. Associates from the world of the movies."

"Movies?"

He was beginning to sound like Little Sir Echo. "What about lady friends?" I said. "He have any?"

This produced a full-blown laugh. It was not a pleasant thing to hear. "*Any?*" he crowed. "Listen, mister, that guy had more broads than he knew what to do with. Every night, nearly, he come home with a different one."

"You must have been keeping a sharp eye on him and his comings and goings."

"I seen him, that's all," he said, in a sulkily defensive tone. "They used to wake me up, with all the ruckus they made. One of them dropped a bottle of something on the sidewalk one night—champagne, I think it was. Sounded like a shell exploding. The broad just laughed."

"The neighbors didn't complain about these shenanigans?"

He gave me a pitying look. "What neighbors?" he said with contempt.

I nodded. The sun wasn't getting any cooler. I took out a handkerchief and swabbed the back of my neck. Around here there are days in high summer when the sun works on you like a gorilla peeling a banana.

"Well, thanks anyway," I said and stepped past him. The air rippled above the roof of my car. I was thinking how hot to the touch the steering wheel was going to be. Sometimes I tell myself I'll move to England, where they say it's cool even in the dog days.

"You ain't the first one asking after him," the old man said behind me.

I turned. "Oh, yeah?"

"Pair of wetbacks come 'round last week."

"Mexicans?"

"That's what I said. Two of them. They was all gussied up, but a wetback in a suit and a fancy necktie is still a wetback, right?"

The sun had been shining on my back and was now shining on my front. I could feel my upper lip getting damp. "You speak to them?" I asked.

"Naw. They drove up in some kind of car I never seen the likes of before, must have been made down there. High and wide as a whorehouse bed, and a canvas roof with holes in it."

"When was this?"

"Two, three days ago. They prowled around the place for a

while, looking in the windows like you did, then got in the car again and moseyed off." Another dry spit. "I don't care for wet-backs."

"You don't say."

He gave me a surly look, then sniffed.

I turned away again and started toward my hot car. Again he spoke—"You think he's coming back?"—and again I stopped. I felt like the wedding guest trying to unhook himself from the Ancient Mariner.

"Doubt it," I said.

He gave another sniff. "Well, he ain't much missed, I guess. Still, I liked him."

He had smoked the cigarette down to about a quarter inch of stub, which now he dropped into the grass. "You didn't ought to do that," I said, getting into the car.

When my fingers touched the steering wheel, I was surprised they didn't sizzle.

= 3 =

Instead of going back to the office, I tootled around the corner to Barney's Beanery in search of something cool to pour into myself. Barney's was a bit too self-consciously bohemian for my taste—too many folks hanging about there with *artist* written all over them. That tired old sign reading, "Fagots—Stay Out" was still behind the bar. That's a thing I've noticed about Barney's kind of people: they're not very good at spelling. Barney must have been thinking of some other word with one *g*, like *bigot*. But the barkeep was a decent guy who had lent a tolerant ear to my late-night grousings on more occasions than I cared to remember. He called himself Travis, but whether that was his first name or his last I couldn't say. Big fellow with hairy forearms and an elaborate tattoo on his left bicep showing a blue anchor entwined with red roses. I doubted he was ever a seaman, though. He was very popular with the "fagots," who, despite the warning sign, kept on coming here—because of the sign, maybe. He used to tell a funny story about Errol Flynn and something he did here at the bar one night with a pet snake he kept in a bamboo box, but I can't remember the punch line.

I sidled onto a stool and ordered a Mexican beer. There was a bowl of hard-boiled eggs on the bar; I took one and ate it with a lot of salt. The salt and the dryness of the egg yolk left my tongue feeling like a piece of chalk, so I called for a refill of Tecate.

It was a slow early evening and there were few customers in the place. Travis, not being an overly familiar sort, had given me the barest nod when I came in. I wondered if he knew my name. Probably not. He knew what I did for a living, I was pretty sure of that, though I didn't remember him ever mentioning it. When the place wasn't busy, he had a way of standing with his hands spread on the bar and his big square head lowered, gazing out through the open doorway into the street with a far-off look in his eye, as if he were remembering a long-lost love or a fight one time that he won. He didn't say much. He was either dumb or very wise, I could never decide which. Either way, I liked him.

I asked him if he knew Peterson. I didn't think Barney's would be Peterson's kind of place, but I thought it was worth a try anyway. "Lives over on Napier," I said. "Or did, until recently."

Travis slowly came back from whatever section of memory lane he had been wandering down. "Nico Peterson?" he said. "Sure, I know him. Used to come in in the afternoon sometimes, drink a beer and eat an egg, just like you."

This was the second time I had been linked with Peterson—Clare Cavendish had said he was tall like me—and however weak the link was, I didn't welcome it. "What sort of guy is he?" I asked.

Travis flexed his muscleman's shoulders in a shrug. He was wearing a tight black sweatshirt, out of which his thick short neck stuck up like a fireplug. "Playboy type," he said. "Or that's how he presents himself. Ladies' man, with that mustache and the oiled hair combed in a nice wave. Funny, too—he can always make them laugh."

"He brought his girls here?"

Travis heard the skepticism in my voice; Barney's was hardly the place to romance stylish ladies in. "Now and then," he said, with a wry half-smile.

"One of them tallish, blond hair, black eyes, a particularly memorable mouth?"

Travis gave me his cautious smile again. "That could be any of them."

"Has an air, this one. Nicely spoken and very elegant—too elegant for Peterson, probably."

"Sorry. If they're as good-looking as you make her sound, I don't look too close. It's distracting."

He was a real professional, Travis. But it occurred to me that maybe there was a reason he didn't notice women, and that he too didn't much like the sign behind the bar, for his own, private reasons.

"When was he last in?" I asked.

"Haven't seen him in a while."

"A while being . . . ?"

"Couple of months. Why? Is he missing?"

"He seems to have gone off somewhere."

Travis's eye took on a faintly merry light. "That a crime nowadays?"

I studied my beer glass, rotating it on its base. "Somebody is looking for him," I said.

"The lady with the memorable mouth?"

I nodded. As I said, I liked Travis. Despite his size, there was something clean and neat about him, something trim and shipshape; maybe he had been a sailor, after all. I'd never felt I could ask. "I was over at his house," I said. "Nothing there."

A customer was signaling from the far end of the bar, and Travis went off to serve him. I sat and thought about this and that. For instance, why was the first sip of beer always so much better than the second? This was the kind of philosophical speculation I was prone to, hence my reputation as the thinking man's detective. I thought a bit about Clare Cavendish, too, but, like Travis said, I found her distracting and instead went back to the beer question. Maybe temperature was the answer. It wasn't that the second sip was going to be all that much warmer than the first, but that the mouth, having had that first cool rinse, knew what to expect the second time around and adjusted accordingly, so the element of surprise was absent, with a consequent falling off in the pleasure principle. Hmm. It seemed a reasonable explanation, but was it sufficiently comprehensive to satisfy a stickler like me? Then Travis came back and I was able to take off my thinking cap.

"I just realized," he said, "you're not the first to ask after our friend Peterson."

"Oh?"

"A week or two ago, a couple of Mexicans were in here wanting to know if I knew him."

That same two again, no doubt, in their car with the holes in the roof. "What sort of Mexicans?" I asked.

Travis gave me a sort of wistful smile. "Just Mexicans," he said. "Businessmen, they looked like."

Businessmen. Right. Like my man from New York with the pinkie ring. "They say why they were looking for him?"

"Nope. Just asked if he was a customer here, when he'd last been in, and so on. I couldn't tell them any more than I've told you. It didn't improve their mood."

"A gloomy pair, were they?"

"You know Mexicans."

"Yes—not the most scrutable people in the world. They stay around long?"

He gestured at my glass. "One of them drank a beer, the other had a glass of water. I had the impression they were men on a mission."

"Oh? What sort of mission?"

Travis considered the ceiling for a moment. "Can't say. But they had that serious look that made their eyes shine—you know what I mean?"

I didn't, but nodded anyway. "You think this mission they were on might have had serious consequences for our Mr. Peterson?"

"Yeah," Travis said. "One of them kept on toying with a pearl-handled six-shooter while the other picked his teeth with his knife."

I wouldn't have taken Travis for the ironic type. "Funny, though," I said. "Peterson doesn't seem the kind of guy to be involved with Mexican businessmen, somehow."

"Lot of opportunities, south of the border."

"You're right, there are."

Travis picked up my empty glass. "You want another?"

"No thanks," I said. "I wouldn't want to go wild."

I paid the man and climbed down from the stool and went out into the evening. It was a little cooler now, but the air tasted of car exhaust, and the day's grit had laid down a grainy deposit between my teeth. I had passed Travis my card and asked him to give me a call if he happened to hear any news of Peterson. I wouldn't be waiting by the phone, but at least now Travis knew my name.

I drove home. The lights in the houses up in the hills were coming on, making it seem later than it was. A sickle moon hung low on the horizon, embroiled in a bank of mud-blue murk.

I still had the house in Laurel Canyon. The woman who owned it had gone on an extended visit to her widowed daughter in Idaho and decided to stay there—for the potatoes, maybe. She had written to say I could have the house for as long as I liked. It left me feeling pretty settled on Yucca Avenue, in my hillside roost with the eucalyptus trees across the street. I didn't know how I felt about that. Did I really want to spend the rest of my days in a

rented house where about the only things I could call my own
were my trusty coffeepot and a chess set of faded ivory? There
was a woman who wanted to marry me and take me away from
all this, a beautiful woman, like Clare Cavendish, and rich like her,
too. But I was bent on staying footloose and fancy-free, even if it
didn't feel quite like that. Yucca Avenue is not exactly Paris, which
is where the poor little rich girl was nursing her bruised heart, last
time I'd heard from her.

The house was about the right size for me, but on certain evenings, such as this one, it felt like the White Rabbit's place. I
brewed a strong pot of coffee and drank a cup of it and prowled
around the living room for a while, trying not to carom off the
walls. Then I drank another cup and smoked another cigarette,
ignoring the dark blue night gathering in the window. I thought
of laying out one of Alekhine's less terrifying openings and seeing
where I could go with it, but I didn't have the heart. I'm not a
chess fiend, but I like the game, the concentrated coolness of it, the
elegance of thought it calls for.

The Peterson business was weighing on my mind, or at least
the part of the business that involved Clare Cavendish. I was still
convinced there was something fishy in her approach to me. I
couldn't say why, but I had the distinct sense that I was being set
up. A beautiful woman doesn't walk in off the street and ask you
to find her missing boyfriend; it doesn't happen that way. But what
way does it happen? For all I knew, there might be offices like
mine all over the country that beautiful women walked into
every other day and asked poor saps like me to do exactly that. I
didn't believe it, though. For a start, the country surely couldn't
boast many women the likes of Clare Cavendish. In fact, I doubted
there was even one more like her. And if she was really on the
level, how come she was involved with a lowlife like Peterson?
And if she was involved with him, why wasn't she the slightest bit
embarrassed about throwing herself on the mercies—I was going

to say "into the arms" but stopped myself in time—of a private
detective and imploring him to find the flown bird? All right, she
didn't implore.

I decided that in the morning I would do some digging around
in the history of Mrs. Clare Cavendish née Langrishe. For now I
had to content myself with placing a call to Sergeant Joe Green at
Central Homicide. Joe had once briefly entertained the notion of
charging me as an accessory to first-degree murder; that's the kind
of thing that will create a bond between two people. I wouldn't say
Joe was a friend, though—more a wary acquaintance.

When Joe answered, I said I was impressed that he was working
so late, but he only breathed hard into the receiver and asked what
I wanted. I gave him Nico Peterson's name and number and address.
None of it was familiar to him. "Who is he?" he asked sourly.
"Some playboy involved in one of your divorce cases?"

"You know I don't do divorce work, Sarge," I said, keeping my
tone light and easy. Joe had an unpredictable temper. "He's just a
guy I'm trying to trace."

"You got his address, don't you? Why don't you go knock on
his door?"

"I did that. No one home. And no one has been home for some
time."

Joe did some more breathing. I considered telling him he
shouldn't smoke so much but thought better of it. "What's he to
you?" he asked.

"A lady friend of his would like to know where he's taken himself off to."

He made a noise that was halfway between a snort and a chuckle.
"Sounds like divorce business to me."

You've got a one-track mind, Joe Green, I said, but only to myself.
To him I repeated that I didn't handle divorces and that this had
nothing to do with one. "She just wants to know where he is," I
said. "Call her sentimental."

"Who is she, this dame?"

"You know I'm not going to tell you that, Joe. There's no crime involved. It's a private matter."

I could hear him striking a match and drawing in smoke and blowing it out again. "I'll have a look in the records," he said at last. He was getting bored. Even the tale of a woman and her missing beau couldn't hold his jaded interest for long. He was a good cop, Joe, but he'd been in the business a long time and his attention span was not broad. He said he would call me, and I thanked him and hung up.

He telephoned at eight the next morning, while I was frying up some nice slices of Canadian bacon to have with my toast and eggs. I was about to tell him again that I was impressed by the hours he kept, but he interrupted me. While he spoke I stood by the stove with the wall phone's receiver in my hand, watching a little brown bird flitting about in the branches of the tecoma bush outside the window above the sink. There are moments like that when everything seems to go still, as if someone had just taken a photograph.

"The guy you were asking about," Joe said, "I hope his lady friend looks good in black." He cleared his throat noisily. "He's dead. Died on"—I heard him riffling through papers—"April nineteenth, over in the Palisades near that club they got there, what's it called. Hit-and-run. He's in Woodlawn. I've even got the plot number, if she'd like to go visit him."

4

I don't know why they call it Ocean Heights, since about the only thing high about it would be the maintenance costs. The house wasn't all that big, if you consider Buckingham Palace a modest little abode. Langrishe Lodge, it was called, though I couldn't imagine anything less like a lodge. It was made of pink and white stone, lots of it, and had turrets and towers, and a flag flying proudly on a flagpole on the roof, and about a thousand windows. It looked pretty ugly to me, but I'm no judge of architecture. Off to the side there were big green trees, some variety of oaks, I thought. The short drive led straight to an oval of gravel in front of the house that you could have run a chariot race on. It struck me that I was in the wrong trade, if a pile like this was what you got for making women smell nice.

During the drive over I had been thinking of what Clare Cavendish had said about liking music. I hadn't picked up on it, hadn't asked her what kind of music she preferred, and she hadn't offered to tell me, and somehow that was significant. I mean, it was significant that we had let it go. It wasn't the most intimate

thing she could have told me, not like her shoe size or what she
wore or didn't wear to bed at night. All the same, it had weight, the
weight of something precious, a pearl or a diamond, that she had
passed from her hand into mine. And the fact that I had taken it
from her without comment, and that she had been content for me
to say nothing, meant it was something held in secret between
us, a token, a promise for the future. But then I decided that this
was probably all hooey, just a case of wishful thinking on my part.

When I had parked the Olds on the gravel, I noticed a sporty-
looking young man coming toward me across the lawn. He was
swinging a golf club and knocking the heads off daisies with it.
He wore two-tone golf shoes and a white silk shirt with a floppy
collar. His dark hair was floppy too, a wing of it falling over his
brow so that he had to keep pushing it out of his eyes with a nervous flick of a pale and slender hand. He walked in a willowy sort
of way, meandering a little, as if there were a weakness somewhere
in the region of his knees. When he got close I saw with a shock
that he had Clare Cavendish's almond-shaped black eyes—they
were much too pretty for him. I saw too that he wasn't nearly as
young as he'd seemed at a distance. I guessed he was in his late
twenties, though with the light behind him he could have passed
for nineteen. He stopped in front of me and looked me up and
down with a faint sneer. "You the new chauffeur?" he asked.

"Do I look like a chauffeur?"

"I don't know," she said. "What do chauffeurs look like?"

"Leggings, cap with a shiny peak, insolent stare of the prole-
tarian."

"Well, you haven't got the leggings or the cap."

He had, I noticed, an expensive smell, cologne and leather and
something else, probably that perfumed tissue paper they pack
Fabergé eggs in. Or maybe he liked to dab on a bit of his ma's
finest. He was a precious lad, all right. "I'm here to see Mrs. Cavendish," I said.

"Are you now." He snickered. "Then you must be one of her beaux."

"What do they—?"

"Rugged, blue-eyed types. On second thought, you're not that kind of material either." He glanced past me at the Olds. "They come in scarlet coupés"—he pronounced it the French way—"or the odd Silver Wraith. So who are you?"

I took a bit of time to light a cigarette. For some reason this seemed to amuse him, and he did that mean little laugh again. It sounded forced; he so much wanted to be a tough guy. "You must be Mrs. Cavendish's brother," I said.

He gave me a wide-eyed theatrical stare. "Must I?"

"Some part of the family, anyway. Which are you, pampered pet or black sheep?"

He lifted his nose a disdainful inch into the air. "My name," he said, "is Edwards, Everett Edwards. Everett Edwards the Third, as it happens."

"You mean there've been two of you already?"

He relented a bit then and grinned, rolling his shoulders in a boyish shrug. "Stupid name, isn't it," he said, biting his lip.

I did my own kind of shrug. "We don't get to choose what we're called."

"What about you—what are you called?"

"Marlowe."

"Marlowe? Like the playwright." He struck a histrionic pose, leaning sideways from the hips and pointing toward the sky with a trembling hand. "*See, see, where Christ's blood streams in the firmament!*" he cried, making his lower lip quiver. I had to smile.

"Tell me where I can find your sister, will you?" I said.

He let his arm fall and straightened up to his former slouch. "She's here somewhere," he said. "Try the conservatory." He pointed. "It's around that way."

He couldn't keep that sulky look out of his eyes. He was just an overgrown kid, spoiled and bored. "Thanks, Everett the Third," I said.

As I walked away he called after me, "If you're selling insurance, you're wasting your time." He snickered again. I hoped for his sake it was something he would grow out of—when he got into his fifties, maybe, and started wearing three-piece suits and sporting a monocle.

I crunched across the gravel and took the way he had pointed to, along by the side of the house. Stretching off to my left, the garden was the size of a small public park, only much better kept. The sweet smell of roses was carried to me on a breeze, along with the scent of cut grass and a briny whiff of the nearby ocean. I wondered what it would be like to live in a place like this. I glanced in through the windows as I walked past them. The rooms, what I could see of them, were large, lofty, and impeccably furnished. What if you wanted to flop in front of the television set with a bucket of popcorn and a couple of cans of beer and watch a ball game? Maybe they had specific places in the basement for that kind of thing, billiard rooms, romper rooms, dens, whatever. I suspected that in Langrishe Lodge, the real business of living would always be carried on somewhere else.

The conservatory was an elaborate affair of curved glass and steel framing attached to the back of the house like a monstrous suction cup and reaching up two or three stories. There were giant palms inside, pressing their heavy fronds against the panes as if appealing to be let out. A pair of French doors stood wide, and in the opening a white gauze curtain undulated languidly in the gently stirring air. Summer in these parts isn't harsh and punishing like it is over in the city; these folks have their own special season. I stepped across the threshold, batting the curtain aside. In here the air was heavy and dense and smelled like a fat man after a long, hot bath.

At first I didn't spot Clare Cavendish. Partly hidden by a low-leaning swath of palm leaves, she was sitting on a delicate little wrought-iron chair, before a matching wrought-iron table, writing in a leather-bound diary or notebook. She wrote with a fountain pen, I noticed. She was dressed for tennis, in a short-sleeved cotton shirt and skimpy white skirt with pleats, ankle socks, and pipe-clayed bucks. Her hair was pinned back with barrettes at both sides. I had not seen her ears before. They were very pretty ears, which is a rare thing, ears being in my estimation just a little less weird-looking than feet.

She heard me approach, and when she glanced up a look came into her eyes that I couldn't quite figure. Surprise, of course—I hadn't called to say I was coming—but something else, too. Was it alarm, sudden dismay even, or did she just not recognize me for a second?

"Good morning," I said, as lightly as I could.

She had shut her book quickly, and now, more slowly, she fitted the cap to her fountain pen and laid it on the table with slow deliberation, like a statesman who has just finished signing a peace treaty, or a declaration of war. "Mr. Marlowe," she said. "You startled me."

"Sorry. I should have phoned."

She stood up and took a step backward, as if to put the table between her and me. Her cheeks were a little flushed, as they had been yesterday when I'd asked her to tell me her first name. People who blush easily have it tough, always being liable to give themselves away at the drop of a brick. Once again I had trouble not looking at her legs, though somehow I saw that they were slim, shapely, and honey-hued. A crystal jug containing a tobacco-colored drink stood on the table, and now she touched a fingertip to the handle. "Some iced tea?" she asked. "I can ring for a glass."

"No, thanks."

"I'd offer you something stronger, only it seems a little early . . ." She glanced down and bit her lip, in just the same way Everett the

Third had. "Have you made some progress in your inquiries?" she asked.

"Mrs. Cavendish, I think maybe you should sit down."

She gave her head a tiny shake, smiling faintly. "I don't—" she began. She was looking past my shoulder. "Oh, there you are, darling," she said, her voice sounding a shade too loud, with too much forced warmth in it.

I turned. A man was standing in the open doorway, holding the curtain aside with a raised hand, and for a moment I thought that he, like Everett the Third, might be about to deliver a ringing line from some old play. Instead he dropped the curtain and ambled forward, smiling at nothing in particular. He was a well-built fellow, not tall, slightly bow-legged, with broad shoulders and large square hands. He was dressed in cream jodhpurs, calf-skin boots, a shirt so white it glowed, and a yellow silk cravat. Another sporty type. It was beginning to look like they did nothing here but play games.

"Hot," he said. "Damned hot." As yet he had not so much as glanced in my direction. Clare Cavendish began to reach toward the jug of iced tea, but the man got there first, picked up the glass, half filled it from the jug, and emptied it in one swallow, his head thrown back. His hair was fine and straight and the color of pale oak. Scott Fitzgerald would have found a place for him in one of his bittersweet romances. Come to think of it, he looked a bit like Fitzgerald: handsome, boyish, with something in him that was fatally weak.

Clare Cavendish watched him. She was biting her lip again. That mouth of hers, it really was a thing of beauty. "This is Mr. Marlowe," she said. The man gave a start of pretend surprise and looked this way and that, holding the empty glass in his hand. At last he fixed on me and frowned slightly, as if he hadn't noticed me before, as if I had been indistinguishable from the palm leaves and the gleaming glass all around. "Mr. Marlowe," Clare Cavendish went on, "this is my husband, Richard Cavendish."

He beamed at me with a mixture of indifference and disdain. "Marlowe," he said, turning the name over and examining it, as if it were a small coin of scant value. His smile became brighter still. "Why don't you put down your hat."

I had forgotten I was holding it. I glanced around. Mrs. Cavendish stepped forward and took the hat from me and laid it on the table beside the glass jug. Inside the triangle formed by the three of us, the air seemed to crackle soundlessly, as if a current of static electricity were passing back and forth in it. Yet Cavendish appeared to be entirely at ease. He turned to his wife. "Have you offered the man a drink?"

Before she could reply, I said, "She did, and I declined."

"You declined, did you?" Cavendish chuckled. "You hear that, sweetheart? The gentleman declined." He poured more tea into the glass and drank it off, then put the glass down, grimacing. I noticed he was an inch or two shorter than his wife. "What kind of business are you in, Mr. Marlowe?" he asked.

This time Clare got in ahead of me. "Mr. Marlowe finds things," she said.

Cavendish ducked his head and gave her a sly, upward glance, thrusting his tongue hard into his cheek. Then he looked at me again. "What kind of things do you find, Mr. Marlowe?" he asked.

"Pearls," his wife said quickly, again meaning to cut me off, though I hadn't yet thought of a reply. "I lost that necklace you gave me—misplaced it, I mean."

Cavendish considered this, looking at the floor now, smiling pensively. "What's he going to do," he asked, addressing his wife without looking at her, "crawl around the bedroom floor, peer under the bed, poke his finger into mouse holes?"

"Dick," his wife said, and there was a pleading note in her voice, "it's not important, really."

He gave her an exaggerated stare. "Not important? If I weren't a gentleman, like Mr. Marlowe here, I'd be tempted to tell you how much that little trinket cost. Of course"—he turned to me, his voice becoming a drawl—"if I did, she'd tell you it was her money I bought it with." He glanced at his wife again. "Wouldn't you, sweetie?"

There was nothing to say to that, and she just looked at him, her head lowered a little and the soft plump apex of her upper lip thrust out, and for a second I saw what she must have looked like when she was very young.

"It's a matter of retracing your wife's steps," I said, in the plodding tone I've learned to mimic from all the years I've spent around cops. "Checking the places she went to over the past few days, the stores she was in, the restaurants she visited." I could feel Clare's eyes on me, but I kept mine on Cavendish, who was looking off through the open doorway and nodding slowly. "Yeah," he said. "Right." He glanced about the place again, blinking distractedly, touched the rim of the empty glass on the table with a fingertip, then sauntered out, whistling to himself.

When he was gone, his wife and I just stood there for a while. I could hear her breathing. I imagined her lungs filling and emptying, the tender pinkness of them, in their frail cage of glistening white bone. She was the kind of woman to make a man think thoughts like that. "Thank you," she said at last, the barest murmur.

"Don't mention it."

She laid her right hand lightly on the back of the wrought-iron chair, as if she were feeling a little weak. She wasn't looking at me. "Tell me what you've found out," she said.

I needed a cigarette but didn't think I should light up in this lofty glass edifice. It would be like smoking in a cathedral. The urge reminded me of what I had brought with me. I took the ebony cigarette holder from my pocket and laid it on the table, next to my hat. "You left it at my office," I said.

"Oh, yes, of course. I don't use it much, only for effect. I was nervous, coming to see you."

"You could have fooled me."

"It was myself I needed to fool." She was watching me intently. "Tell me what you've found out, Mr. Marlowe," she said again.

"There's no easy way to put this." I looked at my hat on the table. "Nico Peterson is dead."

"I know."

"He died two months ago in a hit-and-run over on—" I stopped, and stared at her. "What did you say?"

"I said I know." She smiled at me, holding her head to one side in that slightly sardonic way, just as she had done the previous day, when she had sat in my office with her gloves folded across her lap and the ebony holder held at an angle, without her husband there to give her the jitters. "Maybe *you* should sit down, Mr. Marlowe."

"I don't understand," I said.

"No, of course you don't." She turned aside and put her hand to the glass her husband had drunk from, moved it an inch to one side and then returned it to where it had been, standing on its own ring of dampness. "I'm sorry, I should have told you."

I got out my cigarettes—the air in here had suddenly stopped feeling sanctified. "If you already knew he was dead, why did you come to me?"

She turned back and gazed at me in silence for a moment, judging what she would say, how she should put it. "The thing is, Mr. Marlowe, I saw him the other day, in the street. He didn't look dead at all."

5

I liked the idea of the outdoors. I mean I liked the thought of it being there: the trees, the grass, birds in the bushes, all that. I even liked looking at it, sometimes, from the highway, say, through a car windshield. What I didn't much care for was being out in it, unprotected. There was something about the feeling of the sun on the back of my neck that made me uneasy—I didn't just get hot, I got worried, in a twitchy sort of way. There was also the sense of being watched by too many eyes, trained on me from among leaves, from between fences, out of the mouths of burrows. When I was a kid I hadn't been much interested in nature. Streets were where I did my boyhood wanderings and experienced my youthful epiphanies; I don't think I'd have recognized a daffodil if I saw one. So when Clare Cavendish suggested a walk in the garden, I had to make an effort not to show how little the prospect excited me. But of course I said yes. If she had asked me to go on a hike in the Himalayas, I'd have put on a pair of mountain boots and followed her.

After she had pulled the pin and tossed me that grenade about

having seen the supposedly dead Peterson, she had gone off to
change, leaving me to stand at one of those curved glass walls
looking out at the little puffs of white cloud sailing in from the
ocean. As she was excusing herself, she had laid three fingers
briefly on my wrist, where I could still feel them. If I'd thought
before there was something fishy about this whole business, I had
a hundred-pound marlin to grapple with now.

After fifteen minutes or so and a couple more cigarettes, she came
back dressed in a white linen suit with box shoulders and a calf-
length skirt. She may have been Irish, but she had all the poise
and cool grace of an English rose. She was wearing flat shoes,
which made me taller than she was by an extra couple of inches,
but I still had that feeling of looking up at her. She wore no jew-
elry, not even a wedding ring.

She came up behind me quietly and said, "You probably don't
feel like walking, do you? But I have to get outside—my mind
works better in the open air."

I might have asked why she needed to have her thinking appa-
ratus in tip-top working order, but I didn't.

There was this to be said for the grounds of Langrishe Lodge:
they were about as far from a wilderness as they could get and
still be covered in greenery, or what would have been greenery
if the summer hadn't turned most of it brown. We set off along
a gravel path that led away from the house at a right angle and
headed straight as a stretch of railroad toward that stand of trees
I'd seen from the road and, farther off, a few flashes of indigo that
I knew must be the ocean. "All right, Mrs. Cavendish," I said.
"Let's hear it."

I had put more of a grating note into it than I'd meant to, and
she gave me a quick sideways glance, her cheeks coloring a little
in that way I was getting used to. I frowned and cleared my

throat. I felt like a kid on his first date, everything I did a false move.

We had gone a dozen paces before she spoke. "Isn't it strange," she said, "the way you can recognize people instantly, no matter where you are or what the circumstances? You're walking through Union Station in a rush-hour crowd and you glimpse a face a hundred yards ahead, or maybe not even a face, just the set of someone's shoulders, the tilt of a head, and immediately you know who it is, even if it's a person you haven't seen for years. How is that?"

"Evolution, I guess," I said.

"Evolution?"

"The need to distinguish friend from foe, even in the depths of the forest. We're all instinct, Mrs. Cavendish. We think we're sophisticated, but we're not—we're primitives."

She gave a faint laugh. "Well, maybe evolution will make something of us someday."

"Maybe. But you and I won't be around to see it."

For a moment the sunlight seemed shadowed, and we walked on in a somber silence. "Nice, the oaks," I said, nodding toward the line of trees ahead of us.

"Beeches."

"Oh. Beeches, then."

"Shipped from Ireland, believe it or not, twenty years ago. Where nostalgia is concerned, my mother will spare no expense. They were saplings then, and look at them now."

"Yes, look at them now." I needed a cigarette again, but again the surroundings frowned on the thought. "Where did you see Nico Peterson?" I said.

She did not reply immediately. As she walked, she looked at the tips of her sensible shoes. "In San Francisco," she said. "I was there on business—for the firm, you know. It was on Market Street, I was in a taxi, and there he was, walking along the sidewalk in that way he did, in a hurry, off"—she let out that faint laugh again—"off to see someone, no doubt."

"When was this?"

"Let me think." She thought. "Friday, last week."

"Before you came to see me, then."

"Of course."

"You're sure it was him?"

"Oh, yes, I'm sure."

"You didn't try to talk to him?"

"He was gone before I could think what to do. I suppose I could have told the driver to turn the taxi around, but the street was crowded—you know what San Francisco is like—and I didn't think there'd be much hope of catching him. Besides, I was sort of numb and felt paralyzed."

"From the shock?"

"No, the surprise. Nothing Nico did could ever shock me, really."

"Even coming back from the dead?"

"Even coming back from the dead."

At a distance, across the greensward, a horseman appeared, going at a fast clip. He raced along for a little way, then slowed up and disappeared under the trees. "That was Dick," she said, "riding Spitfire, his favorite."

"How many horses has he got?"

"I don't really know. Quite a few. They keep him occupied." I glanced at her and saw her mouth tighten at the corner. "He does his best, you know," she said, in a tone of weary candor. "It's not easy, being married to money, though of course everyone thinks otherwise."

"*Did* he know about you and Peterson?" I asked.

"I told you, I can't say. Dick keeps things to himself. I hardly ever know what he's thinking, what he's aware of."

We had reached the trees. The path veered off to the left, but instead of following it, Clare took me by the elbow and led me forward, into the copse, I guess you'd call it; it took a spot like Langrishe Lodge to get me trawling through my vocabulary for the right words for things. The ground underfoot was dry and dusty. Above us the trees made a parched, muttering sound— thinking of their native land, I supposed, where the air, it's said, is ever damp and the rain falls with the lightness of something being remembered.

"Tell me about you and Peterson," I said.

She was watching the uneven ground, stepping over it with care.

"There's so little to tell," she said. "The fact is, I'd almost forgotten him. I mean, I'd almost stopped remembering him, or missing him. There wasn't very much between us when he was alive—when we were together, that is."

"Where did you meet?"

"I told you—the Cahuilla Club. Then I saw him again, a few weeks later, in Acapulco. That was when"—again that faint rush of blood to her cheeks—"well, you know."

I didn't know, but I could guess. "Why Acapulco?"

"Why not? It's one of those places one goes to. Nico's kind of place."

"Not yours?"

She shrugged. "Few places are my kind of place, Mr. Marlowe. I bore easily."

"Still, one goes there." I tried to keep the sourness out of my voice but didn't succeed.

"You mustn't despise me, you know," she said, trying to make it sound playful.

For a moment I felt slightly woozy, like you do when you're young and a girl says something that makes you think she's interested in you. I pictured her down there in Mexico, on the beach, in a one-piece bathing suit, reclining in a deck chair under an umbrella with a book, and Peterson walking by and stopping, pretending to be surprised to see her, and offering to fetch her something tall and cool from the fellow in the sombrero selling drinks from a shack under the palms up behind the beach. And at that moment, as we stepped out on the far side of the trees, as if my thoughts had conjured it, there was the ocean, with long, lazy waves rolling in, and the sandpipers scurrying, and a smoke-stack off on the horizon trailing behind it a motionless plume of white vapor. Clare Cavendish sighed and, seeming hardly aware that she was doing it, linked her arm in mine. "Oh, Lord," she said, with a sudden fervent throb in her voice, "how I love it here."

We had come out of the trees, onto the beach. The sand was close-packed, and walking on it was not difficult. I knew how out of place I must look, in my dark suit and hat. Clare made me stop and held on to my forearm with one hand as she leaned down to take off her shoes. I thought about what would happen if she was to lose her balance and fall against me, so that I had to catch her in the crook of my arm. It was the kind of fool thought that would come into a man's head on such occasions. We walked on. She linked her arm through mine again. She was carrying her shoes in her other hand, dangling from the tips of two fingers. There should have been music, a big whoosh of soupy violins, and some guy with a vowel at the end of his name crooning about the sea and the sand and the summer wind and *you* . . .

"Who was it that told you about me?" I asked. I wasn't really all that interested, but I wanted to talk about something besides Nico Peterson for a while.

"A friend."

"Yes, you said—but what friend?"

She bit her lip again. "Someone you know quite well, actually."

"Oh?"

"Linda Loring."

That came like a smack in the chops. "You know Linda Loring?" I asked, trying not to sound too surprised—trying not to sound anything. "How?"

"Oh, from here and there. Ours is a very small world, Mr. Marlowe."

"You mean the world of the rich?"

Was she blushing again? She was. "Yes," she said, "I suppose that is what I mean." She paused. "I can't help it that I have some money, you know."

"It's not my business to blame anyone for anything," I said, too quickly.

She smiled and looked sideways into my eyes. "I thought that's precisely what your business was," she said.

My mind was still on Linda Loring. A butterfly the size of a chicken was flapping its wings somewhere in the region of my diaphragm. "I thought Linda was in Paris," I said.

"She is. I spoke to her on the telephone. We call each other now and then."

"To check up on the latest gossip among the international set, I suppose."

She smiled and squeezed my arm against her side reprovingly. "Something like that."

We came to a sort of lean-to, like a bus shelter, standing at the edge of the soft sand where the beach met the low dunes. Inside it there was a bench made from a few roughly cut planks, well weathered by the salt wind. "Let's sit for a moment," Clare said.

It was pleasant there, in the shade, with a nice breeze coming up from the water. "This must be a private beach," I said.

"Yes, it is. How did you know?"

I knew because if it had been public, a shelter like this would have been so fouled and littered we wouldn't have dreamed of sitting in it. Clare Cavendish, I told myself, was one of those people the world shields from its own awfulness.

"So you told Linda about Nico disappearing and then suddenly resurrecting himself, right?" I said.

"I didn't tell her as much as I've told you."

"You haven't told me very much."

"I've admitted to you that Nico and I were lovers."

"You think a girl like Linda wouldn't have guessed that? Come on, Mrs. Cavendish."

"I wish you'd call me Clare."

"Sorry, but I don't think I can do that."

"Why not?"

I disengaged my arm from hers and stood up. "Because you're my client, Mrs. Cavendish. All this"—I waved a hand to take in the shelter, the beach, those busy little birds down at the water's edge where the pebbles hissed in the wash as if they were on the boil—"all this is very nice, and pretty, and friendly. But the fact is, you came to me with some story about your boyfriend disappearing and you being anxious to trace him, poor thing though he was. Then it turns out Mr. Peterson had done the biggest disappearing trick of all, which you, for whatever reasons of your own, failed to tell me about. Then you introduce me to your husband and indicate how unhappy he makes you—"

"I—"

"Let me finish, Mrs. Cavendish, then you can have your say. I come to your lovely home—"

"I didn't invite you here. You could have phoned and asked me to call in to your office again."

"That's true, that's very true. But here I came, the bearer of bad news, news that would be a shock to you, as I thought, only to discover that you already knew what I had to say. Then you take me for a pleasant stroll in your delightful garden, you link your arm in mine and lead me onto your private beach and tell me you know my friend Mrs. Loring, who recommended my services to you after you didn't tell her why you needed them—"

"I *did* tell her!"

"You half told her." She tried to speak again, but I held a hand in front of her face. She was gripping the seat at both sides and looking up at me with an expression of desperation I didn't know whether to believe in or not. "Anyway," I said, feeling tired suddenly, "none of that matters. What matters is, what exactly do you want from me? What is it you think I can do for you—and why do you feel you have to pretend to be on the verge of falling in love with me to get me to do it? I'm for hire, Mrs. Cavendish. You come to my office, you tell me your troubles, you pay me some money, I go out and try to solve your problem—that's how it works. It's not complicated. It's not *Gone with the Wind*—you're not Scarlett O'Hara and I'm not what's-his-name Butler."

"Rhett," she said.

"What?"

She had lost her stricken look and had turned her eyes away from mine and was gazing down the beach, toward the waves. She had a way of batting things aside, things she didn't like or didn't want to deal with, that always left me hanging. It's the kind of knack that only a lifetime soaked in money can teach you. "Rhett Butler is the character you mean," she said. "It's also, by coincidence, my brother's pet name."

"You mean Everett the Third?"

She nodded. "Yes," she said, "we call him Rett—without the *h*." She smiled to herself. "I can't imagine anyone less like Clark Gable." Now she looked at me again, with a puzzled frown. "How do you know him?" she asked. "How do you know Everett?"

"I don't. He was mooching about the lawn when I arrived. We exchanged a few friendly insults and he pointed me in your direction."

"Ah. I see." She nodded, still frowning. Again she looked off in the direction of the ocean. "I used to bring him here to play when he was little," she said. "We'd spend whole afternoons, paddling in the surf, building sand castles."

"He told me his name is Edwards, not Langrishe."

"Yes. We have different fathers—my mother married again, when she came here from Ireland." She pulled down the corners of her mouth in a wry smile. "It wasn't a success, the marriage. Mr. Edwards turned out to be what the novelists used to call a fortune hunter."

"Not just the novelists," I said.

She inclined her head in an ironic little nod of acknowledgment, smiling. "Anyway, in the end Mr. Edwards checked out— worn down, I suppose, by the effort of pretending to be what he wasn't."

"Which was? Apart from a fortune hunter, that is."

"What he wasn't was fair and honest. What he was, well, I don't think anyone knew what he really was, including himself."

"So he left."

"He left. And that's when my mother brought me into the firm, young though I was. I turned out to have a talent for selling perfume, to the surprise of all, especially me."

I sighed and sat down beside her. "You mind if I smoke?" I asked.

"Please, go ahead."

I produced my silver case with the monogram on it. I've never found out whose monogram it is—I bought the case in a pawnshop. I opened it and offered it to her. She shook her head. I lit up. It's pleasant, smoking by the sea; the salt air gives a fresh tang to the tobacco. Today, for some reason, it reminded me of being young, which was strange, since I hadn't grown up by the ocean.

Once again, eerily, she seemed to read my thoughts. "Where are you from, Mr. Marlowe?" she asked. "Where were you born?"

"Santa Rosa. A nowhere town north of San Francisco. Why do you ask?"

"Oh, I don't know. Somehow it always seems important to know where someone comes from, don't you think?"

I leaned back against the rough wood wall of the shelter and rested the elbow of my smoking arm in the palm of my left hand. "Mrs. Cavendish," I said, "you puzzle me."

"Do I?" She seemed amused. "Why is that?"

"I said already—I'm the hired help, but you're talking to me like someone you've known all your life, or someone you'd like to know for the rest of it. What gives?"

She pondered this for a while, her eyes lowered; then she looked at me from under her lashes. "I suppose it's that you're not at all what I expected."

"What did you expect?"

"Someone hard and smart-mouthed, like Nico. But you're not like that at all."

"How do you know? Maybe I'm just putting on a show for you, pretending to be a pussycat when really I'm a skunk."

She shook her head, closing her eyes briefly. "I'm not that poor a judge of men, despite evidence to the contrary."

She had not moved at all, not that I'd noticed, yet somehow her face was closer to mine than it had been. There seemed nothing for it but to kiss her. She didn't resist, but she didn't respond, either. She just sat there and took it, and when I drew back she smiled a little and looked wistful. I was suddenly very conscious of the sound of the waves, of the pebbles hissing and the gulls crying. "I'm sorry," I said. "I shouldn't have done that."

"Why not?" She spoke very softly, almost in a whisper.

I got to my feet and dropped the cigarette on the sand and put my heel on it. "I think we should go back," I said.

As we returned through the trees, she took my arm again. She seemed quite at ease, and I had to wonder if that kiss had really happened. We came out onto the lawn, and there was the house before us in all its ghastly grandeur. "Hideous, isn't it," Clare said, reading my thoughts again. "It's my mother's house, you know, not mine and Richard's. That's another reason for Richard's moroseness."

"Because he has to live with his mother-in-law?"

"Can't be pleasant for a man, or for a man like Richard, anyway."

I stopped and made her stop with me. I had sand in my shoes and salt grit in my eyes. "Mrs. Cavendish, why are you telling me these things? Why are you treating me like we're on the most intimate of terms?"

"Why did I let you kiss me, you mean?" Her eyes sparkled; she was laughing at me, though not unkindly.

"All right, then," I said. "Why did you let me kiss you?"

"I suppose I wanted to see what it would be like."

"And what was it like?"

She thought for a moment. "Nice. I liked it. I'd like you to do it again, sometime."

"I'm sure that could be arranged."

We walked on, her arm in mine. She was humming to herself. She seemed happy. This, I thought, is not the woman who walked into my office yesterday and examined me coldly from behind her veil, sizing me up; this is someone else.

"One of the movie people built it," she said. She was talking about the house again. "Irving Thalberg, Louis B. Mayer—one of those moguls, I forget which one. They shipped the stone in from Italy, somewhere in the Apennines. Good thing the Italians can't see what was done with it."

"Why do you live here?" I asked. "You told me you're rich— you could move somewhere else."

I glanced at her. A little shadow had settled on her smooth brow. "I don't know," she said. She was silent for a few paces, then spoke again: "Maybe I can't face the prospect of being alone with my husband. He's not particularly good company."

It wasn't for me to comment on that, so I didn't.

We were approaching the conservatory. She asked if I would come in. "Maybe you'd like a drink now?"

"I don't think so," I said. "I'm a working man, with a job to do. Is there anything else you want to tell me about Nico Peterson before I apply my bloodhound nose to his trail?"

"I can't think of anything." She picked a fragment of leaf from the sleeve of her linen jacket. "I'd just like you to trace him for me," she said. "I don't want him back. I'm not sure I wanted him in the first place."

"Why did you get him, then?"

She made a clown's lugubrious face. I liked the way she did it, making fun of herself. "He represented danger, I suppose," she said. "As I told you, I get bored easily. He made me feel alive for a while, in a slightly soiled sort of way." She gave me a level look. "Can you understand that?"

"I can understand it."

She laughed. "But you don't approve."

"It's not for me to approve or otherwise, Mrs. Cavendish."

"Clare," she said, again in that breathy whisper. I just stood there, feeling stolid and craggy-faced, like a cigar-store Indian. She gave a sad little shrug, then shoved her hands into the pockets of her jacket and drew in her shoulders. "I'd like you to find out where Nico is," she said, "what he's doing, why he pretended to be dead." She looked off across the smooth green lawn, toward the trees. Behind her there was another, ghostly version of the two of us reflected in the glass of the conservatory. She said, "It's strange to think of him, you know, being somewhere right now, doing something. I'd got used to believing he was dead, and I find it hard to adjust."

"I'll do what I can," I said. "He shouldn't be too difficult to trace.

He doesn't sound like a professional, and I doubt he'll have covered his tracks too well, especially since he won't be expecting anyone to be looking for him, him being dead, supposedly."

"What will you do? How will you go about it?"

"I'll have a look at the coroner's report. Then I'll talk to some people."

"What kind of people? The police?"

"The cops tend not to be very helpful to someone who's not one of their own. But I know one or two guys down at headquarters."

"I wouldn't like to think of it being generally known that it's me who's looking for him."

"You mean you don't want your mother to find out."

Her face went hard, which was not an easy thing for that face to do. "I'm thinking more of the business," she said. "Any kind of scandal would be very bad for us—for Langrishe Fragrances. I hope you understand."

"Oh, I understand, all right, Mrs. Cavendish."

From somewhere nearby there came a scream, eerily thin and piercing. I stared at Clare. "A peacock," she said. Of course: there had to be a peacock. "We call him Liberace."

"Does he do that often? Scream like that?"

"Only when he's bored."

I turned to go, then stopped. How beautiful she was, standing in the sun in her cool white linen, with all that shining glass and candy-pink stone behind her. I could still feel the softness of her mouth on mine. "Tell me," I said, "how did you hear about Peterson's death?"

"Oh," she said, perfectly casual, "I was there when it happened."

6

I was almost at the gate when I met Richard Cavendish walking a big chestnut stallion up the drive. I drew the car to a stop and rolled down the window.

"Hello there, sport," Cavendish said. "Leaving us already?" He didn't look like a man who had been riding hard for the past hour. His oaken hair was untousled, and his jodhpurs were as pristine as when he'd first walked into the conservatory. He wasn't even sweating, not so you'd notice. The horse was the one that looked frazzled; it kept rolling its eyes and tossing its head and tugging at the reins, which rested in its master's hand as lightly as a child's jump rope. Excitable creatures, horses.

Cavendish leaned down toward the window and rested a forearm on the door frame and smiled broadly at me, showing two rows of small white even teeth. It was one of the emptiest smiles I'd ever had flashed at me. "Pearls, eh?" he said.

"That's what the lady said."

"That's what she said, yes, I heard her." The horse was nuzzling at his shoulder now, but he took no notice. "They're not as valuable as she thinks they are. Still, I imagine she's attached to them. You know what women are like."

"Not sure that I do, where pearls are concerned."

He was still smiling. He hadn't believed the story of the lost necklace for a second. I didn't much care. I knew Cavendish—he was a type I was familiar with: the handsome, polo-playing smoothie who marries a rich girl and then proceeds to make her life hell whining about what a tough time he has spending her money and how wounding it is to his pride.

"Nice horse," I said, and as if it had heard me, the animal rolled an eye my way.

Cavendish nodded. "Spitfire," he said. "Seventeen hands, strong as a tank."

I made a funnel of my lips as if to whistle, but didn't. "Impressive," I said. "You play polo on him?"

He gave a little laugh. "Polo is played on ponies," he said. "Can you imagine trying to get at a ball on the ground from this guy's back?" He rubbed his chin with a forefinger. "You don't play, I take it."

"What do you mean?" I said. "Where I come from, the polo stick is never out of our hands."

He studied me, letting his smile dismantle itself in lazy stages. "You're quite a joker, aren't you, Marlowe."

"Am I? What did I say?"

He went on looking at me for a while. When he narrowed his eyes, a fan of fine wrinkles opened at the outer corner on each side. Then he straightened, smacked a palm on the door frame, and stepped back. "Good luck with the pearls," he said. "Hope you find them."

The horse tossed its head and flapped its lips in that funny way they do. The sound it made was very like a sarcastic laugh. I put the car in gear and let out the clutch. "Tally ho," I said and drove off.

Half an hour later I was in Boyle Heights, parking outside the Los Angeles County Coroner's Office. I wondered how many times I'd plodded up those steps. The building was a wild piece of art nouveau architecture and looked more like a gin palace than a government building. It was cool inside, though, and restfully quiet. About the only sound to be heard was the clicking of an unseen lady clerk's high heels as she walked down a corridor on one of the floors somewhere above me.

The public desk was manned, if that was the word, by a bouncy little brunette in an unignorably tight sweater. I passed my detective's license in front of her like a magician showing the playing card he's about to palm. Most of the time they don't bother to look and assume I'm from police headquarters, which is fine by me. She said it would take an hour to call up the file on Nico Peterson. I said in an hour I'd be watering my cactuses. She gave me an uncertain smile and said she'd see if the process could be speeded up.

I paced the corridor for a while, smoked a cigarette, then stood at a window with my hands in my pockets and watched the traffic on Mission Road. It's an exciting life, being a private detective.

The sweater girl was as good as her word and came back in under fifteen minutes with the file. I took it to a bench by the window and flipped through the papers. I hadn't expected them to tell me much, and I wasn't wrong, but you have to start somewhere. The deceased had been struck by a vehicle, driver unknown, on Latimer Road, Pacific Palisades, in the County of Los Angeles, at some time between eleven P.M. and midnight on the night of April 19. He had suffered numerous injuries with long names, including a "gross comminuted fracture of the right side of the skull" and multiple lacerations of the face. The cause of death was our old friend blunt force trauma—pathologists love blunt force trauma; the very sound of it makes them rub their hands. There was a photograph taken at the scene of the accident. How black and glossy blood looks in the light of a flashbulb. Driver Unknown had done some job on Nico Peterson. He resembled an ill-used side of beef trussed up in a sharkskin suit. I heard myself heave a little sigh. Death be not proud, said the poet, but I don't see why the Reaper shouldn't feel a certain sense of accomplishment, given the thoroughness of his work and his unchallenged record of successes.

I handed the file back to the little lady and thanked her nicely, though all I got in return was a distracted smile; she had other things to think about. It crossed my mind to ask her if she had plans for lunch, but no sooner had the notion formed than I dropped it. Thoughts of Clare Cavendish weren't going to be neutralized that easily.

On the street, I stepped into a phone booth and called Joe Green at Central Homicide. He answered on the first ring. "Joe," I asked, "don't they *ever* give you time off?"

He let out his rattly sigh. Joe reminds me of one of the larger seagoing mammals—a porpoise, maybe, or a big old elephant seal. After twenty years on the force, dealing every day with murderers, drug pushers, kiddie rapists, what have you, he's become a shapeless wad of weariness and melancholy and the occasional sudden rage. I asked if I could buy him a beer. I could hear him turning suspicious. "Why?" he growled.

"I don't know, Joe," I said. An angry-looking young woman wearing ski pants and a scarlet halter, with a kid in a stroller, was waiting outside the booth, glaring at me to finish my call and let her have the phone. "Because it's summer," I said, "and it's lunchtime, and it's hotter'n hell, and besides, there's something I want to talk to you about."

"More about the Peterson stiff?"

"That's right."

He waited a moment, then said, "Yeah, why not. Meet me at Lanigan's."

When I opened the door of the booth, the air from inside met the outside heat with a soundless thump. As I stepped out, the young mother swore at me and pushed past and grabbed the receiver. "Don't mention it," I said. She was too busy dialing to swear at me again.

Lanigan's was one of those pretend-Irish places with shamrocks painted on the mirror behind the bar and photographs of John Wayne and Maureen O'Hara in glowing Technicolor framed on the walls. Among a shelf of bottles there was a quart of Bushmills wearing a tam-o'-shanter. Scotland, Ireland—what's the difference? The bartender seemed the genuine article, though, short and gnarled, with a head like an oversized potato and hair that had once been red. "What'll yiz have, boys?" he said.

Joe Green was wearing a wrung-out suit of gray linen that at some time in the past had probably been white. When he took off his straw hat, the rim of it left a livid groove across his forehead. He yanked a big red handkerchief from the breast pocket of his jacket and mopped his brow. This brow had by now extended so far up his skull that he would very soon be officially bald.

We sat slumped in front of our beers with our elbows on the bar. "Jesus," Joe said, "how I hate summer in this town."

"Yes," I said, "it's bad."

"You know what gets me?" He lowered his voice. "You know the way your boxer shorts bunch up in your crotch, hot and damp, like some damn poultice?"

"Maybe you're wearing the wrong kind," I said. "Consult Mrs. Green. Wives know about these things."

He threw me a sidelong look. "Oh, yeah?" He had the eyes of a bloodhound, loose-lidded and mournful and deceptively stupid-looking.

"So I'm told, Joe," I said. "So I'm told."

We drank our beers in silence for a while, avoiding our own eyes in the mirror in front of us. Pat the bartender was whistling the tune of "Mother Machree"—he was, I could hardly believe it. Maybe he was paid to do it, bringing the true lilt of the Old Sod to the City of the Angels.

"What you dig up on the Peterson bird?" Joe asked.

"Not much. I had a peek at the coroner's report. Mr. P. took some pounding that night. You ever get a lead on who it was that ran him down?"

Joe laughed. His laugh sounded like a plunger being pulled out of a toilet. "What do you think?" he said.

"Latimer Road wouldn't have been busy at that hour."

"It was a Saturday night," Joe said. "They come and go at that club there like rats at the back of a diner."

"The Cahuilla?"

"Yeah, I think that's what it's called. Could have been one of a hundred cars that flattened him. And of course nobody saw nothing. You been to that place?"

"The Cahuilla Club is not my kind of spot, Joe."

"Guess not." He chuckled; this time it was a smaller plunger coming out of a smaller toilet. "This mystery broad you're working for—she go there?"

"Probably." I put my teeth together and gave them a grind; it's a bad habit I have when I'm working up the nerve to do something I think I shouldn't do. But there comes a moment when you have to level with a cop, if he's going to be of any use to you. Sort of level, anyway. "She thinks he's still alive," I said.

"Who, Peterson?"

"Yes. She thinks he didn't die, that it wasn't him who got mashed on Latimer Road that night."

That made him sit up. He swivelled his big pink head and stared at me. "Jeez," he said. "What gives her that idea?"

"She saw him, the other day, she says."

"She *saw* him? Where?"

"In San Francisco. She was in a taxi on Market Street and there he was, large as life."

"Did she talk to him?"

"They were going in opposite directions. By the time she got over the surprise, she was way past."

"Jeez," Joe said again, in a tone of happy wonderment. Cops love it when things get turned on their head; it adds a pinch of spice to their dull working day.

"You know what that means," I said.

"What does it mean?"

"You may have a homicide on your hands."

"You figure?"

Mrs. Machree's boy was standing by the cash register dreamily poking a matchstick in one of his ears. I signaled him for another couple of glasses.

"Think about it," I said to Joe. "If Peterson didn't die, who did? And was it really an accident?"

Joe turned this over for a minute, paying special attention to the dirty underside of it. "You think Peterson set it up so he could disappear?"

"I don't know what to think," I said.

Our fresh beers arrived. Joe was still thinking hard. "What do you want me to do?"

"I don't know that, either," I said.

"I can't just do nothing. Can I?"

"You could maybe have the body exhumed."

"Dug up?" He shook his head. "It was cremated."

I hadn't thought of that, but I should have, of course. "Who identified Peterson?" I asked.

"Dunno. I can check." He picked up his glass, then put it down again. "Christ, Marlowe," he said, more rueful than angry, "every time I talk to you, it's nothing but trouble."

"Trouble's my middle name."

"Ho ho."

I moved my beer glass an inch to the side and then back again to where it had been, standing in its own ring of froth. I thought of Clare Cavendish doing the same thing a couple of hours before. When a woman gets into your head, there's nothing that won't remind you of her. "Look, Joe, I'm sorry," I said. "Maybe none of this is for real. Maybe my client only imagined it was Peterson she saw. Maybe it was a trick of the light or she'd had one martini too many."

"You going to tell me who she is?"

"You know I'm not."

"If it turns out she's right, and this guy ain't dead, you'll have to name her."

"Maybe so. But for now there's no case, so I don't need to tell you anything."

Joe sat way back on his stool and gave me a long look. "Listen, Marlowe, *you* called *me*, remember? I was having a nice peaceful morning, nothing on my desk 'cept a schoolgirl that's been missing for three days, a gun heist at a filling station, and a double murder over in Bay City. It was going to be a breeze of a day. Now I have to worry whether this guy Peterson arranged for some poor schmuck to be run over so he could vamoose."

"You could forget I told you anything. Like I say, there may be nothing in it."

"Yeah—like that high school kid may be visiting her grandma in Poughkeepsie, and it may be by accident those two guineas in Bay City got a slug each in the noggin. Sure. The world is full of things that only look serious on the surface."

He slid down from the stool and took his straw hat from where it had been sitting on the bar. Joe's face turns the color of liver when he's annoyed. "I'll run some more checks on Peterson's death, or whoever it was that died, and let you know. In the meantime, you go and hold your lady client's hand and tell her not to worry about her boyfriend Lazarus, that if he's alive you'll track him down or your name ain't Doghouse Reilly."

He turned and strode off, whacking his hat against his thigh. That went well, Marlowe, I told myself. Nice work. The bartender came and asked mildly if everything was all right. Oh, sure, I told him, everything's fine.

I drove back to the office, bought a hot dog from a stand at the corner of Vine, and ate it at my desk with a bottle of soda. Then I sat for a long time with my feet up and my hat on the back of my head, smoking. Anyone looking in at me would have said I was engaged in some hard thinking, but I wasn't. In fact, I was trying not to think. How much I might have loused things up by calling Joe Green I couldn't say, mostly because I didn't want to say. Had I betrayed Clare Cavendish's trust in me by telling Joe about her spotting Peterson when he was supposed to be dead? It was hard to see it otherwise. But sometimes, when you're getting nowhere, you have to give the wasps' nest a wallop. But shouldn't I have waited, shouldn't I have followed Peterson's trail further before I brought Joe in on the affair?

I put a hand to my forehead and gave little groan. Then I opened the drawer in my desk that's supposed to hold document files and got out the office bottle and poured myself a stiffish one into a paper cup. When you know you've goofed, there's nothing for it but to blitz a few million brain cells.

I was contemplating another belt from the bottle when the telephone rang. How is it that, after all these years, the damned machine can still make me jump? I expected it would be Joe, and

I was right. "That stiff had Peterson's wallet in his pocket," he said. "Plus he was identified at the scene by the manager of—what did you say that club is called?"

"The Cahuilla."

"Don't know why I keep forgetting it. The manager is a Floyd Hanson."

"What do you know about him?"

"If you mean have we got anything on him, we don't. The Cahuilla is a hoity-toity outfit and wouldn't hire anyone with a record to head it up. You know the Sheriff's a member there, plus a couple of judges and half the business bigwigs in town. You poke a finger in there, you're liable to get the end of it bitten off."

"Anything in the file about a disturbance there the night Peterson, or whoever he was, got run over?"

"No. Why?" I could hear Joe getting suspicious again.

"I heard Peterson was tanked that night and kicked up a fuss in the bar," I said. "It got so bad they threw him out. Next thing, someone found him on the side of the road as dead as a side of mutton."

"The someone being one of the hat-check girls on her way home with her boyfriend. The boyfriend had picked her up at the end of her shift."

"Anything there?" I asked.

"Naw. Couple of kids. They went back and got Hanson, the manager. He called us."

I thought about this for a while.

"You there?" Joe said.

"I'm here. I'm thinking."

"You're thinking you're wasting your time on this, right?"

"I'll call my client."

"You do that." He was chuckling when he hung up.

I drank another little drink from my trusty bottle, but it didn't go down well. It was too hot for bourbon. I took my hat and left the office and went down in the elevator and out onto the street. The idea was to clear my head, but how do you do that when the air is as hot as the inside of a furnace and tastes like iron filings? I walked up the sidewalk a ways, keeping in the shade, then back again. The whiskey was making my head feel like it was full of putty. I went back up to the office and lit a cigarette and sat staring at the phone. Then I called Joe Green again and told him I had spoken to my client and convinced her she was wrong about having seen Peterson.

Joe laughed. "That's frails for you," he said. "They get a notion in their pretty little heads and make you run in circles for a while, then it's *Oh, I'm tow towwy, Mr. Marwo, I must have been wong.*"

"Yeah, I guess that's it," I said.

I could hear Joe not believing a word I was telling him. He didn't care. All he wanted was to close the file on Nico Peterson and put it back on the dusty shelf he'd taken it down from.

"She pay you anyway?" he asked.

"Sure," I lied.

"So everybody's happy."

"Don't know if that's the word, Joe."

He laughed again. "Keep your nose clean, Marlowe," he said and hung up. Joe is an all-right guy, despite his temper.

═ 7 ═

I could have left it there. I could have done what I'd said to Joe I'd done, could have phoned Clare Cavendish and told her she must have been mistaken, that it couldn't have been Nico Peterson she had seen up in San Francisco that day. But why would that convince her? I had nothing new to give her. She was already aware that the dead man on Latimer Road had been wearing Peterson's clothes and had Peterson's wallet in his breast pocket. She knew, too, as she had told me before I'd parted from her in the leafy shade of Langrishe Lodge, that this fellow Floyd Hanson had identified the body. She had been at the Cahuilla that night, she had seen Peterson, drunk and loud, being escorted off the premises by a couple of Hanson's goons, and she'd still been there an hour later when the hat-check girl and her boyfriend came in to tell everybody about finding Peterson dead at the side of the road. She had even gone out and seen the body being loaded into the meat wagon. Despite all that, she was certain it was Peterson she had spotted on Market Street a couple of months after he was supposed to have died. What could I say that would make her change her mind?

I still had the feeling there was something wrong with all this, that there was something I wasn't being told. Being suspicious becomes a habit, like everything else.

I was pretty idle for the rest of that day, but I couldn't get the Peterson business out of my head. Next morning I went to the office and made a few telephone calls, checking on the Langrishes and the Cavendishes. I didn't turn up much. About the most interesting thing I found out about them was that despite their money, there were no skeletons in their closets, at least none that anyone had ever heard rattling. But it couldn't be that straightforward, could it?

I went down in the elevator and crossed the road to where I'd parked the Olds. I had left it in the shade, but the sun had fooled me and angled around the corner of the Permanent Insurance Company building and was shining full on the windshield and, of course, the steering wheel. I opened all four windows and drove off fast to get a breeze going, but it didn't help. What would have happened, I wondered, if somehow the English Pilgrims and not the Spaniards had landed first on this coast? I guess they'd have prayed for rain and low temperatures and the Lord would have heeded them.

It was cooler at the Palisades, where the ocean was close. I had to ask directions a couple of times before I found the Cahuilla Club. The entrance was up a leafy road at the end of a long high wall with bougainvillea blossoms spilling over it. The gates weren't electrified, as I'd expected they would be. They were tall, ornate, and gilded. They were open, too, but just inside them a striped wooden pole blocked the way. The gatekeeper stepped out of his

little hut and gave me a cheesy look. He was a young fellow in a
spiffy beige uniform and a cap with braid on the peak. He had a
pin head on top of a long neck and an Adam's apple that bobbed
up and down like a Ping-Pong ball when he swallowed.

I said I was there to see the manager.

"You got an appointment?" I told him no, and he screwed up
his mouth in a funny way and asked my name. I showed him my
card. He frowned at it for a long time, as if the information it con-
tained was written in hieroglyphics. He did that thing with his
mouth again—it was a kind of soundless gagging—and went into
the lodge and spoke briefly on the phone, reading from my card,
then came back and pressed a button and the barrier came up.
"Keep to the left, where it says 'Reception,'" he said. "Mr. Hanson
will be waiting for you."

The drive wound its way beside a long, high wall with hanging
masses of bougainvillea. The blossoms here came in a variety of
shades, pink, crimson, a delicate mauve. Someone sure was fond
of the stuff. There were other things growing, gardenias, and hon-
eysuckle, the odd jacaranda, and orange trees filled the air with
their sweet-sharp fragrance.

The reception area was a log cabin affair with lots of squinty
little windows and a red carpet in front of the door. I stepped
inside. The air had a piney tang, and flute music was playing softly
through hidden speakers in the ceiling. There was no one at the
desk, a large and venerable item with stacks of drawers with brass
handles and a rectangle of green leather set into the top, the kind
of thing an Indian chief might have signed away his tribal lands on.
Various items of Americana stood about: a full-length Indian head-
dress on a special stand, an antique silver spittoon, an ornate sad-
dle on another stand. On the walls were mounted bows and arrows
of various designs and sizes, a pair of ivory-handled pistols, and
framed photographs by Edward Curtis of noble-looking braves

and their dreamy-eyed squaws. I was having a close-up gander at one of these studies—tepees, a campfire, a circle of women with papooses—when I heard a soft step behind me.

"Mr. Marlowe?"

Floyd Hanson was tall and slim, with a long, narrow head and oiled black hair brushed smoothly back and with a fetching touch of gray at each temple. He wore high-waisted white slacks with a crease you could cut your finger on, tasseled loafers, a white shirt with a laid-back collar, and a sleeveless sweater in a pattern of big gray diamonds. He stood with his left hand in the side pocket of his slacks and regarded me with a quizzical eye, as if there was something faintly comical about me that he was too polite to laugh at. I suspected it wasn't personal, that this was how he looked at most things that came under his careful scrutiny.

"That's me," I said. "Philip Marlowe."

"What can I do for you, Mr. Marlowe? Marvin, our gateman, tells me you're a private investigator—is that so?"

"Yes," I said. "I used to work for the DA's office, a long time ago. I'm freelance now."

"Are you. I see."

He waited another moment, calmly regarding me, then put out his right hand for me to shake. It was like being given a sleek, cool-skinned animal to hold for a moment or two. The most striking thing about him was a quality of stillness. When he wasn't moving or speaking, something inside him seemed to switch off automatically, as if to conserve energy. I had the feeling that nothing the world could come up with would surprise or impress him. As he stood there looking at me, I found it hard not to fidget. "It's about an accident that occurred around here a couple months ago," I said. "A fatal accident."

"Oh?" He waited.

"Fellow called Peterson got run down by a hit-and-run driver."

He nodded. "That's right. Nico Peterson."

"Was he a member of the club?"

This brought on a cold smile. "No. Mr. Peterson wasn't a member."

"But you knew him—I mean, enough to identify him."

"He came here often, with friends. Mr. Peterson was a gregarious type."

"Must have been a shock for you, seeing him on the road like that, all bashed up."

"Yes, it was." His gaze seemed to roam over my face; I could almost feel it, like the touch of a blind man's fingers exploring my features, fixing me in his mind. I started to say something, but he interrupted me. "Let's take a stroll, Mr. Marlowe," he said. "It's a pleasant morning."

He moved to the door and stood to one side of it, ushering me through with an upturned palm. As I stepped past him, I thought I caught him giving me another faint smile, amused and mocking.

He was right about the morning. The sky was a vault of clear blue shading to purple at the zenith. The air was laden with mingled fragrances of tree and shrub and blossom. A mockingbird somewhere was going through its repertoire, and among the shrubbery there was the soft hushed hiss of water sprinklers at work. Los Angeles has its moments, if you're rich and privileged enough to be in the places where they happen.

From the clubhouse we walked down a smooth, curved path that led past yet more hanging clusters of bougainvillea. Here the profusion of colors was dazzling, and though they didn't seem to have much of a scent the air was heavy with the damp presence of the blossoms. "These flowers," I said, "they seem to be the signature of the place."

Hanson gave this a moment or two of judicious consideration.

"Yes, I suppose you could say that. It's a very popular plant, as I'm sure you know. In fact, it's the official flower of San Clemente, and of Laguna Niguel, too."

"You don't say."

I could see him deciding to ignore the sarcasm. "Bougainvillea has an interesting history," he said. "I wonder if you know it?"

"If I did, I've forgotten."

"It's native to South America. It was first described by one Philibert Commerçon, a botanist accompanying the French admiral Louis-Antoine de Bougainville on an around-the-world voyage of exploration. However, it's thought that the first European to see it was Commerçon's mistress, Jeanne Baret. He had smuggled her aboard dressed as a man."

"I thought that kind of thing only happened in swashbuckling novels."

"No, it was quite common in those days, when sailors and passengers could be away from home for years on end."

"So this Jeanne—what did you say her last name was?"

"Baret. With a *t*."

"Right." I couldn't hope to match his French pronunciation, and so I didn't try. "This girl discovers the plant, her boyfriend writes it up, yet it gets called after the admiral. Seems less than fair."

"I suppose you're right. The world in general does tend to be a little on the unfair side, don't you find?"

I said nothing to that. His affected, phony British accent was beginning to get on my nerves.

We came into a clearing shaded by eucalyptus trees. I happened to know a bit about the eucalyptus—unranked angiosperm, species of myrtle, native to Australia—but I didn't think it worth parading my knowledge before this cool customer. He would probably just do another of his twitchy, dismissive little smiles. He pointed beyond the trees. "The polo grounds are over there. You can't see them from here." I tried to look impressed.

"About Peterson," I said. "Can you tell me something of what happened that night?"

He continued to walk along beside me, without saying anything or even registering that he had heard the question, and looking at the ground ahead of him, the way Clare Cavendish did when we were strolling together across the lawn at Langrishe Lodge. His silence left me with the dilemma of whether to ask the question again and probably make a fool of myself. There are people who can do that, who can put you on edge just by staying quiet.

At last he spoke. "I'm not sure what you want me to tell you, Mr. Marlowe." He stopped and turned to me. "In fact, I'm wondering what exactly is your interest in this unfortunate business."

I stopped too, and scuffed the dirt of the pathway with the toe of my shoe. Hanson and I were facing each other now, but not in any confrontational way. Generally he seemed not to be the confrontational type; neither, for that matter, am I, unless I'm pushed.

"Let's say there are concerned parties who've asked me to look into it," I said.

"The police have already done that pretty thoroughly."

"Yes, I know. The problem is, Mr. Hanson, people tend to have a wrong idea of the police. They go to the movies and see these cops with slouch hats and guns in their hands relentlessly pursuing bad guys. But the fact is, the police want a quiet life just like the rest of us. Mostly their aim is to get things cleared up and squared away, to write a neat report and file it along with stacks and stacks of other neat reports and forget all about it. The bad guys know this and make their arrangements accordingly."

Hanson looked at me, nodding a little, as if in time with his thoughts. "And who, in this instance, would the bad guys be?" he asked.

"Well, the driver of the car, for a start."

"Only for a start?"

"I don't know. There are aspects of Nico Peterson's death that raise certain questions."

"Which questions?"

I turned away from him and walked on. After a few steps, however, I realized he wasn't following me, and I drew to a halt and looked back. He was standing on the path with his hands in the pockets of his slacks, gazing toward the line of eucalyptus trees with his eyes narrowed. I was beginning to see that he was a man who did a lot of thinking. I walked back to him. "You identified the body," I said.

"Not really. Not officially, anyway. I think his sister did that, the next day, downtown at the morgue."

"But you were at the scene. You called the cops."

"Yes, that's true. I saw the body. It wasn't a happy sight."

We moved on together then. By now the sun had burned off all traces of morning mist and the light was sharp and the air so clear that far-off sounds traveled through it as smoothly as javelins. From somewhere nearby I could hear the slither and crunch of a gardener's spade delving into what sounded like dryish clay. It struck me how lucky Hanson was to have a job that put him every day in these surroundings, among trees and flowering plants and watered grass, under a sky as blue and clean and bright as a baby's eye. Yes, there were people who had all the luck, and then there was the rest of us. Not that I could have worked here: too much raw nature everywhere.

"Somebody else came on the body first," I said, "is that right?"

"Yes, a young lady called Mary Stover. She was a hat-check girl here at the club. Her boyfriend had come to collect her at the end of her shift and drive her home. They'd barely turned onto Latimer Road when they saw Mr. Peterson's body. They came back and told me of their grim find."

Funny how easily even people as sophisticated as Hanson will fall into the jargon of dime novels. Their grim find, indeed.

"Is it possible for me to talk to Miss Stover?" I asked.

He frowned. "I'm not sure. She married her young man shortly afterward, and they moved together to the East Coast. Not New York. Boston, maybe? I'm afraid I can't remember."

"What's her married name?"

"Ah. There you have me. Only met the young man that one time. Introductions were perfunctory, in the circumstances."

Now it was my turn to do some heavy thinking. He watched me with a gleam of amusement. He seemed to be getting a lot of mild fun out of our encounter. "Well," I said, "I guess she won't be too hard to track down." I could see he knew this was just talk, and knew I knew it, too.

We walked on again. Around a bend in the path, we came on an elderly Negro turning the clay in a bed of roses—his was the spade I had heard at work a minute ago. He wore faded denim overalls, and his hair was a close cap of tight gray kinks. He gave us a quick, furtive glance, the whites of his eye showing, and I thought suddenly of Richard Cavendish's high-strung horse looking down at me through the window of my car.

"Good morning, Jacob," Hanson called out. The old man did not reply, only gave him another nervous-eyed look and went on with his work. When we had passed, Hanson said quietly, "Jacob doesn't talk much. He just appeared at the gate one day, frightened and starving. We've never succeeded in getting him to tell us where he came from or what had happened to him. Mr. Canning ordered that he be taken in, of course, and given shelter and something to do."

"Mr. Canning?" I said. "Who's he?"

"Oh, you don't know? I thought you'd have found out everything like that, being an investigator. Wilber Canning is the founder of our club here. That's Wilber with an *e*. In fact, his name is Wilberforce—his parents called him after William Wilberforce, the great English parliamentarian and leader of the abolitionist movement."

"Yeah," I said, in as dry a tone as I could muster, "I think I've heard of him, all right."

"I'm sure you have."

"William Wilberforce, I mean."

"Mr. Canning is a dedicated humanitarian, as were his parents before him. His father set up the club, you know. Our aim is to help, insofar as we can, the less fortunate members of society. The elder Mr. Canning's employment policy, which still holds today, directed that a certain number of positions be reserved for—well, for those in need of help and protection. You've met Jacob and Marvin, our gateman. If you're around for long enough, you'll come across some other deserving individuals who've found sanctuary here. The Cahuilla Club has an excellent reputation among the migrant fraternity."

"That's very impressive, Mr. Hanson," I said. "You make this place sound like a cross between a rest home and a rehabilitation center. That wasn't the impression I had of it, somehow. But no doubt folks like Nico Peterson really appreciate the philanthropic spirit of the place."

Hanson smiled tolerantly. "Not everyone subscribes to Mr. Canning's benevolent principles, of course. Besides, as I said, Mr. Peterson was not a member."

Without my realizing it, we had come full circle, and now suddenly we were back at the clubhouse. We weren't at the front door, though, the one I'd entered by earlier, but somewhere along the side of the building. Hanson opened a door with a full-length glass panel in it and we stepped into a wide, low room with chintz armchairs standing about, and little tables on which stacks of magazines were laid out neatly like roof shingles, and a stone fireplace about as roomy as the living room in my house on Yucca Avenue. A fireplace like that would surely get a lot of use in Pacific Palisades. There was a faint after-smell of cigars and fine old brandy. I could see Wilberforce Canning and his fellow patricians gathered here in the evening after dinner, discussing the lamentable decline in public morality and planning good works. In my imagination, they wore frock coats, knee breeches, and powdered wigs. I get fanciful sometimes; I can't help it.

"Sit down, Mr. Marlowe," Hanson said. "Care for some tea? I usually have a cup at this time of the morning."

"Sure," I said, "tea is fine."

"Indian or China?"

"Indian, I guess."

"Darjeeling all right?"

At that point, I wouldn't have been surprised if some fruity type in white shorts and a blazer had come bounding through the door, inquiring with a lisp if anyone was for tennis. "Darjeeling is just dandy," I said.

He pressed a bell push beside the fireplace—really, just like on the stage—while I lowered myself into one of the armchairs. It was so deep my knees nearly gave me an uppercut. Hanson lit a cigarette with a silver lighter and then positioned himself with an elbow on the mantelpiece and his ankles crossed and looked down at me, way below him. His expression, somewhat pained but forbearing, was that of a dutiful father compelled to have a serious talk with a wayward son. "Mr. Marlowe, did someone hire you to come here?" he asked.

"Someone like who?"

He seemed to wince; it was probably my grammar. Before he could reply, a door opened and an ancient party in a striped vest insinuated himself into the room. He looked so bloodless it was hard to believe he was alive. He was short and stocky and had gray cheeks and gray lips, and a bald gray pate over which a few long strands of oily gray hair were carefully plastered. "You rang, sir?" he said in a quavering voice; his British accent was the real thing. The Cahuilla Club was turning out to be some place, an Indian museum with a dash of Merrie Olde England thrown in.

"A pot of tea, Bartlett," Hanson said loudly, the old fellow being deaf, evidently. "The usual." He turned to me. "Cream? Sugar? Or would you prefer lemon?"

"Just the tea will be fine," I said.

Bartlett nodded, swallowed, gave me a watery glance, and shuffled out.

"What were we saying?" Hanson asked.

"You wanted to know if someone hired me to come and talk to you. I asked who you thought such a someone might be."

"Yes," he said, "that's right." He tapped the tip of his cigarette on the rim of a glass ashtray beside his elbow on the mantelpiece. "What I meant was that I can't think who would be interested enough in the case of Mr. Peterson and his sad end to go to the trouble of hiring a private investigator to open it all up again. Especially since, as I say, the police have already been through the whole thing with a fine-tooth comb."

I chuckled. I can do a good chuckle, when I try. "Combs the cops use tend to be gap-toothed, and clogged up with stuff you wouldn't want to investigate too closely."

"All the same, I can't think why you're here."

"Well, you see, Mr. Hanson," I said, shifting around in the depths of the chair in an effort to maneuver myself into something like a dignified position, "violent death always leaves loose ends. It's a thing I've noticed."

He was watching me again out of that lizard-like stillness. "What kind of loose ends?"

"You mean in Mr. Peterson's case? Like I say, there are aspects of his death that raise certain questions."

"And I asked, what kind of questions?"

There's nothing like quiet relentlessness; the noisy kind never works as well.

"Well, for instance, the question of Mr. Peterson's identity."

"His identity." It wasn't a question. His voice had become as soft as a breeze over a battlefield after a particularly bloody engagement. "What question about his identity could there be? I saw him there on the road that night. There was no mistaking who it was. Plus, his sister was shown his corpse the next day and expressed no doubts."

"I know, but the point is—and here we're at the nub of the thing—someone spotted him recently in the street, and he wasn't dead at all."

There are are silences and silences. Some you can read, some you can't. Whether Hanson was surprised by what I'd just said, whether he was astounded by it, or whether he was only saying nothing the better to let himself think, I didn't know. I watched him—a hawk wouldn't have done it more sharply—but still I couldn't decide.

"Let me get this straight," he began, but just then the door opened again and Bartlett the butler came in backward at an ape-armed stoop, carrying a wide tray on which there were cups and saucers and a silver teapot and little silver jugs and white linen napkins and I don't know what all. He came forward and set the tray down on one of the small tables, sniffed, and padded out. Hanson leaned down and poured the tea into two cups—through a silver strainer, no less—and handed one to me. I balanced it on the arm of the chair. I had a vision of myself knocking it by accident with my elbow and sending the scalding stuff flooding into my lap. I should have had an aunt when I was small, one of those fierce ones in bombazine, with a lorgnette and a mustache, who would have coached me in how to comport myself in social situations like this.

I could see Hanson preparing to claim again, in that studied,

jaded way of his, that he'd forgotten what we were talking about.
"You wanted to get something straight," I said, prompting him.
He had taken up position by the fireplace again and was slowly
stirring a silver spoon around in his tea, stirring and stirring.

"Yes," he said, then paused—more thinking. "You say someone saw Mr. Peterson in the street recently."

"That's right."

"Claimed to have seen him, that is."

"The person was pretty certain."

"And this person is . . . ?"

"Someone who knew Mr. Peterson. Someone who knew
him well."

At that his eye took on a weaselly sharpness, and I wondered if
I'd said too much. "Someone who knew him well," he repeated.
"Would that be a female someone?"

"Why do you ask?"

"Women tend to be more prone than men to that kind of
thing."

"What kind of thing?"

"Seeing a dead man walking in the street. Imagining they did."

"Let's just say this person was an associate of Mr. Peterson's," I
said, "and leave it at that."

"And this is the person who hired you to come here and make
inquiries?"

"I didn't say that. I don't say that."

"Does that mean you're operating on a secondhand report? On
hearsay?"

"It was said, and I heard it."

"And did you believe it?"

"Belief is not part of my program. I take no position. I just do
the inquiring."

"Right." He drew the word out, giving it a sort of sighing fall.
He smiled. "You haven't touched your tea, Mr. Marlowe."

I took a sip, to be polite. It was nearly cold already. I couldn't remember the last time I'd drunk tea.

A shadow moved in the glass panel of the door we had entered by, and looking up I spotted there what I took to be a boy, thin and sharp-faced, peering in at us. Seeing me see him, he shifted quickly and was gone. I turned to Hanson. He didn't seem to have noticed the figure at the door.

"Who did you call that night," I asked, "after you'd seen the body?"

"The police."

"Yes, but what police? Downtown or the Sheriff's office?"

He scratched his ear. "I don't think I know," he said. "I just called the operator and asked for the police. A squad car came, and a motorcycle policeman. I think they were from Bay City."

"You remember any of their names?"

"I'm afraid not. There were two plainclothes officers and the motorcyclist in uniform. They must have told me their names, I suppose, but if they did I've forgotten them. I wasn't in a frame of mind to register such things very clearly. I hadn't seen a dead man since my time in France."

"You were in the war?"

He nodded. "The Ardennes—Battle of the Bulge."

That brought on a silence, and it seemed almost that a breath of icy mountain air passed through the room. I sat forward in the armchair and cleared my throat. "I don't want to take up too much more of your time, Mr. Hanson," I said. "But can I ask you again if you're sure, if you're absolutely certain, that the man you saw lying dead on the road that night was Nico Peterson?"

"Who else would it have been?"

"I've no idea. But can you say you're certain?"

He fixed me with those cool dark eyes. "Yes, Mr. Marlowe, I'm certain. I don't know who it was that your employer saw in the street subsequently, but it wasn't Nico Peterson."

I lifted the cup and saucer carefully from the arm of the chair and put them back on the tray, then got myself to my feet, my kneecaps creaking. Sitting in that chair had been like squatting in a very small, very deep bath. "Thanks for seeing me," I said.

"What will you do next?" he asked. He seemed genuinely curious.

"I don't know," I said. "I could try to find that hat-check girl— Stover, was it?"

"Mary Stover, yes. Frankly, I suspect you'd be wasting your time."

"You're probably right."

He, too, put his teacup on the tray, and together we moved to the door where the butler had exited. Again Hanson stood back and ushered me through. We walked along a corridor with wall lights in ironwork brackets and a pale gray carpet so deep I swear I could feel the nap tickling my ankles. We passed through another smoking room, where there were more Indian artifacts on the walls and more Curtis prints. Then we were in another corridor, where the air was warmly heavy and smelled of liniment. "The pool is through there," Hanson said, indicating a blank white door, "and then the gymnasium."

As we were walking past it, the door opened and a woman in a white terry-cloth robe came out. She wore rubber beach shoes, and a big white towel was wrapped around her head like a turban. I registered a broad face and green eyes. I felt Hanson beside me hesitate an instant, but then he quickened his pace, touching a hand to my elbow and moving me on with him.

This time a young woman with blue-framed glasses was sitting behind the reception desk. She greeted her boss with a simpering smile; me she ignored. "There've been some calls for you, Mr. Hanson," she said. "I have one on hold, from a Mr. Henry Jeffries."

"Tell him I'll call him back, Phyllis," Hanson said, doling out one of his tight little smiles. He turned to me, offering his hand again. "Goodbye, Mr. Marlowe. It was interesting to talk to you."

"Thanks for taking the time."

We walked to the door and stepped outside, onto the square of red carpet. "I'd wish you luck in your inquiries," he said, "only I don't think they're going to get anywhere."

"It certainly seems that way." I looked about at the trees, the sparkling lawn, the banks of multicolored blossoms. "Nice place to work," I said.

"Yes, it is."

"Maybe I'll come around some evening, shoot a game of pool—or snooker, I guess you'd say—maybe sample the house brandy."

He couldn't resist a faint smirk. "Do you know any members?"

"As a matter of fact, I do, sort of."

"Have them bring you along. You'd be very welcome."

Like hell, I thought, but I smiled nicely enough, tipped a finger to the brim of my hat, and walked away.

I was puzzled. What had been going on, exactly, for the past hour? The guided tour of the grounds, the history of the bougainvillea plant, the lecture on philanthropy, the tea ceremony—what had all that been about? Why had Hanson given so much ear time to a gumshoe asking nosy questions about a not very significant death on a nearby road? Was he just a guy with not enough to do, whiling away part of a lazy morning by entertaining a representative of the sordid world beyond the gilded gates of the Cahuilla Club? Somehow I wasn't convinced that this was the case. And if it wasn't, what did he know that he'd chosen not to tell me?

I had left the Olds parked under a tree, but of course the sun had moved again, as it insists on doing, and the front half of the car was quietly baking away. I opened all the doors and moved into the shade and smoked a cigarette while I waited for the air inside to cool off a bit.

As I stood there, I began to get the feeling that I was being watched. It was like the sensation you have when you're lying on a warm beach and a cool breeze passes over your bare shoulder blades. I looked all around but could see no one. Then, behind me, I heard a quick step—it was the quickness of it that made me jump. I turned, and there was the little fellow I had seen shortly before when he had looked in through the glass door at Hanson and me. He wasn't a boy, I saw now; in fact, I estimated he was somewhere in his fifties. He wore a uniform of khaki pants and a khaki shirt with short sleeves. He had a little wizened face and clawlike hands, and eyes so pale they seemed to have no color at all. He kept his face half turned away and regarded me sidelong. He seemed very tense, like some timid wild thing, a fox, or a hare, that had approached me out of curiosity and was ready to dart off at the slightest movement I might make.

"Morning, pilgrim," I said, in friendly fashion.

At this he nodded to himself, with a crafty little smile, as if what I had said was exactly what he had expected me to say, as a way to fool him and lull him into a false sense of security. "I know you," he said, in a rusty sort of voice, almost a whisper.

"Do you?"

"Course I do. I seen you with Hook."

"You're wrong there," I said. "Don't know any Hook."

He smiled again, pinching his lips together. "Sure you do."

I shook my head, guessing he was another one of Mr. Canning's waifs and strays. I dropped the cigarette onto the dry leaves at my feet and stepped on it, then shut three doors of the car and climbed in at the fourth, behind the hot wheel. I rolled down the window. "Got to be going," I said. "Nice talking to you."

Still keeping himself half turned away from me, he sidled up to the car. "You got to be careful with that Hook," he said. "Watch he don't press-gang you into service."

I put the key in the ignition and pressed the starter. There's something grand and thrilling about the rolling burble of a big V-8 engine when it's idling; it always makes me think of one of those turn-of-the-century New York society ladies, the statuesque ones with bustles and hats and soft pale prominent throats. When I gunned the engine, the thing turned into Teddy Roosevelt, all noise and bluster.

"Hasta la vista, muchacho," I said, giving the little guy a tight wave. He put a hand on the window frame, though, and wouldn't let me go.

"He's Captain Hook," he said, "and we're the Lost Boys." I stared at him—his face was about half a foot away from mine—and suddenly he laughed. It was one of the strangest laughs I've ever heard, a high-pitched whinny, desperate and mad. "That's right," he said, "ain't it? Him, Hook—us, them boys. Hee hee hee!"

He shuffled away then, still moving crabwise, laughing to himself and shaking his head. I gazed after him for a moment, then pressed on the gas and drove down to the gate. Marvin saluted me and raised the barrier, pulling his face all up to one side in that gagging way of his. I drove through and slewed the car to the right and sped off, feeling released, like a sane man escaping from an asylum.

8

When I got back to my office in the Cahuenga Building, there was a message waiting for me with my phone service. The operator who gave it to me was the one with the nasal whine—her voice always makes it seem as if I've got a wasp trapped in my ear. "A Mrs. Anguish called," she said.

"A Mrs. what? Anguish?"

"That's what she said. I wrote it down. Says will you meet her at the Ritz-Beverly at noon."

"I don't know anyone called Anguish. What kind of name is that?"

"I wrote it down, I have it here on my pad. Mrs. Dorothea Anguish, the Ritz-Beverly Hotel, twelve o'clock."

A light bulb went on, which should have gone on sooner—my mind was still at the Cahuilla Club. *"Langrishe,"* I said. "Dorothea *Langrishe.*"

"That's what I said."

"Right." I sighed and put down the receiver. "Thanks, Hilda," I growled. That's not the operator's name, but it's what I call her, after I've hung up. She sounds like a Hilda, don't ask me why.

The Ritz-Beverly was a swish joint and took itself very, very seriously. The doorman wore a claw-hammer coat and an English-style bowler hat; he looked as if he'd turn up his nose at anything under a ten-dollar tip. The black-marble lobby was half the size of a football field, and in the middle of it there was a cut-glass vase of giant calla lilies standing on a big round table. The heavy scent of the flowers tickled my nostrils and made me want to sneeze.

Mrs. Langrishe had asked me to meet her in the Egyptian Room. This was a bar with bamboo furniture and statues of Nefertiti look-alikes holding torches aloft and table lamps with shades made from stuff that could have been papyrus but was obviously just paper. A painted map of the Nile took up all of one wall. The river had Arab boats on it and crocodiles in it, and over it flew white birds—I think they're called ibises—while along the banks there were, of course, painted pyramids and a sleepy-looking Sphinx. All this was impressive, in an overdone sort of way; but it was still a bar.

I had the image of Clare Cavendish in my mind and expected the mother to be the original of the daughter. Boy, was I mistaken. I heard her before I saw her. She had the voice of an Irish long-shoreman, raucous, loud, and hoarse. She was sitting at a little gilt table under a big potted palm, telling a waiter in a white jacket how to make tea. "First of all, you have to boil the water—d'ye know how to do that? Then you scald the teapot—give it a good scalding, mind—and put in a spoonful for each cup and an extra one for the pot. Then leave it for three minutes to draw. Think of a soft-boiled egg—three minutes, no more, no less. Then you're ready to pour. Now, have you got that? Because this stuff"—she pointed to the teapot—"is as weak as maiden's water and tastes about the same."

The waiter, a sleek Latin type, had gone pale under his smooth tan. "Yes, madam," he said in a cowed voice and hurried off, carrying the offending tea and its pot at arm's length; if he'd been less of a professional, he'd have mopped his brow.

"Mrs. Langrishe?" I said.

She was very small and very fat. Under her clothes, she might have been sitting in a barrel with holes cut in it for her arms and legs to stick out through. Her face was round and pink, and she wore a henna wig set in short, springy waves. The only thing in her of Clare that I could recognize was her eyes; those lustrous black irises ran in the family. She was squeezed into a two-piece suit of pink satin and had on clunky white shoes and a hat that must have been concocted, on an off day, by the same milliner who'd made the little black job Clare had been wearing the first time I met her. She looked up at me and arched a painted-on eyebrow. "Are you Marlowe?"

"That's right," I said.

She pointed to a chair beside her. "Sit down there now, I want to have a good look at you."

I sat. She scanned my face closely. I'll say this for her: she smelled nice, as you'd expect—every time she moved, her suit, that was made of a stuff I think is called taffeta, gave off crackling noises and a waft of perfume came out of the folds. "You're doing a job for my daughter, is that so?" she said.

I took out my case and matches and lit a cigarette. No, I hadn't forgotten to offer her one, but she had waved it aside. "Mrs. Langrishe," I said, "how did you know about me?"

She chuckled. "How did I track you down, you mean? Aha, that'd be telling, wouldn't it." The waiter came back with the teapot and nervously filled her cup. "Look at that, now," she said to him. "That's the way it should be, strong enough to trot a mouse on."

He smiled with relief. "Thank you, madam," he said and glanced at me and went away.

Mrs. Langrishe slopped milk into the tea and added four lumps of sugar. "They won't let me do this at home," she said darkly, putting down the sugar tongs. She scowled. "Doctors—pah!"

I said nothing. I wouldn't have thought there was anything anyone would be capable of not letting this lady do.

"Will you have a cup?" she said. I politely said no. Two intakes of tea in one day was more than I could face. She drank from her cup, holding the saucer under her chin. I had the impression that she smacked her lips. "There was talk of a lost necklace," she said.

"Is that so?"

"Did Clare—did Mrs. Cavendish tell you that?"

"No."

Then it had to have been the husband. I leaned back in the chair and smoked my cigarette, making myself look relaxed. People tend to think private dicks are stupid. I suppose they figure we were too dumb to make it on to the police force and be real detectives. In some instances, they're not wrong. And sometimes it comes in handy to play the numbskull. It gets folks relaxed, and relaxed folks get careless. However, I could see that wasn't going to be the case with Mrs. Dorothea Langrishe. She may have looked like the Irish Washerwoman and sounded like a navvy, but she was as sharp as the pin in her hat.

She put down the cup and saucer and glanced around the room with a scathing eye. "Look at this place," she said. "A cathouse in Cairo it could be, by the look of it. Not, mind you, that I've ever been to Cairo," she added merrily. She picked up the menu—it had been made to look like an ancient scroll, with fake hieroglyphics in the margins—and held it close to her nose, squinting at it. "Ach," she said, "I can't read that, I forgot my specs. Here"—she thrust the menu into my hands—"tell me, have they any cakes?"

"They have all kinds of cakes," I said. "Which one would you like?"

"Have they chocolate cake? I like chocolate." She put up a fat little hand and waved, and the waiter came. "Tell him," she said to me.

I told him: "The lady will try a slice of Triple-Cocoa Fondant Delight."

"Very good, sir." He went away again. He hadn't asked if I wanted anything. He must have known I was the help, just like him.

"It's not about pearls at all that Clare hired you, is it," Mrs. Langrishe said. She was rooting in her purse and brought out at last a small magnifying glass with a bone handle. "My daughter is not the kind of woman who loses things, especially things like pearl necklaces."

I looked at one of the slave girl statues. Her eyes, heavily outlined in black, were tear-shaped and unnaturally long, reaching halfway around the side of her head with its helmet of gold hair. The sculptor had given her a nice bosom and a nicer rear end. Sculptors are like that; they aim to please—to please the men in the room, that is. "I want to ask you again, Mrs. Langrishe," I said, "how did you hear about me?"

"Ah, don't bother your head about that," she said. "It wasn't hard to find you." She gave me a teasing glance. "You're not the only one able to conduct an investigation, you know."

I wasn't going to be diverted. "Did Mr. Cavendish tell you I'd been at your house?"

The slice of Triple-Cocoa Fondant Delight arrived. Mrs. Langrishe, her little eyes turning to greedy slits, examined it under her magnifying glass, intent as Sherlock himself. "Richard is not a bad fellow," she said, as if I'd criticized her son-in-law. "Bone-idle, of course." She ate a forkful of her cake. "Oh, now, that's good," she said. "Mm-mmm."

I wondered what the doctors would say if they saw her gobbling down this toxic delight. "Anyway," I said, "are you going to tell me why you've asked me here?"

"I told you—I wanted to get a look at you."

"Forgive me, Mrs. Langrishe, but now that you've had a look, I think—"

"Oh, stop," she said placidly. "Get down off your high horse. I'm sure my daughter is paying you handsomely"—I might have told her that, in fact, her daughter hadn't paid me a dime so far—"so you can spare a few minutes for her poor old mother."

Patience, Marlowe, I told myself; patience. "I can't talk to you about your daughter's business," I said. "That's between her and me."

"Sure it is. Did I say it wasn't?" She had a dab of cream on her chin. "But she is my daughter, and I can't help wondering why she'd need to hire a private detective."

"She told you—"

"I know, I know. The precious pearl necklace that she lost." She turned to me. I tried not to look at that blob of white on her chin. "What kind of a fool do you take me for, Mr. Marlowe?" she asked, almost sweetly, with a sort of smile. "It's nothing to do with pearls. She's in some sort of trouble, isn't she. Is it blackmail?"

"I can only say it again, Mrs. Langrishe," I repeated wearily, "I'm not in a position to discuss your daughter's business with you."

She was still watching me, and now she nodded. "I know that," she said. "I heard you the first time."

She put down her fork, gave a sated sigh, and wiped her mouth with her napkin. I was toying with the thought of ordering a drink, something with bitters and a sprig of green stuff in it, but decided against it. I could imagine Mrs. Langrishe fixing a sardonic eye on the glass.

"Know anything about perfume, Mr. Marlowe?" she asked.

"I know it when I smell it."

"Sure, sure. But do you know anything about the manufacture of it? No? I thought not." She settled back in her chair and did a sort of shimmy inside her pink suit. I felt a lecture coming and put myself as best I could into what I thought would seem a receptive attitude. What was I doing here? Maybe I'm too much of a gentleman for my own good.

"Most people in the perfume business," Mrs. Langrishe said, "base their products on attar of roses. My secret is that I use only what is called rose absolute, which is got not by distillation but by the solvents method. It's a far superior product. Know where it comes from?"

I shook my head; it was all I was required to do: listen, nod, shake my head, be attentive.

"Bulgaria!" she crowed, in the tone of a poker player slapping down a straight flush. "That's right, Bulgaria. They do the harvesting in the morning, before the sun is up, which is when the flowers are at their most fragrant. It takes at least two hundred and fifty pounds of petals to produce an ounce of rose absolute, so you can imagine the cost. Two hundred and fifty pounds for one ounce— think of that!" Her gaze turned dreamy. "I made my fortune on a flower. Can you credit it? The damask rose, *Rosa damascena.* 'Tis a beautiful thing, Mr. Marlowe, one of God's gifts bestowed upon us for nothing, out of His great good bounty." She sighed again, contentedly. She was rich, she was happy, and she was full of Triple-Cocoa Fondant Delight. I envied her a little. Then her look darkened. "Tell me what my daughter hired you for, Mr. Marlowe, will you? Will you do that?"

"No, Mrs. Langrishe, I won't. I can't."

"And I suppose you won't take money. I'm very rich, you know."

"Yes. Your daughter told me."

"You could name your price." I just looked at her. "God, Mr. Marlowe, but you're a fierce stubborn man."

"I'm not," I said. "I'm just your ordinary Joe, trying to earn a buck and stay honest. There are thousands like me, Mrs. Langrishe—millions. We do our dull jobs, we go home tired in the evenings, and we don't smell of roses."

She said nothing for a while, only sat and looked at me with a half-smile. I was glad to see she'd wiped the cream off her chin. It hadn't done anything for her, that blob of cow fat. "Have you heard of the Irish Civil War?" she asked.

That threw me for a second. "I knew of a guy once that fought in some Irish war," I said. "I think it was the War of Independence."

"That came first. Wars of independence usually do, before a civil war. It's the way of these things. What was your friend's name?"

"Rusty Regan. He wasn't a friend—in fact, I never met him. He got killed, by a girl. It's a long story, and not a very edifying one."

She wasn't listening. I could see by her look that she was off somewhere in the far past. "My husband was killed in that war," she said. "He was with Michael Collins's men—do you know who he was, Michael Collins?"

"Guerrilla fighter? Irish Republican Army?"

"That's the one. They murdered him, too."

She picked up her empty teacup, looked into it, put it down again.

"What happened to your husband?" I asked.

"They came for him in the middle of the night. I didn't know where they were taking him. It wasn't till the day after that he was found. They'd brought him down to the strand at Fanore, a lonely spot in those days, and buried him up to his neck far out in the sand. They left him there, facing the sea, watching the tide come in. It takes a long time, at Fanore, to reach high water. He was discovered when the tide went out again. They wouldn't let me see the body. I suppose the fish had already been at him. Aubrey, he was called. Aubrey Langrishe. Wasn't that a queer name for an Irishman? There weren't many Protestants that fought in the Civil War, you know. No, not many."

I let a beat go past, then said, "I'm sorry, Mrs. Langrishe."

She turned to me. "What?" I think she'd forgotten I was there.

"The world's a cruel place," I said. People are always telling me about the terrible things that have happened to them and their loved ones. I felt sorry for this sad old lady, but a man gets weary, acting sympathetic all the time.

"I was seven months gone when he died," she said wistfully. "So Clare never knew her father. I think it has affected her. She pretends it didn't, but I know." She reached out and put a hand on mine. It gave me a shock, being touched like that, but I tried not to show it. The skin of her palm was warm and brittle and felt like—well, like papyrus, or what I imagined papyrus would feel like. "You'd want to go carefully, Mr. Marlowe," she said. "I don't think you know who you're dealing with."

I wasn't sure which one she meant, herself, or her daughter, or someone else. "I'll be careful," I said.

She took no notice. "People can get hurt," she said, in an urgent voice. "Badly hurt." She let go of my hand. "Do you know what I mean?"

"I've no intention of harming your daughter, Mrs. Langrishe," I said.

She was looking into my eyes in a funny way that I couldn't make out. I had the feeling she was laughing at me a little but that at the same time she wanted me to understand what she was warning me of. She was a tough old dame, she was probably ruthless, she probably underpaid her workers, and she could probably have me killed, if she wanted to. All the same, there was something about her that I couldn't help liking. She had fortitude. That wasn't a word I felt called on to use very often, but in this case it seemed right.

She stood up then, reaching inside her suit jacket to yank up a
fallen strap in there. I got to my feet too and brought out my wallet. "That's all right," she said, "I have an account here. Anyway,
you didn't have anything. You'd have liked a drink, I suppose."
She gave a cackle of laughter. "I hope you weren't waiting for me
to ask you. No use being shy around me, Mr. Marlowe. Every man
for himself, I say."

I smiled at her. "Goodbye, Mrs. Langrishe."

"Oh, by the way, while I have you here, maybe you can help
me. I'm in need of a chauffeur. The last fellow was a terrible rogue
and I had to get rid of him. Do you know anybody who would fit
the bill?"

"Offhand, no. But if I think of anyone, I'll let you know."

She was looking at me with a speculative eye, as if she were
trying to see me in a uniform and a cap with a peak.

"Too bad," she said. She pulled on a pair of white cotton gloves,
the kind you can buy at Woolworth's. "You know, my name is
really Edwards," she said. "I married again, over here. Mr. Edwards
subsequently took his leave of me. I prefer Langrishe. It has a certain ring to it, wouldn't you say?"

"Yes," I said. "Yes, it has."

"I'm not really Dorothea, either. I was christened Dorothy and
was always called Dottie. That wouldn't look too good on a perfume bottle, would it—Dottie Edwards?"

I had to laugh. "I guess not," I said.

She looked up at me, grinning, and crooked an index finger
and gave me a knock with her knuckle on the breastbone, through
my tie. "Remember what I say, Marlowe," she said. "People get
hurt, unless they keep a sharp lookout." Then she turned and waddled away.

9

I drove over to the Bull and Bear for a bite to eat—watching Ma Langrishe feed her face with chocolate cake had made me hungry, and anyway, it was lunchtime. As I dawdled along the Strip, steering with one finger on the wheel, I again considered calling up Clare Cavendish and telling her I wanted out. She hadn't sent back the signed contract, and no filthy lucre had changed hands yet, so I was free to wave goodbye. But it's not easy to let go of a woman like that, until you're forced to, and it's not easy then, either. I recalled her sitting in my office in her hat with the veil on it, smoking her Black Russian through that ebony holder, and knew I couldn't do it, that I couldn't break the link with her, not yet.

I can't decide which are worse, bars that pretend to be Irish, with their plastic shamrocks and shillelaghs, or Cockneyfied joints like the Bull. I could describe it, but I haven't the heart; think dartboards and wooden beer pulls and a framed pink-tinted photo of the young Queen Elizabeth—the present one, that is—on a horse.

I sat at a table in a corner and ordered a roast beef sandwich and a tankard of ale. They served it warm, just like they do down Lambeth way; as to the sandwich, you sure take a sober view of matters while chewing on a slab of overcooked beef as tough as an Englishman's tongue. Where was I to go from here in the quest for Nico Peterson? If he really was alive, there had to be someone who knew where he was and what he was up to. But who? Then I remembered Clare Cavendish mentioning a movie actress Peterson had worked with, or for. What was her name? Mandy something—Mandy Rogers, yes, the poor man's Jean Harlow. She might be worth talking to. I took a sip of my beer. It was the color of shoe polish and tasted like soap suds. I thought, how come Britannia rules the waves, if this is what she gives her sailors to drink?

I got up from the table and crossed to the phone booth and dialed an old pal of mine, Hal Wiseman. Hal was in the same line of work as I was, only he was on the payroll at Excelsior Studios. He had a fancy title there—chief security officer, something like that—and took it easy, and why shouldn't he. He spent his time babysitting starlets and keeping the younger actors on the straight and narrow, or on the not too crooked and not too wide, at least. Now and then he had to use his contacts at the Sheriff's office to get one of Excelsior's stars off a dope rap or to ease a studio exec out from under a charge of drunk driving or wife beating. It wasn't a bad life, he said. While I waited for him to answer, I busied myself trying to work a piece of gristle from between my upper molars with my tongue. The roast beef of Old England sure is tenacious.

At last he picked up.

"Hello, Hal."

He recognized my voice straight off. "Hiya, Phil, how's it swinging?"

"Just fine."

"You at a cocktail party or something? I hear the sound of revelry in the background."

"I'm at the Bull and Bear, eating lunch. No revelers here, just the usual crowd. Listen, Hal, you know Mandy Rogers?"

"Mandy? Yeah, I know Mandy." He'd gone cautious all of a sudden. Hal was no oil painting—kind of a cross between Wallace Beery and Edward G. Robinson—which made his success with women hard to explain, if you weren't a woman. Maybe he was a great conversationalist. "Why do you ask?"

"There's a guy who did some work with her," I said. "Agenting work. Name of Nico Peterson."

"Never heard of him."

"You sure?"

"Sure I'm sure. What's this about, Phil?"

"You think you could get me a meeting with Miss Rogers?"

"What for?"

"I want to talk to her about Peterson. He got killed one night a couple months ago, over in Pacific Palisades."

"Oh, yeah?" I could hear Hal continuing to close up, slowly, like a giant clam. "What kind of killed did he get?"

"Hit-and-run."

"So?"

"So I've got a client who's paying me to look into Peterson's death."

"Something in it that don't meet the eye?"

"Could be."

There was a silence. I could hear him breathing; it might have been the sound of his mind working, in long, slow beats. "What's Mandy Rogers got to do with it?"

"Nothing at all. Only I need some background on Peterson. He's kind of an enigma."

"Kind of a what?"

"Let's say there are things about him that don't meet the eye."

Some more breathing, some more thinking. Then he said, "I guess Mandy will talk to you." He gave a snuffly laugh. "It ain't as if she's too busy these days. Leave it to me. You still at the same office, that flytrap on Cahuenga? I'll call you."

I went back to my table, but when I looked at the half-eaten sandwich and the half-drunk pint of tepid beer I lost heart, and instead of sitting down I dropped a bill beside my plate and left. A big purple cloud had come up from somewhere and covered the sun, and the light in the street had turned surly and had a livid cast. Maybe it was going to rain. That would be a nice novelty, in summer, in these parts.

Hal, who was a man of his word, telephoned in the afternoon. Mandy Rogers would meet me at the studio; I should come over there now. I took my hat, locked the office, and went down to the street. That cloud was still hanging over the city, or maybe it was another one just like it, and raindrops the size of silver dollars were splashing on the pavement. I sprinted across the road and made it into the car just as the shower got going in earnest. It may not rain here often, but when it rains, it rains. The wipers on the Olds needed replacing, and I had to crouch over the wheel with my nose nearly touching the windshield so I could see the road.

Hal was waiting for me at the gates of the studio, sheltering in the gateman's cabin. He came out with his jacket pulled over his head and jumped in beside me. "Goddamn," he said, "three steps and I'm soaked—look at me!" Did I mention that Hal is a sharp dresser? He was wearing a pale linen double-breasted suit, a green shirt and green silk tie, brown-and-white two-toned wingtips. Also a gold link bracelet, two or three rings, and a Rolex watch. He was doing well for himself; maybe I should look into the movie business.

"Thanks for doing this, Hal," I said. "I appreciate it."

"Yeah, well." He scowled, brushing at the raindrops on the padded shoulders of his jacket.

Movie lots are strange places. You feel like you're in a waking dream, meeting cowboys and showgirls, ape-men and Roman centurions, all of them just walking along like any other bunch of workers on their way to the office or the factory. They looked even stranger than usual today, since most of them had umbrellas up. The umbrellas had the studio logo on them, a bright yellow sun rising out of a crimson lake and the words "Excelsior Pictures" emblazoned in gilt scrollwork. "Was that James Cagney we just passed?" I asked.

"Yeah. He's on lease from Warner Brothers, doing a fight picture for us. The movie is crap, but Cagney will carry it. That's what stars are for. Take a left here."

"You know the word *blasé*, Hal? French word."

"No. What's it mean?"

"It means you've seen it all and don't care for any of it anymore."

"I get it," he said sourly. He was still tut-tutting over a few spots of damp on the lapels of his suit. "You see how *you'd* feel, wiping the puke off the back seat of your car at four in the morning after you've sprung yet another star of the silver screen out of the drunk tank and dumped him at his mansion in Bel-Air. And then there's the dames—they're worse. Ever met Tallulah Bankhead?"

"Can't say I have."

"Count yourself lucky. Stop here."

We were at the commissary. A blond kid in a zipped-up windbreaker hopped out from the doorway with an Excelsior umbrella and escorted Hal inside—I was left to duck the rain as best I could. "Give Joey here the key," Hal said. "He'll look after your car for you." Joey flashed me a big smile; he'd had a dental job done that

I bet his old ma in Peoria or wherever had sacrificed her life's savings for. Everyone in Hollywood is a hopeful.

It was midafternoon and there was hardly anyone in the place. Opposite the long counter where the food was served there was a big picture window looking out on a grass slope with palm trees and a small ornamental lake. The rain was making the water in the lake look like a bed of nails. Mandy Rogers sat at a table by the window, posing with a hand to her chin and gazing out soulfully at the sad gray day and thinking great thoughts. "Hey there, Mandy," Hal said, laying a hand on one of her shoulder blades. "This is the guy I told you about—meet Philip Marlowe."

She made a show of tearing herself away from her reverie and turned her saucer eyes up to me and smiled. I've got to say, film people have a special something, no matter how small-time they are. They spend so much of their days looking into things—cameras, mirrors, the eyes of their fans—that they get a smooth, all-over glaze, as if they'd been smeared with a special kind of honey. In the female of the species, the effect can take your breath away when you get treated to it up close.

"Mr. Marlowe," Mandy Rogers said, offering me one of her little white hands to shake. "Charmed, I'm sure." Her voice dispelled some of the magic. It was so high-pitched and piercing she could have etched her name on the window with it.

"Thanks for seeing me, Miss Rogers," I said.

"Oh, call me Mandy, please."

I was still holding on to her hand, which she was making no attempt to retrieve.

"Take a seat, Phil," Hal said drily. "You look like you're going to faint."

Was I that much affected? Mandy Rogers was no Rita Hayworth. She was on the short side, not exactly slim, a bottle blonde with a butterfly mouth and a chubby little chin. Her eyes were nice, though, big and round and baby blue. She was wearing a scarlet dress that was tight and low in the bodice and full in the skirt. Only in a film studio could a girl get away with a dress like that in the middle of the afternoon.

At last she took back her hand, and I sat down on a metal chair. Out of the corner of my eye I saw through the window a bluebird flit down from one of the palm trees and land on the wet grass.

"Okay," Hal said, "I'm going to leave you two together. Mandy, you keep an eye on this guy—he's not as harmless as he looks." And he gave me a soft punch on the shoulder and went away.

"He's such a nice person," Mandy sighed. "And you can't say that of everybody in this business, you know."

"I'm sure that's true, Miss Rogers."

"*Mandy,*" she said, shaking her head at me and smiling.

"All right—Mandy."

There was a bottle of Coke on the table in front of her, with a straw sticking out of it. "Is it true, what Hal says?" she asked. "Are you so dangerous?"

"Naw," I said. "I'm a pushover, you'll see."

"He tells me you're a private detective. That must be exciting."

"So much so I can hardly bear it."

She gave me her hazy smile, then picked up the bottle and sucked up some Coke through the straw. For that moment she could have been just any kid sitting at a soda fountain, drinking a bottle of pop and dreaming of being a big star one day. I liked how, when she leaned over the straw and looked down, the upper set of her eyelashes almost rested on the soft curve of her cheek. I wondered how much she owed to how many men in this town already.

"Nico Peterson was your agent," I said, "yes?"

She put down the bottle. "Well, he wanted to be. He did get me some work. I was in *Riders of the Red Dawn*—did you see it?"

"Not yet," I said.

"Oh, it's gone now. Joel McCrea was supposed to be in it, but something happened and he couldn't do it. I played the rancher's daughter."

"I'll catch it when it comes around again."

She put her head on one side, smiling. "You're sweet," she said. "Are all private investigators like you?"

"Not all of them, no." I offered her a cigarette from my silver case, but she shook her head, pursing her lips demurely. I could see her as the rancher's daughter, dainty one minute and feisty the next, in a gingham skirt and button boots, with a big bow in her hair. "What can you tell me about Mr. Peterson?" I asked.

"What would you like to know?" She bit her lip and gave her bubbly blond hair a toss. Since I'd first set eyes on her, five minutes or so previously, she had tried out half a dozen parts, from bobby-soxer to big-eyed siren. But she was still just a kid.

"When did you last see him?"

She pressed an index finger to her mouth at one side, making a dimple there, and turned her eyes up to the ceiling. I could see the direction in the script: *She pauses, thinking.* "I guess about a week before he died," she said. "He was working on getting me into the new Doris Day movie—you know Miss Day's real name is Kappelhoff? They say Rock Hudson is going to be in it too." Her fresh little face clouded over for a moment. "I guess I won't get the part now. Oh, well."

A young guy came by the table. He wore a short white apron and was carrying a tray. He might have been the kid brother of the one who had held the umbrella over Hal when we got out of the car in the rain. I could have worked up a thought about the movies being a machine for devouring the young and the eager, but instead I asked for a cup of coffee. "You got it, sir!" the young guy said, and flashed a smile at Mandy and went off.

"Nico, was he a good agent?" I asked. "I mean, was he successful?"

Mandy gave that some thought, too. "He wasn't one of the big

MARLOWE   101

ones," she said. "He was just starting out, like me—only of course
he was older. I'm not sure what he did before he was an agent."

"Did you see him socially?"

She wrinkled her nose, which was as near to a frown as that
sweet, clear face could come. "You mean, did he try to—? Oh, no.
Ours wasn't that kind of relationship."

"I meant, did he take you out to places, places where you'd
meet people?"

"What sort of people?"

"Well, producers, directors, studio heads."

"No, he was always too busy. He always had someone to see."

"Yes, so I hear."

"Do you?" She was suddenly sharp. "Who from?"

"No one in particular," I said. "Everyone talks, in this town."

"You can say that again."

She was looking out the window, and her eyes had narrowed. I
really didn't want to know more than I already did about Mandy
Rogers, the ups and the—more likely—downs of her career so far.
Yet I heard myself asking, "Where are you from, Mandy?"

"Me?" She seemed genuinely surprised by the question. For a
moment she was confused, and when she was confused, I could
see, she stopped acting. Suddenly she looked tentative, uncertain,
maybe even a bit alarmed. "I was born in Hope Springs, Iowa. I
guess you've never been there. Nobody has, really. Hope Springs
is the kind of place people leave."

The young waiter came with my coffee. Again he ogled Mandy,
who gave him an absentminded smile in return. She was thinking
still of Hope Springs and all the things, or all the nothings, she'd
left behind her there.

"How did you hear of Nico's death?" I asked.

She thought about it, then shook her head. "You know, I can't
remember. Isn't that strange? There must have been talk about it
here at the studio. Someone must have told me."

I looked toward the window. The bluebird flew up to its perch in the palm tree again. When it got there I couldn't see it any longer, in the shadows under the fronds. That's happiness for you: there one minute, gone the next. At least the rain was easing off.

Mandy took another sip of Coke. The bottle, now almost empty, made a loud gurgle, and Mandy glanced at me quickly, as if she was afraid I'd laugh.

"Did you ever meet Nico's friends?" I asked. "A girlfriend, maybe?"

She gave a little tinkly laugh. "Oh, he had plenty of those."

"You didn't meet any of them?"

"I saw him a couple of times with a woman, but I don't think she was his girlfriend."

"What did she look like?"

"I didn't see her very well. Once it was at a party and he was leaving with her. Another time I saw them in a bar, but that night *I* was leaving. A tall woman. Dark hair. Nice face, too—big, you know, squarish, but nice."

"Why do you think she wasn't his girlfriend?"

"They didn't have that air. She wasn't really *with* him—you know what I mean? Maybe she looked a bit like Nico, too—maybe they were related, I don't know." She fiddled with the straw in the empty Coke bottle. "Is it one of his girlfriends you're working for?"

I wondered what Hal had told her about me and my search for Nico Peterson, dead or alive. For my part, I hadn't told Hal much—there wasn't much to tell—so I supposed he must have made something up. Hal is like that. Despite his rough demeanor, he has a colorful imagination and loves to embroider the dull old truth. Mandy Rogers probably thought I was acting for some woman Nico had jilted before he died. And come to think of it, I thought, maybe I am.

"What was Nico like?" I asked.

"What was he like?" Mandy frowned. Peterson, I could see, hadn't been anyone Mandy had given much thought to before today, even if he had got her a part in *Riders of the Red Dawn*. "Gee, I don't think I knew him all that well. He was just a guy on the make. I liked him, I suppose—not in *that* way, of course. I mean, he wasn't even a friend, just a business associate." She paused, then said, "He asked me one time to come to Mexico with him." She looked away and even blushed a little.

"Did he?" I said, trying not to sound too interested. "Where in Mexico?"

She was doing that lip-biting thing again. Who was she trying to be? Doris Kappelhoff, maybe, in one of her girl-in-buckskin roles.

"Acapulco. He often went down there, or so he told me. He knew people—I could tell he meant people who were rich."

"But you didn't go."

She widened her eyes and made an O of her mouth. "Of course I didn't! I suppose you think I'm the usual Hollywood tramp, ready to go anywhere, with anyone."

"No, no," I said soothingly. "I don't think anything of the kind. I just thought, since he was older than you and so on, he might have been offering to take you on a nice trip with him, as a friend."

She smiled, a grim, tight little smile. "Nico had girlfriends," she said, "but he didn't have girls who were friends. You know what I mean?"

A guy came in who looked so much like Gary Cooper that it couldn't have been him. He wore riding breeches and leather leggings and a red bandanna knotted around his suntanned neck, and had a holster with a six-shooter in it strapped to his hip. He took up a tray and walked along the counter, eyeing the serving pans of food.

"You've been a real help, Miss Rogers," I said, giving her my liar's smile.

"Have I?" She looked startled. "How did I do that?"

"In my business," I said, lowering my voice as if I were confiding a trade secret, "there's nothing that's not important, nothing that doesn't help to build up a picture."

She was looking at me with her lips parted and a knot of puzzlement between her eyebrows. "A picture of what?" she asked, speaking, like me, in a murmur.

I pushed my dead coffee cup away and picked up my hat. The rain outside had stopped, and it looked like the sun was toying with the possibility of coming out. "Let's just say, Mandy," I said, with a slow wink, "I know more now than I did when I came in."

She nodded, still gazing at me, still wide-eyed. She was a sweet girl, in her way. I couldn't help fearing for her future, in the career she'd chosen for herself. "Can I come talk to you again," I said, "if I think of some more questions you might know the answers to?"

"Sure," she said. Then she remembered who she was supposed to be, and moistened her lips with the tip of her tongue and leaned her head back lazily, showing off her snowy throat; I guessed Barbara Stanwyck in *Double Indemnity*, which was one I *had* seen. "Come around anytime," she said. "Hal will tell you where to find me."

On the way out, I passed the table where the rangy guy with the red bandanna was hunched over a plate of chili con carne, spooning the food into himself as if he thought someone might creep up and reach over his shoulder and steal it from him. He really was a dead ringer for the Coop.

═ 10 ═

I hadn't known where I was headed until I got there. The air was
fresh, after the rain, and had a melancholy fragrance. I had the car
window down, enjoying the cool breeze on my face. I was thinking of Mandy Rogers, and of all the other kids like her who had
come out here to the coast, drawn by the promise of one day getting to play opposite Doris and Rock in some mindless concoction
of schmaltzy songs and mink coats and white telephones. There
was bound to be a boy in Hope Springs who still pined for her. I
could see him, clear as the rinsed light over the Hollywood Hills,
a gawky fellow with hands like shovels and ears that stuck out. Did
she ever think of him, there among the cornfields, eating his heart
out over the memory of her? I felt sorry for him, even if she didn't.
I was in that frame of mind; it was that kind of hour, after the rain.

I parked at the start of Napier Street and walked to Peterson's
house. I didn't want another encounter with the old buzzard across
the way, and I figured that if I drove up he would probably recognize the Olds—his type remembers cars more than it does people.
His shack was shut up, and there was no sign of him anywhere.

This time I didn't go to Peterson's front door, but made my way around to the back, the wet grass squeaking under my shoes.

The yard was overgrown, and there were gone-to-seed acacia bushes and some kind of creeper, with a sickly yellow flower, that had run riot and was strangling everything within reach. Here, just like at the front, a couple of wooden steps led up to the porch. The windows were dusty. A tabby cat that had been sleeping by the door opened one eye and looked at me, then got up slowly and padded away, its tail lazily twitching. What is it cats know about us that makes them disdain us so?

I tried the door, but it was locked. That was hardly a surprise. Luckily, I happened to have on my key ring a handy implement given to me in my days at the DA's office, which I'd managed to hold on to when I'd left the job, and which has proved invaluable ever since. It was molded out of the same blue-black metal they made tuning forks from, and it opened any lock you could care to name, short of the big one at Fort Knox. Having quickly glanced first over my left shoulder and then over my right, I inserted the dingus into the little slit under the doorknob, fiddled around for a bit, with my teeth on edge and one eye shut, then heard the tumblers click, and all at once the knob turned under my hand. The DA nowadays was a fellow called Springer, a political type with big ambitions. I wished I could let him know how my time in his office had continued to help me in my role as a lone crime fighter.

I shut the door behind me and leaned my back against it and stood for a moment, listening. Nothing like the stillness inside a deserted house. There was a faint sweet smell of dry rot in the motionless air. I felt as if the furniture was watching me, like a pack of guard dogs too dispirited to get off their hind legs or even bark. I had no idea what I might be looking for. That smell of mold and the dust everywhere and the gray lace curtains at the windows hanging down dejectedly somehow suggested there would be a body somewhere, in a locked room, lying on a bed in a body-shaped hollow, its eyes, still with a trace of surprise in them, fixed on the dim ceiling.

But the body wasn't here; I knew that. It had lain for a spell in a mangled state at the side of that road in Pacific Palisades, then it had been gathered up and whisked away to the morgue, and then burned, and now was no more than a scattering of random atoms on the air. Over these past days, since Clare Cavendish had first walked into my office, Peterson had become a ghostly presence for me, shimmering and elusive, like one of those slippery floating motes you get in your eye that move every time you try to look at them directly. But what did I care about Peterson, really? Nothing. It wasn't him I cared about.

It was a small house, and I must say Peterson kept it in good order. In fact, it was so tidy it didn't seem lived in. I looked around the living room, poked my head into the bedroom. The bed looked as if a hospital nurse had made it up, with the covers all squared off at the corners and the pillows as smooth as slabs of marble.

I'd gone through a few drawers and opened and shut a few closets when I heard a key being pushed into the front door lock. I had the usual reactions: bristling hairs on the back of my neck, thumping heart, palms suddenly moist. At times like that you know how an animal feels when it hears a twig breaking under a boot heel and looks up to see the huntsman's silhouette against the forest glow. I was leaning over the bureau, with a framed photograph in my hand—an old lady, Peterson's mother I assumed, steel-rimmed glasses on the end of her nose, glaring with disapproval at the camera—and when I looked to the door I saw through the dusty glass panel the outline of a woman's head. Then the door swung open. With slow and careful movements, I replaced the photograph on the bureau.

"Jesus!" the woman said, rearing back and in her fright stamping a heel down hard on the wooden threshold. "Who are you?"

Straight off I knew two things about her: first, that this was the woman Mandy Rogers had seen with Peterson. I couldn't say how I knew it. Sometimes these things just come to you, and you have to accept them. The second thing I realized was that I'd seen her before somewhere. She was a big-jawed, slouchy brunette, with wide hips and a heavy bust. She wore a tight white blouse and a red skirt that was even tighter, and white mules with a high square heel. She looked like the kind of girl who'd have a dinky little pistol in her purse.

"It's all right," I said, holding up what was meant to be a reassuring hand. "I'm a friend of Nico's."

"How did you get in?"

"Back door was unlocked."

I could see her trying to decide whether to stay or get out of there quick. "What's your name?" she demanded, acting tough. "Who are you?"

"Philip Marlowe," I said. "I'm in security."

"What sort of security?"

I gave her one of my lopsided, aw-shucks-it's-only-little-me smiles. "Look, why don't you step inside and shut the door. I'm not going to hurt you."

The smile must have worked. She did step in, she did shut the door. All the same, she didn't take her eyes off me for a second.

"You're Nico's sister, right?" I said.

It was a shot in the dark. I'd recalled Floyd Hanson mentioning that Peterson's sister had identified his body at the morgue. This had to be her. Of course, it could have been one of the many girlfriends I'd heard so much talk about, but somehow I didn't think so. Also at that moment I remembered where I'd seen her before: coming through the door from the swimming pool at the Cahuilla Club, in a terry-cloth robe with a towel wrapped around her head.

Same wide face, same green eyes. That was why Hanson had been thrown for a second when she'd appeared. She was Peterson's sister, and he hadn't wanted me to meet her.

She took a couple of steps sideways now, still watching me, cautious as a cat, and stopped by an armchair and laid a hand on the back of it. She was beside a window, so I got a good look at her. Her hair was almost black, with bronze tints in its depths. There was something vague and undefined about her, as if whoever made her got interrupted before adding the finishing touches and never came back to complete the job. She was one of those women whose sister would be beautiful though she'd just missed it herself. "Marlowe," she said, "is that what you say your name is?"

"That's right."

"And what are you doing here?"

I had to think about that one. "I was looking through Nico's things," I said weakly.

"Oh, yeah? For what? He owe you money?"

"No. He had something of mine."

She curled a lip. "What was that? Your stamp collection?"

"No. Just a thing I need to get back." I knew how lame it sounded, but I was improvising as I went along, and it wasn't easy. I moved away from the bureau. "Mind if I smoke? You're making me nervous."

"Go ahead, I'm not stopping you."

I wished I had my pipe; getting that filled would have given me time to think. I fumbled around with my cigarette case and a box of matches, got out a pill, and lit up, doing it all as slowly as I could. She was still standing there by the armchair, still with her hand on the back of it, still watching me.

"You *are* Nico's sister, aren't you?" I said.

"I'm Lynn Peterson. I don't believe any of this stuff you're telling me. How about you come clean and say who you really are?"

I had to hand it to her, she had guts. I was the intruder, after all, and she had stumbled on me nosing around in her brother's house. I could have been a robber. I could have been a maniac escaped from the loony bin. I could have been anybody. And I could have been armed. But there she was, standing her ground and taking no guff from me. In any other circumstances, I'd probably have asked her to come out with me to some shady bar and see what might have happened after. "All right," I said. "My name is Marlowe, that much is true. I'm a private investigator."

"Sure you are. And I'm Little Red Riding Hood."

"Here," I said, taking one of my cards out of my wallet and passing it to her. She read it, frowning. "I've been hired to look into your brother's death."

She wasn't really listening. Now she started to nod. "I've seen you," she said. "You were with Floyd, at the club."

"Yes," I said, "I was."

"Floyd have something of yours too, that you needed to get back?"

"I was talking to him about Nico."

"Talking to him what about Nico?"

"About the night your brother died. You were there that night, weren't you, at the club?" She said nothing. "Did you see your brother's body?"

"Floyd wouldn't let me."

"But you identified it the next day, at the morgue, right? Your brother's body, I mean. That must have been rough."

"It wasn't much fun."

We let a silence follow that. We were like a pair of tennis players taking a breather between sets. Then she came forward and went to the bureau and picked up the framed photograph of the sour old lady in the wire-rimmed spectacles. "This can't be what you were looking for," she said. She turned to me with a cold smile. "It's Aunt Margie. She reared us. Nico hated her—I don't know why he's got her picture on his bureau." She put the photo down. "I need a drink," she said, and walked past me, out to the kitchen.

I followed her. She'd got a bottle of Dewar's down from a cabinet on the wall and was searching in the freezer for ice cubes. "What about you," she said over her shoulder, "you want a belt?"

I took a couple of tall glasses from a shelf and set them on the counter beside the gas stove. She brought a tray of ice to the sink and ran water on the back of it, and a handful of cubes came loose. She piled them into the glasses. "See if there's a mixer under there," she said. I opened the cupboard she had pointed to and found a couple of miniatures of Canada Dry. I like the *glug-glug-glug* that the soda makes as it tumbles over ice; it's a sound that always cheers me up. I could smell Lynn Peterson's perfume, a sharp, feline scent. That was cheery, too. This chance encounter was turning out not so bad after all.

"Mud in your eye, buster," Lynn said, and clinked the rim of her glass against mine. Then she leaned back with her behind against the sink and gave me the once-over. "You don't look like a shamus," she said, "private or otherwise."

"What *do* I look like?"

"Hard to say. Gambler, maybe."

"I've been known to sit in on the odd game."

"Did you win?"

"Not often enough."

The hooch was spreading its warmth inside me slowly, like sunlight flowing across a summer hillside. "You know Clare Cavendish?" I asked, though perhaps I shouldn't have. "Nico's girlfriend."

She laughed so suddenly she almost choked on her drink. "The ice maiden?" she said hoarsely, staring at me with a disbelieving smile. "His *girlfriend*?"

"So I'm told."

"Well, it must be true then, I suppose." She laughed again, shaking her head.

"She was there that night, too, at the club—the night Nico died."

"Was she? I don't remember." Now she frowned. "She hire you to stick your nose into what happened that night?"

I took another go of Mr. Dewar's best. That inner sunshine was getting sunnier by the minute. "Tell me what happened at the morgue," I said.

She was watching me again, just as she had when she'd first laid eyes on me. "What do you mean, what happened? They brought me into a white room, they lifted back the sheet, and there was Nico, dead as a Thanksgiving turkey. I shed a tear, the cop patted my shoulder, I was led out, and that was that."

"What cop?" I asked.

She lifted her shoulders and let them fall again. "I don't know what cop. He was there, he asked me if this was my brother, I said yes, he nodded, I left. Cops are cops. They all look alike to me."

I half heard, very faintly, a car pulling up in the street out front. I took no notice of it, though I should have. "He didn't give you his name?"

"If he did, I've forgotten. Look, Marlowe, what's this all about?"

I looked away from her. I wondered if I should tell her what Clare Cavendish had told me, about seeing Nico hurrying through the crowds on Market Street up in San Francisco that day? Could I risk it? I was about to speak, not really knowing what I was going to say, when I noticed that she was looking past my shoulder with an odd expression. I turned, just as the back door opened and a guy with a gun in his hand stepped into the room. A Mexican guy. Behind him there was a second Mexican. He had no gun. He looked like he wouldn't need one.

=== 11 ===

I never did find out their names. For the sake of convenience, in my mind I called them Gómez and López. Not that my convenience, or anyone else's, was going to be high on their list of priorities; I knew that straight off. Gómez was the brains, such as they were, and López was the muscle. Gómez was short and squarely built, and on the heavy side, for a Mexican, while López was as lean as a rattlesnake. The old guy across the street had said they were stylish dressers, but his sartorial judgment, I could see, wasn't to be trusted. Gómez wore a powder-blue double-breasted suit with boxy shoulders and a tie with a half-naked bathing beauty painted on it, not very expertly. López's Hawaiian shirt was about the loudest I've ever seen. His white deck pants would have been clean when they were bought, a long time ago. He wore open-toed sandals, and his toes were filthy.

Look, don't get me wrong, I have nothing against Mexicans. They're gentle, kindhearted people, most of them. I like their food and their beer and their architecture. I once spent a very pleasant weekend in Oaxaca, in a fine hotel there, in the company of a friendly lady of my acquaintance. The days were warm and the nights were cool, and at twilight we sat in the Zócalo drinking salty margaritas and listening to the mariachi bands. That's my Mexico. Gómez and López came from a different place. I'd put them down to a barrio in one of the more raucous towns just south of the border. I heard Lynn Peterson catch her breath at the sight of them. I probably caught my own breath. They were quite a sight, after all.

They came through the door in a big hurry. They were impatient fellows in general, as I was to find out. Gómez's gun was a hefty silver-plated automatic that looked as if it would have the firepower of a small howitzer. A man with a gun like that in his paw is not a man to quibble with over petty details. From the negligent way he held it, I could see that he and the gun were chums from way back. López, though, would be a knife man; he had that nervy, wild-eyed look. I recalled Travis, the bartender at the Beanery, making a joke about this pair—it had to have been them—toying with their gun and knife. Some joke. He didn't know how right he'd turn out to be.

At first Gómez didn't even look at Lynn Peterson or me. He stalked straight through the kitchen into the living room, was silent in there for a moment or two, checking the place out, I supposed, then came back. He was a twitchy type, like his partner, and kept sort of throwing himself around inside that roomy suit of his. López meanwhile stood in the open doorway eyeing Lynn Peterson. Gómez gave her his attention too, but it was me he spoke to. "Who are you?"

It was a question I was getting tired of being asked. "Marlowe's the name," I said, then added, "I think there must be some mistake here."

"What kind of mistake?"

"I'm sure we're not who you think we are, Miss Cavendish and I." I felt Lynn Peterson's surprised stare. It was the only name I'd been able to come up with on the spot. "Miss Cavendish is a rental agent. She's showing me the house."

"Why?" Gómez asked. I had the impression he was asking just for the sake of asking, while he thought up some sharper questions, ones with more point.

"Well," I said, "I'm thinking of renting." This amused López, and he laughed. I noticed he had a harelip, badly stitched. "Are you detectives?" I asked. This made López laugh some more. When the gap opened in his lip, a yellowish tooth glinted in there.

"Sure," Gómez said, without even a smile, "we're the cops." He turned his attention to the woman beside me. "Cavendish," he said. "That's not your name. Am I right?" She began to protest, but he waved the barrel of his gun wearily in front of her face, like a huge reproving forefinger. "No, no, no, senorita. You don't lie to me. You do, you pay for it. What's your real name?" She said nothing. He shrugged, the padded shoulders of his jacket tilting to the left. "It don't matter. I know who you are."

He moved away, and in his place López came forward and stood in front of the woman, smiling into her eyes. She flinched from him. His breath probably wasn't the sweetest. Gómez said something in Spanish that I didn't catch, and López scowled. "What's your name, baby?" he crooned softly. "I bet you got a real nice name."

He put a hand under her right breast and hefted it, as if guessing its weight. She jerked herself back, out of his reach, but he followed her, still with his hand out. He wasn't leaving me much choice. I got him by the wrist with one hand and by the elbow with the other and yanked both joints in different directions. It hurt, and he gave a yelp and tore his arm out of my grasp. Sure enough, a knife had appeared in his other hand, the left one. It was a small knife, with a short blade, but I wasn't fool enough not to know what he'd be able to do with it.

"Look, take it easy," I said, letting my voice go high-pitched, trying to sound like a guy whose only interest was renting a house at a nice rate and staying out of trouble. "But keep your hands off the lady."

I could feel Lynn Peterson's fear; it was in the air, like a fox's scent. I happened to have my .38 Special in a spring-loaded holster on my belt at the side. I hoped the Mexicans wouldn't notice it until I had figured out a way to get at it without being shot or sliced first. You see them in the movies, the quick-draw artists; their guns come out like greased lightning, spinning on their index fingers. Unfortunately, that's not how it works in real life.

López was closing in again—on me, this time, not Lynn, his little knife at the ready. But his sidekick said something in Spanish that I didn't catch and waved the automatic at him, and he held off.

"Give me your wallet," Gómez said to me. His English was good, though he spoke it with a Spanish lisp. I held up both my hands.

"Look," I said, "I told you, you're making a—"

That was as far as I got. I hardly saw the gun move before I felt the barrel of it land on my right cheekbone with a dull smack that made my teeth on that side shiver at their roots. Lynn Peterson, beside me, gave a little scream and put a hand to her mouth. I almost went down but caught myself in time and managed to stay on my feet. The skin of my cheek was broken, and I felt warm blood run down and form drops along the line of my jaw. I put up a hand, and it came away smeared with crimson.

I began to speak, but Gómez interrupted again. "Shut up, *hijo de la chingada!*" he said, baring his front teeth but keeping them clenched together. They looked very white against his dark skin. He must have had Indian blood. That's the kind of thought that crosses your mind when you've just been pistol-whipped. It was then or never, I decided. Pretending to reach toward my pocket for a handkerchief, I moved instead to my belt and got the flap of the holster up and my fingers on the spring. That was the last thing I was aware of doing for a long time.

═ 12 ═

It had to have been López who delivered the knockout blow. I don't know what he hit me with—a blackjack, probably—but it got me right on that conveniently placed outcrop of bone at the base of the skull, on the right side. I must have gone down like a felled steer. The kind of unconsciousness I entered was nothing like the kind you drop into when you fall asleep. It was dreamless, for one thing, and there was no sense of time passing—it started and ended at what seemed pretty much the same instant. It felt like a dummy run for death, and if that really is what being dead is like, then the prospect is not so bad. It was the waking up that hurt. I was lying on my face on the floor, the side of my mouth stuck to the linoleum by my own blood and drool. No point saying how my cheekbone felt. An ache is an ache, though this one was a whopper.

I lay there for a while with my eyes open, hoping the room would stop wheeling like a carousel. The light was dim, and I thought it was maybe twilight, but then I heard the rain. My wristwatch had stopped working—I must have banged it on something

when I fell. I wondered how long I'd been out for. A half hour or
so, I thought. I put my hands to the floor and gave myself a heave.
A woodpecker was working in energetic slow motion on that
bone at the base of my skull. I felt around there with my fingertips. The swelling was hard and hot and as big as a boiled egg. I
foresaw the necessity for cold compresses and repeated doses of
aspirin: it was possible to be in pain and bored at the same time.

I still had my wallet, but the holster at my hip was empty.

Then I remembered Lynn Peterson. I looked around the kitchen,
checked the living room. She was gone. I hadn't really expected
her to be here, after the way López had looked at her. I paused to
take a deep breath before going into the bedroom, but she wasn't
there, either. The Mexicans had turned the house upside down,
and it looked as if a tornado had torn through it. They had emptied every drawer, ransacked every closet. The sofa had been sliced
open and its stuffing yanked out, likewise the mattress in the
bedroom. They'd sure been keen to find whatever it was they
were looking for. I had a hunch they hadn't found it.

Who was this guy Peterson? And where the hell was he, if he
was anywhere?

Wondering about Peterson and his whereabouts was a way of
staving off thoughts of Peterson's sister and *her* whereabouts.
That the Mexicans had taken her with them I didn't doubt. They'd
known who she was and hadn't been fooled by my fumbling
attempt to cover up her identity. But where had they taken her? I
had no idea. They could be well on the way to the border already.

I felt weak suddenly and sat down on the disemboweled sofa,
nursing my swollen and blood-caked cheek and trying to figure
out what to do next. I had no leads on the Mexicans, none. I hadn't
even seen their car, the one with the canvas roof with the holes in
it that Mr. Busybody across the way had described. I'd have to call
the cops; there was nothing else to do. I picked up the phone that
stood on a low table by the sofa, but it was dead—the service

would have been cut off weeks ago. I got out a handkerchief and started to wipe off the receiver, then gave up. What was the point? My prints were all over the place, on the knob of the back door, in the kitchen, here in the living room, in the bedroom—everywhere except the attic, if there was an attic. Anyway, why try to hide? I'd already talked to Joe Green about Peterson, and I intended to talk to him again about Peterson's sister, as soon as I worked up the energy to get myself off this sofa and back to the office.

I went out and around by the side of the house. How come it was raining again? It wasn't supposed to rain in June. Seeing that my car wasn't out front, I thought the Mexicans had stolen it, but then I remembered I had parked it down the street. When I got to it, I was wet already and smelled like a sheep—not that I've ever been near enough to a sheep to say what one smelled like. I made a U-turn and got on the boulevard. The rain was coming down now like polished steel rods, though the sky in the west was a cauldron of molten gold. The clock on the dashboard said it was six-fifteen, but that clock had never worked properly. Whatever time it was, the day had begun to end, or if not, my eyes were giving out.

I decided not to go to the office and headed instead for Laurel Canyon. When I got there, the dark was really coming on. The redwood steps up to the front door of my house had never seemed so many or so steep. Inside, I changed my shirt and jacket and went into the bathroom to have a look at my face. There was a dark red gash on my cheekbone, and the skin around it was all the colors of the rainbow and more. I swabbed it with a wet face towel. The cool of the water was soothing. It was going to be a long time before that swelling abated. The good part was that the cut wasn't deep enough to need stitching.

I went into the kitchen and mixed myself an old-fashioned, with brandy and a twist of lime. It took effort, but the effort was good for me and helped me to get myself in some sort of focus. I sat on a straight-backed chair in the breakfast nook—yes, the damned house had a breakfast nook—and sipped my drink and smoked a couple of cigarettes. The pain in my cheekbone was jockeying for the lead with the pain in the back of my head; I was in no condition to judge, but it seemed to be a dead heat.

I took down the receiver of the wall phone and dialed Central Homicide. Joe the Steadfast was at his desk. I told him what had happened at the house on Napier Street, or bits of it. He was skeptical.

"You say two Mexes turned up out of nowhere and kidnapped this broad? Is that what you're telling me?"

"Yes, Joe, that's what I'm telling you."

"Why'd they take her?"

"I don't know."

He was silent for a while. I heard him light a cigarette, I heard him blow out the first draw of smoke. "This Peterson again," he said in disgust. "Jesus Christ, Phil, I thought we'd cleared that one away?"

"So did I, Joe, so did I."

"Then what were you doing at his house?"

I took a second searching for the answer—any old answer. "There were some letters my client wanted collected." I stopped. It was the kind of lie that could get me into worse trouble than I was already in.

"You find them?"

"No."

I knocked back a good hard swallow of my drink. The sugar in it would give me energy, while the brandy would stop me from trying to use that energy to do strenuous things.

"And how come Peterson's sister is involved now?" Joe asked.

"I don't know. She arrived at the house just after I did."

"You knew her before?"

"No, I didn't."

Joe chewed on that for a while. "There's an awful lot here you're not telling me, Phil—that right?"

"I've told you all I know," I said, which we both knew was another lie. "The thing is, Joe, this business with Peterson's sister, it's got nothing to do with my end of things. This is other business, I'm sure of it."

"How can you be sure?"

"I just am. The Mexicans had been at Peterson's place before— they'd been seen scouting around outside the house, looking in the windows, that kind of thing. My guess is Peterson owes them money. They had the look of men who are owed, and owed big."

Another silence. Then: "The Peterson broad, she give you any clue as to why the Mexes were looking for her brother?"

"There wasn't time. She was fixing us a drink when they came in the back door waving guns and looking mean."

"Ooh," Joe cooed, "so the two of you was getting friendly, eh, even though it was the first time you met? Sounds real cozy."

"I got bopped, Joe, first with a gun barrel across the face, then with a blackjack or something on the back of the head. My eyes are still spinning in their sockets. These guys are for real."

"Okay, okay, I get it. But listen, Phil, this ain't my jurisdiction. I'm going to have to call in the Sheriff's office. You understand? Maybe you should have a quiet word with your pal Bernie Ohls over there."

"He's not exactly a pal, Joe."

"Sounds to me like you're going to need any kind of pal you can get, even the not exactly kind."

"I'd rather you called him," I said. "I'd appreciate it. I'm not at my best, and even at my best Bernie tends to get up my nose—or I tend to get up his, depending on the weather and the time of day."

Joe sighed into the mouthpiece. It sounded like a freight train going past my ear. "All right, Phil. I'll call him. But you better have your story straight when he comes knocking on your door. Bernie Ohls is no Joe Green."

You're right, Joe, I wanted to say, *you're certainly right there.* But all I did say was "Thanks. I owe you one."

"You owe me more than that, you son of a bitch," he said, laughing and coughing at the same time. Then he hung up. I lit another cigarette. It was the second time I'd been called a son of a bitch that day. It hadn't sounded any less of an insult in Spanish.

═ 13 ═

I was lying on top of the covers on my bed, drifting in and out of a sort of sleep, when Bernie arrived at my front door. It was as hard to get my head up as it had been in Nico Peterson's kitchen a few hours previously, though the bells that went off inside my skull didn't make quite as bad a din as before. In fact, I'd mistaken the sound of the doorbell for them when Bernie first pressed it. He rang it again almost immediately, and didn't take his finger off the button until he saw the light go on in the living room. "What the hell is all this, Marlowe?" he demanded, barging past me through the doorway.

"Yeah, good evening to you, too, Bernie."

He turned his big livid face and glared at me. "Still the smart lip, eh, Marlowe?"

"I try to keep it buttoned. But you know how lips are."

His face turned a darker shade still. I thought he might pop a gasket. "This feel like a joke to you?" he said in an ominously quiet voice.

"Take it easy, Bernie," I said, putting a hand gingerly to the back of my head. The swelling hadn't gone down any, but the boiled egg had cooled off quite a bit. "Sit down, have a drink."

"What happened to your face?"

"It came in contact with the barrel of a gun. At least the gun wasn't being fired at the time."

"That's going to be some bruise."

I've always been fascinated by the size of Bernie's head. Joe Green may have had a large-sized nut, but it had nothing on this guy's. And there was so much of it on top, from the eyes up. You know that type of English bread they call a cottage loaf, like two loaves, one stuck on top of the other? That was the shape of Bernie's noodle. Plus, it looked as if it was made not of dough but of lightly broiled beef that had been pounded into some sort of shape with a mallet.

He wore the regulation suit of dark blue flannel, no hat, and those black shoes they must make specially for cops, as broad as boats and with a rim of sole about a half inch wide all around. He makes a lot of noise, Bernie, and he has no great love for me, but all the same he's a straight-up fellow, the kind you'd be lucky to have beside you when a scrap breaks out. He's a good cop, too. Would have made captain long ago if the Sheriff hadn't rammed a heel on his neck and kept him from rising. I like Bernie, though I'd never take the risk of telling him so.

"I was drinking an old-fashioned earlier," I said. "You want one?"

"No. Gimme a soda."

While I fixed his drink he prowled the room, grinding the fist of his right hand into the palm of his left, like an old-time pharmacist working a mortar and pestle. "Tell me what happened," he said.

I told him, spinning the same version I'd given Joe Green. When I'd finished I said, "Bernie, will you sit down, please? You're making my headache worse, watching you walk up and down like that."

He took his glass of soda and ice and we sat down opposite each other at the table in the breakfast nook. I had made another brandy-and-sugar mess for myself. It couldn't do me anything but good.

"I put out an all-car alert for Lynn Peterson," he said. "Joe says you said the Mexicans were driving some sort of model made down there, big square jalopy with a canvas roof."

"So I'm told. I didn't see it myself."

Bernie was watching me with one eye half shut. "Who were you told by?"

"Old guy across the street. He's the neighborhood watchman, misses nothing."

"You talked to him today?"

"No—the other day, first time I went over there."

"Snooping on behalf of this nameless guy who's paying you, right?"

"If that's how you want to put it."

It tickled me that he thought my client was a man. Joe Green mustn't have bothered to fill him in on the details. That was good. The less Bernie knew, the better.

"You going to tell me who he is, and why he has you chasing Peterson?" I shook my head slowly; shaking it fast was out of the question, with that knot throbbing away at the back of my skull. "You know you're going to have to tell me sooner or later," he growled.

"If so, it'll be much later, probably after you've found out for yourself. I'm no snitch, Bernie. It's against my code of ethics."

He laughed. "Listen to him!" he hooted. "His code of ethics! What do you think you are, some kind of priest hearing people's confessions and guarding their secrets?"

"You know the score," I said. "I'm a professional, just like you." By now my cheek had swollen up so much I could see the bruised skin when I looked down. Bernie was right: my beauty was going to be marred for some time to come. "Anyway," I went on, "Lynn Peterson and the Mexicans, that's something different from the job I'm on. The two are not connected."

"How do you know?"

"I just do, Bernie," I said wearily. "I just do."

That got his anger going again. He's unpredictable that way: anything can set him off. His meaty face turned a light shade of purple. "Goddamn you, Marlowe," he said, "I ought to run you downtown right now and book you."

It's Bernie's policy, tried and tested over a long career: when in doubt, book 'em.

"Come off it, Bernie," I said, keeping it light. "You've got nothing on me, and you know it."

"What if I choose not to believe in these Mexican bandits and all the rest of the guff you've been feeding Joe Green and me?"

"Why would I make it up? Why would I report a woman missing if she wasn't?"

He banged his soda glass down on the table so hard that one of the ice cubes in it hopped out and skidded across the floor. "Why do you do anything you do? You're the most devious son of a bitch I know—and that's saying something."

I sighed. There it was again: me as the offspring of a female dog. Maybe they all knew something I didn't. My cheekbone and the back of my skull were pounding in unison now; it felt like a pair of jungle drummers were putting in a hard piece of practice inside my head, and I decided it was time to start easing Bernie off the premises. I stood up. "You'll call if you hear anything, won't you, Bernie?"

He stayed seated and looked up at me thoughtfully. "You and this Peterson broad," he said. "You sure you met for the first time today?"

"That's right." It was more or less true: my brief encounter with

her at the Cahuilla Club couldn't be called a meeting, and anyway, that was no business of his.

"It's not like you, Marlowe, to pass up an opportunity—good-
looking woman, empty house with a bedroom in it, that kind of
thing." Bernie's leer is a lot worse than his scowl. "You telling me
you didn't take what was on offer?"

"Nothing was on offer." And besides, what did he mean, it wasn't
like me? What did Bernie know about me in that line? Nothing. I
clenched a fist at my side, where he couldn't see it. He wasn't the
only one who could get mad. "I'm tired, Bernie," I said. "I've had a
hard day. I need to sleep."

He got to his feet, yanking at the waistband of his suit pants.
He was putting on fat and had a belly I hadn't noticed before. Well,
I wasn't getting any younger myself.

"Call if your patrol cars turn up anything, right?" I said.

"Why should I? You said whatever you're up to has nothing to
do with this business of the Mexicans and the missing woman."

"I'd like to know, all the same."

He put his head to one side and gave a sort of shrug. "Maybe
I'll call, maybe I won't," he said.

"Depending on what?"

"On how I feel." He stuck a finger into my chest. "You're trouble,
Marlowe, you know that? I should have nailed you in that Terry
Lennox business, when I had the chance."

Terry Lennox was a friend of mine who'd fled a murder rap—
the woman who got murdered was his wife—and then shot himself in a hotel room in Mexico, or so people like Bernie Ohls were
led to believe. There'd been nothing to nail me on then, either,
and Bernie knew it. He was just trying to get under my skin. I
wasn't going to let him. "Good night, Bernie," I said.

I put out a hand. He looked at it, looked at me, then shook it.
"You're lucky I'm a tolerant man," he said.

"I know that, Bernie." I spoke meekly. No point in making him mad all over again.

Bernie had got in his car and driven up to the turning circle at the end of the road when another set of headlights came raking along from the opposite direction. As Bernie passed the second car, he slowed down and tried to see the driver, then went on. I was starting to shut the front door when the car drew up and stopped at the bottom of my steps. I reached to the holster on my belt but then remembered that I had no gun. Anyway, it wasn't the Mexicans coming to call on me. The car was a red sports job, foreign, an Alfa Romeo, in fact, and there was only one person in it. I knew who it was before she opened the door and got out.

Ever notice how a woman walks up a set of steps? Clare Cavendish did it like they all do, keeping her head down and her eyes on her feet, which she placed neatly one in front of the other on each step going up. It was like watching an ice skater make a line of tiny figure eights.

"Well, hello," I said. She was on a level with me now and raised her head. She smiled. She wore a light coat and a head scarf and had on dark glasses, even though it was dark out. "I see you've come disguised."

Her smile faltered a little. "I wasn't sure," she said in confusion. "I mean, I didn't know if you'd be—I didn't know if you'd be home."

"Well, I am, as you see."

She took off her glasses and looked closely at my face. "What happened to you?" she asked in a breathy rush.

"Oh, this?" I said, touching a finger to my cheek. "Walked into a closet door. Come in."

I stood back and she went past me, still looking with concern at that purple-and-yellow bruise under my eye. I shut the door behind us. She took off the head scarf, and I helped her out of her coat. I smelled her perfume. I asked her what it was called, and she told me it was Langrishe Lace. I had myself convinced by now that I'd know it anywhere. "Care for a drink?" I asked.

She turned to me. She was blushing. "I hope you don't mind my coming," she said. "I expected to hear from you, and when I didn't . . ."

When you didn't, I thought, you decided to get in your little red sports car and come find out what Marlowe is doing to earn the money you're paying him—or not paying him, as it happened. "Sorry," I said. "I didn't have anything for you that was worth sharing. I was intending to call you in the morning, just to check in."

"Would you like me to go?" she asked in a suddenly hopeless voice.

"No," I said. "What gives you that idea?"

She relaxed a little, and smiled and bit her lip. "I don't often find myself at a loss, you know. You seem to have that effect on me."

"Is that good or bad?"

"I don't know. I'm trying to get accustomed to it, so I can judge."

I kissed her then, or she kissed me, or maybe we both had the same idea at the same time. She pressed her hands against my chest, but not to push me away, and I reached around and put my hands on her back and felt her shoulder blades, like a pair of neatly folded, warm wings.

"Have a drink," I said. My voice, I noticed, wasn't too steady.

"Maybe a little whiskey," she said. "With water, no ice."

"The English way," I said.

"The Irish, you mean." She smiled. "But just a drop, really."

She laid her cheek against my shoulder. I wondered if she knew about my talk with her mother. Maybe that was why she'd come, to find out what the old girl had said.

I moved away from her then and went to fix her drink. I poured a whiskey for myself, too, a stiff one. I needed it, though I wasn't sure how well it would mix with the brandy I'd been drinking earlier. When I turned back to her, she was looking around, taking it all in—the worn carpet, the drab furniture, the anonymous pictures in their cheap frames, the chessboard set up for a solitary game. You don't realize how narrow the space you're living in is until someone else steps inside it.

"So," she said, "this is your house."

"I rent it," I said, and heard how defensive it sounded. "From a Mrs. Paloosa. She moved to Idaho. Most of the stuff is hers—or the late Mr. Paloosa's." *Shut up, Marlowe, you're babbling.*

"And you have a piano," she said.

It stood in a corner, an old upright Steinway. I'd got so used to it being there that I'd stopped noticing it. She walked across and lifted the lid.

"Do you play?" I asked.

"A little." She blushed again, faintly.

"Play something for me."

She turned and gave me a startled look. "Oh, I couldn't do that."

"Why not?"

"Well, it would be—it would be vulgar. Besides, I'm not good enough to play for anyone but myself." She shut the lid. "And I'm sure it's out of tune."

I drank some of my whiskey. "Why don't we sit down," I said. "The couch is not as unfriendly as it looks."

We sat. She crossed her legs and rested the tumbler on her knee. She'd hardly touched the whiskey. Away in the distance, a police siren set up its wailing. I lit a cigarette. There are certain moments when you feel like you've been led to the edge of a cliff and abandoned there. I cleared my throat, then had to do it again because I really needed to. I was wondering how she'd got my address. I couldn't remember giving it to her—why would I have, anyway? I felt a little niggle of unease. Maybe it was all that space yawning below me, just beyond the cliff's edge.

"I know my mother spoke to you," Clare said. She was blushing again. "I hope it was all right. She can be a little overpowering."

"I liked her," I said. "I wasn't sure how she knew about me."

"Oh, Richard told her, of course. He tells her everything. Sometimes I feel as if he's married to her instead of to me. What did she say? Do you mind my asking?"

"I don't mind at all. She wanted to know why you'd hired me."

"You didn't tell her?" She sounded alarmed. I looked at her stonily and said nothing. She dropped her eyes. "Sorry," she said, "that was stupid of me."

I stood up and went to the drinks cabinet and poured myself another slug of whiskey. I didn't sit down again. "You know, Mrs. Cavendish," I said, "I'm all confused here. Maybe I shouldn't confess it, but I am."

"Aren't you ever going to call me Clare?" she asked, looking up at me out of those great eyes, those very kissable lips of hers parted a little.

"I'm working on it," I said.

I turned away and did a bit of pacing, just like Bernie a while ago. Clare watched me. "Why are you confused?" she asked finally.

"Because I can't figure it out. I don't know what to think. Why do you want to track down Nico Peterson? Did you care for him that much? From even the little I've learned about him, he doesn't seem your type at all. And even if you were crazy about him, wouldn't you be perhaps a tad disillusioned that he tricked you by pretending to be dead? And why would he do that, anyway? Why would he need to disappear?"

I was standing in front of her again, looking down. I noticed that the knuckles of her hand that was holding the glass were white. "You've got to give me some help, Mrs. Cavendish, if I'm to keep on searching for him, and if I'm going to call you Clare."

"What kind of help?" she asked.

"Any kind you can come up with."

She nodded distractedly, looking around the room again. "Have you got family?" she asked.

"No."

"Parents?"

"I said no. Lost them early."

"No brother, sisters? Cousins, even?"

"Cousins, maybe. I don't keep in touch."

She shook her head. "That's sad."

"What's sad about it?" I said, sudden anger making my voice go husky. "To you a solitary life is unimaginable. You're like one of those big fancy cruise ships, clambered all over by sailors, stewards, engineers, fellows in crisp uniforms with braid on their caps. You have to have all this maintenance, not to mention beautiful people dressed in white playing games on the deck. But see that little skiff heading off toward the horizon, the one with the black sail? That's me. And I'm happy out there."

She set the glass on the arm of the couch, taking a lot of care to make sure it was balanced right, then got to her feet. There was hardly more than a couple of inches separating us. She put up a hand and touched the bruise on my cheek with her fingers. "So hot," she murmured, "your poor skin, so hot." I could see little silvery flecks deep in the irises of her black eyes. "Is there a bed somewhere in this house?" she asked softly. "Do you think Mrs. Paloosa would mind if we lay down in it for a while, you and me?"

That throat of mine needed an awful lot of clearing tonight. "I'm sure she wouldn't," I said thickly. "Who's going to tell her, anyway."

14

There was a lamp in the bedroom, on the bedside table, with roses painted on the shade. The painting was pretty crude, done by an amateur. I'd been meaning to get rid of the thing, but somehow I never had. It wasn't that I was attached to it. It was a piece of kitsch, like so many of the other things Mrs. Paloosa stuffed her house with. She was a collector of knickknacks, Mrs. P. Or maybe *accumulator* is a better word—she'd accumulated all this crap, and now I was stuck with it. Not that I noticed it much. Most of it had faded into the background, and I hardly registered it anymore. That lamp, though, was the last thing I saw at night, when I switched it off, and in the darkness an image of it would stay printed on the back of my eyes for quite a while. What was it Oscar Wilde said about the wallpaper in the room where he was dying? One of us will have to go.

Now I lay on my back, with my face turned sideways on the pillow, staring at those roses. They looked as if they were painted with thick globs of strawberry jam that subsequently dried out and lost its sheen. I'd just made love to one of the most beautiful

women I'd ever been allowed to get my arms around, but never-
theless I wasn't at ease. The fact was, Clare Cavendish was out of
my league, and I knew it. She had class, she had money to burn,
she was married to a polo player, and she drove an Italian sports
car. What the hell was she doing in bed with me?

I didn't know she was awake, but she was. She must have been
reading my thoughts again, because she asked, in her sultry way,
"Do you sleep with all your clients?"

I turned my head toward hers on the pillow. "Only the female
ones," I said.

She smiled. The best and loveliest smiles have a hint of melancholy in them. Hers was like that. "I'm glad I came over tonight,"
she said. "I was so nervous, and then you looked so coldly at me
when I arrived, I thought I should turn around and leave."

"I was nervous, too," I said. "I'm glad you stayed."

"Well, I've got to go now."

She kissed me on the tip of my nose and sat up. Her breasts
were so small they were hardly there when she was lying down.
The sight of them made my mouth go dry. They were sort of flat
along the top and plump underneath, and the tips of them were
turned up in a delightful way that made me smile. "When will I
see you again?" I asked. On these occasions, there's nothing original to say.

"Soon, I hope."

She had turned sideways and was sitting on the side of the bed
with her back to me, putting on her stockings. It was a beautiful
back, long, slim, tapered. I wanted a cigarette, but I don't smoke
in bed after lovemaking, ever.

"What will you do now?" I asked.

She looked at me over her bare shoulder. "What do you mean?"

"It's two o'clock in the morning," I said. "You're hardly in the
habit of coming home at that hour, are you?"

"Oh, you mean will Richard be wondering where I am? He's

out somewhere, with one of his girls, I imagine. I told you: we have an understanding."

"*Arrangement,* I think, was the word you used."

She was facing away from me again, fiddling with fasteners. "Arrangement, understanding—what's the difference?"

"Call me a quibbler, but I think there is a difference."

She stood up and stepped into her skirt and zipped it at the side. I like to watch women getting dressed. Of course, it's not as much fun as watching them getting undressed. It's more of an aesthetic experience. "Anyway," she said, "he's out and won't know what time I came home. Not that he'd care."

I'd noticed before how she spoke of her husband, matter-of-factly, without bitterness. That marriage, it was clear, had died and been buried a long time ago. But if she thought even an estranged husband wasn't capable of being jealous any longer, she didn't know men.

"What about your mother?" I asked. I was sitting up myself now.

She was fastening the buckle of a big leather belt, but she stopped and looked at me in puzzlement. "My mother? What about her?"

"Won't she hear you coming in?"

She laughed. "You've been to the house," she said. "Didn't you notice how big it is? We each have a wing to ourselves, her on one side, Richard and me on the other."

"What about your brother—where does he hang out?"

"Rett? Oh, he sort of floats."

"What does he do?"

"How do you mean? Is my other shoe on that side of the bed? God, we did fling ourselves about, didn't we."

I leaned over the side, found her shoe, gave it to her. "I mean, does he work?" I asked.

This time she threw me an arch look. "Rett doesn't need to *work,*" she said, as if explaining something to a child. "He's the apple of his mother's eye, and that's all he needs to do, stay apple-cheeked and sweet."

"He didn't seem very sweet to me."

"He didn't need to, to you."

"You don't much like him, I can see."

She paused again, thinking about it. "I love him, of course—he's my brother, after all, even if we have different fathers. But no, I don't think I like him. Maybe I will, if he grows up one day. But I doubt that's going to happen. Or not while Mother is alive, anyway."

It seemed rude, sitting there in bed while she was busily preparing herself to face the world, even if it was the world of night, so I got up and started getting dressed myself.

I had my shirt on when she stepped close and kissed me. "Good night, Philip Marlowe," she said. "Or good morning, I suppose that should be." She began to turn away, but I held her by the elbow.

"What did your mother say about talking to me?" I asked.

"What did she say?" She shrugged. "Not much."

"I'm wondering why you didn't ask me what she said. You're not curious?"

"I did ask you."

"But not like you really wanted to know."

She turned around to face me and gave me a level look. "All right, then, what did she say?"

I grinned. "Not much."

She didn't grin back. "Really?"

"She told me how perfume is made. And she told me about your father, how he died."

"That's a cruel story."

"One of the cruelest. She's a tough lady, to get over a thing like that and go on to do all she's done."

Her mouth tightened a little. "Oh, yes. She's tough, all right."

"Do you like *her*?"

"Don't you think you've asked me enough questions for one night?"

I held up my hands. "You're right," I said, "I have. It's just . . ."

She waited. "Well? It's just what?"

"It's just that I don't know whether to trust you or not."

She smiled coldly, and for a second I saw her mother in her, her tough mother. "Make a Pascalian wager," she said.

"Who's Pascal?"

"Frenchman. Long time ago. Philosopher, of a sort." She walked out to the living room. I followed her. I was barefoot. She picked up her purse and turned to me. Anger had made her go pale. "How can you say you don't trust me?" she said and nodded toward the bedroom door. "How can you, after *that*?"

I went and poured myself yet another whiskey, my back turned to her. "I didn't say I don't trust you, I said I don't know whether to trust you or not."

This made her so angry that she actually stamped her foot. I had an image of Lynn Peterson stopping in the doorway of her brother's house and doing the same thing, for a different reason. "You know what you are?" she said. "You're a pedant. Do you know what a pedant is?"

"A peasant with a lisp?"

She was fairly glaring at me. Who'd have thought eyes of that color could generate such fire? "And what you're not is a comic."

"I'm sorry," I said. It probably didn't sound as if I meant it. "I'll get your coat."

I held it open for her. She just stood there, still glaring at me, a little muscle rippling in her jaw. "I see I was wrong about you," she said.

"In what way?"

"I thought you were—oh, never mind."

She put her arms into the coat sleeves. I could have made her

turn around; I could have embraced her, could have said I was
sorry and said it so there was no question but that I meant it.
Because I was sorry. I could have bitten off my tongue. She was
maybe the loveliest thing that had happened so far in my life, love-
lier even than Linda Loring, and here I was, with my big mouth,
questioning her trustworthiness and making cheap cracks. That's
Marlowe for you, the Indian who throws away a pearl richer than
all his tribe.

"Listen," I said, "something happened today."

She turned back to me, looking worried suddenly, and wary.
"Oh?" she said. "What?"

I told her how I had gone to Peterson's house, how Lynn had
come in while I was searching the place, how the Mexicans
had arrived, and the rest of it. I made it short, with no frills. While
I was speaking, she kept her eyes fixed on my mouth, as though
she were lip-reading.

When I finished she stood motionless, blinking slowly. "But
why," she said in a dead-sounding voice. "Why didn't you tell me
all this before now?"

"There were other things going on."

"My God." She paused, shaking her head. "I don't understand
you. All this evening when"—she waved a hand in a helpless
gesture—"the bedroom, all that—how could you not tell me—how
could you keep it from me?"

"I wasn't 'keeping it from you,'" I said. "What was happening,
with you and me, just seemed more important."

She shook her head again in angry disbelief. "Who were they,"
she asked, "these Mexicans?"

"They were after Nico. I had the impression he had something
of theirs or owed them something—money, I suppose. You know
anything about that?"

She made another gesture with her hand, impatiently dismissive this time. "Of course not." She glanced in desperation about

the room, then looked at me again. "Is that what happened to your face?" she asked. "Was it the Mexicans who did that to you?" I nodded. She thought about this, trying to add things up, to figure them out. "And now they have Lynn. Will they harm her?"

"They're a pretty tough pair," I said.

She put a hand to her mouth. "My God," she repeated, in the barest whisper. It was all too much for her; she was having difficulty even taking it in. "And the police," she said, "the police came?"

"Yes. A fellow I know, out of the Sheriff's office. That was him driving away when you arrived."

"He was here? Did you tell him about me?"

"Of course I didn't. He has no idea who you are, who I'm working for. And he never will, unless he puts me in front of a grand jury, and he's not going to do that."

She was blinking again, even more slowly than before. "I'm frightened," she murmured. But as well as the fear there was a kind of wonderment in her voice, the wonderment of a person who can't understand how she could get herself into such a mess.

"There's no need for you to be scared," I said. I tried to touch her arm, but she drew back quickly, as if my fingers would soil the sleeve of her coat.

"I must go home now," she said coldly and turned away.

I walked behind her down the redwood steps. The cold blast coming back from her should have hung icicles in my eyebrows. She climbed into the car and had hardly slammed the door shut before she had the engine going. She drove off in a cloud of exhaust smoke that got into my mouth and stung my nostrils. I climbed the steps, clearing my throat, yet again. Nice work, Phil, I said to myself in disgust; nice work.

I was on the last few steps when the phone started to ring. Whoever it was, at this time of night, wouldn't be calling with glad tidings. I got to the phone just as the bell stopped. I swore.

I swear a lot when I'm home alone. It sort of humanizes the place, I don't know how.

I finished my drink, then carried my glass into the kitchen along with Clare's and washed them both at the sink and set them upside down on the rack to dry. I was tired. My face ached, and the tom-toms had started up again at the back of my head.

I was still complimenting myself bitterly on the nice job I'd done tonight with Clare when the phone rang again. It was Bernie Ohls. Somehow I'd known it was going to be Bernie.

"Where the hell were you?" he barked. "I thought you must be dead."

"I stepped out for a minute to commune with the stars."

"Very romantic." He paused—for effect, I suppose. "We found the dame."

"Lynn Peterson?"

"No—Lana Turner."

"Tell me."

"Get up here and see for yourself. Encino Reservoir. Come along Encino Avenue, take a right when you see the 'No Entry' sign. And bring your smelling salts—it ain't a pretty sight."

= 15 =

I drove with the window open. The cool night air was soft on my swollen cheek, but not as soft as Clare Cavendish's fingers had been, earlier, before I'd ruined everything and sent her off into the night, frightened and angry. I couldn't get her out of my head. It was just as well, since thinking of her meant I didn't have to think about Nico Peterson's sister and what was likely to be waiting for me at the reservoir. I also didn't care to dwell on the fact that I'd made a bad mistake by getting those two Mexicans mad at me. If I hadn't, if I'd kept cool and found a way around them, maybe I could have prevented them from taking the woman. Unlikely, but not impossible. But that was something to feel guilty about another time, not now.

It wasn't much of a drive up to Encino, and even though the streets wer. empty I dawdled along, not at all anxious to get there before I had to. Terry Lennox used to live in Encino, in a big fake English mansion on a couple of acres of choice real estate. That was in the days when his wife was still alive and he was

married to her again—they'd got together twice, which must be
some kind of definition of double trouble.

I still missed Terry. He was a disaster area all to himself, but
he was my friend, and in this world, in my world, that's a rare
thing—I don't do friendship easily. I wondered where he was now
and what he was up to. Last I'd heard of him, he was in Mexico
somewhere, spending his late wife's money. There probably wasn't
too much of it left by now, I thought, Terry being the kind of
spender he was. I told myself that one of these days I'd drink a
gimlet in his honor again over at Victor's. It used to be our haunt,
Terry's and mine, and I went there a couple of times and raised a
toast to him when I thought he was dead. Terry had us all fooled,
for a while.

I was so tired I nearly drove smack into the "No Entry" sign.
I turned right and straightaway saw the lights up ahead. There
were two patrol cars parked nose to nose at the side of the road,
as well as Bernie's beat-up Chevy and an ambulance with its back
doors open and the light pouring out. It was a strange scene, out
here in these lonely parts, under the sentinel pines.

I pulled in, and when I got out of the car my lower back nearly
seized up, I was so stiff after that drive. I thought longingly of my
bed, even without Clare Cavendish in it. I'm getting too old for
this kind of work.

Bernie was standing with a guy in a white coat who I thought
might be either a medic or one of the coroner's men. At their feet
there was something body-shaped, covered up with a blanket. I
had a cigarette going, but I dropped it on the ground and trod
on it. After I had gone a few steps I had to backtrack and make
sure it was fully out. It would be one thing to burn down West
Hollywood, as the old guy on Nico Peterson's street had warned
me I was in danger of doing, but Encino was a different matter.
A blaze in Encino would knock a large hole in the funds of half
the insurance companies in Los Angeles County and beyond. Terry

Lennox's house—or, rather, his wife's house—had been worth a hundred grand or more. But I needn't have worried—the ground was soaked after all that recent rain, and everything smelled sodden and resinous.

Not far from Bernie were three or four cops in uniform and a couple of plainclothes guys in hats, playing the beams of their flashlights over the ground. Pine needles glinted in the light. I had the impression that no one's heart was in the search. A couple of Mexicans in a car would be long gone across the border by now, and no number of clues would be likely to lead to them.

"What took you so long?" Bernie said.

"I made a few stops to admire the scenery and think poetic thoughts."

"Sure you did. Come on—what have you been doing since I was at your place?"

"Catching up on my needlepoint," I said. I looked at the blanket-covered body on the ground. "That her?"

"According to her driver's license. Identification ain't going to be easy." He lifted back a corner of the blanket with the toe of one of those clumpy shoes of his. "Don't ya think?"

The Mexicans had done a job on her, all right. She had a lot more face than when I'd last seen her; it was swollen like a pumpkin and black and blue all over. The features weren't all in the right place, either. Plus, a sort of deep second mouth had been carved into her throat, under her chin. That would have been López, with his little knife. For a second I saw Lynn again in my mind, standing by the sink in Peterson's house with the ice tray in her hands and turning to tell me where to look for the bottles of Canada Dry.

"Who found her?" I asked.

"Couple of kids in a car looking for a quiet place to do some serious necking."

"How did she die?"

Bernie gave a sort of laugh. "Look at her—what do you think?"

The guy in the white coat spoke: "There's a deep continuous transverse wound to the anterior triangles of the neck, cutting both venous and arterial structures, not compatible with life."

I stared at him. He was an old guy; he'd seen it all and seemed tired, like me.

"Sorry," Bernie said offhandedly, "this is Dr.— What'd you say it was?"

"Torrance."

"This is Dr. Torrance. Doc, meet Philip Marlowe, ace detective." He turned to me. "What he means is, her throat was cut. By the time it happened, I'd say it was a mercy." He put an arm through mine, turned me with him, and we walked off a little ways. "Tell me the truth, Marlowe," he said quietly. "This dame mean something to you?"

"I met her today—yesterday—for the first time. Why?"

"The doc says these guys had a lot of fun with her. You know what I mean? That was before they started on her with the lit cigarettes and the knuckle-dusters and the knife. I'm sorry."

"I'm sorry too, Bernie. But it's no good—you're not going to get anywhere with this line. I never met her but the once, and we'd barely exchanged a dozen words before the Mexicans burst in."

"You were having a drink with her."

I rescued my arm from his. "That wouldn't have put us in the market for an engagement ring. I have drinks with all kinds of people, all the time. I bet you do, too."

He stood back and looked at me. "She must have been a fine-looking broad, before the Mexes got at her."

"Bernie, leave it." I sighed. "I didn't know Lynn Peterson, not in the way you're suggesting."

"Okay, you didn't know her. She walks in on you while you're shaking down her brother's house—"

"For Christ's sake, Bernie, I wasn't 'shaking it down'!"

"Anyway, she walks in on you, next thing two Mexes come in after her, bop you on the head, and hightail it with her in their evil clutches. Now she's dead on the side of a lonely road in Encino. If you were me, you think you'd say, 'It's fine, Phil, don't worry about it, toddle off about your business, I'm sure you're not connected in any way with this unfortunate lady's murder, even though you were searching for her supposed-to-be-dead brother'? Well, would you?"

I sighed again. It wasn't just because I'd had my fill of Ohls's insinuations—I was bone tired. "All right, Bernie," I said. "I know you're only doing your job, it's what they pay you for. But you're going to waste a whole lot of time, and make yourself annoyed and upset, if you keep on trying to link me with this."

"You *are* linked with it," Bernie almost shouted. "You're the one who went snooping around looking for this Peterson party, and now his sister is dead. What's that if not a link?"

"I know she's dead. You just showed her to me, and Albert Schweitzer over there spelled it out in gory detail. But listen to me, Bernie: it's got nothing to do with me. You really have to believe that. I'm what they call an innocent bystander." Bernie snorted. "I am, honest," I said. "It happens, you know that. You're at the teller's window in the bank and two robbers run in behind you and snatch every last dime in the vault and shoot the manager dead before making off with the loot. The fact that you were doing a bit of business there, putting money in your account or taking some out, that doesn't mean you're connected to the robbery. Does it?"

Bernie thought it over, biting the side of his thumb. He knew I was right, but in a case like this, all cops hate letting go of the one possible lead they think they have. At last he gave a disgusted snarl and flapped a hand at me as if he were swatting a fly. "Go on," he said, "get out of here. I'm sick of you, you sanctimonious clown."

It wasn't nice, being called names. Sanctimonious I could take, but to be cast in the role of Coco of the red nose and the size twenty shoes, that was another thing. "I'm going home now, Bernie," I said, keeping my voice nice and quiet, even respectful. "I've had a long and difficult day, and I need to lay my sore head down and rest. If I find out anything about Nico Peterson, or his sister, or any of his family or friends, and if I think it would be pertinent to this case, I promise I won't keep it from you. All right?"

"Go boil your head," he said. Then he turned away from me and walked back to where Torrance the medic was directing the stowing of Lynn Peterson's broken body into the back of the ambulance.

=== 16 ===

I thought that was the end of the business. Bernie drew a blank on the Mexicans, as I knew he would. He said he'd contacted a friend of his in the border police in Tijuana about the possible whereabouts of Gómez and López, but the friend hadn't been any help. A couple of things surprised me about this. First, that Bernie had a friend, and in Tijuana, of all places. Second, that there were border police down there. So that's what those guys are at the crossing, the ones in khaki shirts with sweat-stained armpits who look at you with bored eyes and wave you through, hardly bothering to take the toothpicks out of their mouths. I must remember to show them more respect, next time I drift down Mexico way.

Anyway, I don't know how much of an effort Bernie made trying to track down Lynn Peterson's killers. She hadn't been anyone much, not like Clare Cavendish, for instance. It turned out Lynn had been a dancer and had worked around the clubs in Bay City. I knew a bit about that kind of life, the grift and the grind of it. I could imagine how it had been for her. The guys with curly hair on the backs of their hands trying to paw you all the time. The night managers who applied their own, unofficial conditions of employment. The drink and the drugs, the bleary late-night weariness, and ash-colored dawns in cheap hotel rooms. I had liked her, the little I'd seen of her. She'd deserved better out of life, and out of death.

I had to make myself stop thinking about the two Mexicans. The kind of smoldering rage I felt against them burns into the soul. You have to cut your losses and move on. The gash on my cheek was healing nicely, and the lump at the back of my skull had shrunk to no more than the size of a pigeon's egg.

A couple of days later, I went to Lynn's funeral. It was held at a mortician's in Glendale, I don't know why—maybe that's where she had been living. She'd been cremated, like her brother. The ceremony took about three minutes. There were only two mourners present, me and a distracted old girl with wire-wool hair and a pinched-up lipstick mouth painted crookedly over her real one. Afterward I tried to talk to her, but she shied away from me as if she thought I might be a brush salesman. She said she had to get home, that her cat would be hungry by now. When she wasn't speaking, she kept moving that painted-on mouth in a sort of silent mumble. I wondered who she was—not Lynn's mother, I was fairly sure of that. An aunt, maybe, or maybe just her landlady. I wanted to ask her about Lynn, but she wouldn't stay, and I didn't try to keep her. A hungry cat has to be fed.

I drove back to the office and parked the Olds. Outside the door of the Cahuenga Building a skinny young guy in a red-and-green checked jacket and a porkpie hat peeled himself away from the wall and stepped in front of me. "You Marlowe?" He had a thin, sallow face with prominent cheekbones and eyes of no particular color.

"I'm Marlowe," I said. "Who are you?"

"The boss wants to talk to you." He glanced past my shoulder to where a big black car was parked at the curb.

I sighed. When a guy like that stops you dead on the way to your place of work and informs you that his employer desires an interview with you, you know it's trouble. "And who's your boss?" I asked.

"Just get in the car, willya?" He opened the right-hand flap of his jacket an inch or two and let me see something black and shiny in there, tucked snugly into a shoulder holster.

I strolled over to the car. It was a Bentley, right-hand drive. Someone must have imported it from England. The kid with the persuader under his arm opened the rear door and stood back to let me climb inside. As I leaned down I thought for a second he was going to put his hand on the top of my head, the way the cops do in the movies, but something in my eye told him not to go too far. He shut the door behind me. It made a rich, heavy clunk, like the door of a bank vault closing. Then he went back to his perch by the wall.

I had a look around the car. There was a lot of chrome and highly polished walnut. The pale cream upholstery had that new-leather smell that's always particularly strong in these expensive English models. In front, sitting at the wheel, was a black man wearing a chauffeur's cap. He hadn't made a move when I got in but had kept looking straight ahead, through the windshield, though I did catch his eye in the rearview mirror for a second. It wasn't a friendly eye.

I turned to the fellow beside me. "So," I said. "What do you want to talk about?"

He smiled. It was a warm, expansive smile, the smile of a happy and successful man. "You know who I am?" he asked pleasantly.

"Yes," I said, "I know who you are. You're Lou Hendricks."

"Good!" The smile grew broader still. "I hate the bother of introductions, don't you?" He had a plummy, put-on British accent. "Such a waste of precious time."

"Sure," I said, "jolly tedious, for busy chaps like us."

He didn't seem to mind being mocked. "Yes," he said easily, "you're Marlowe, all right, I've heard of your smart mouth."

He was a large man, large enough to seem to be filling one whole side of the rear section of this overlarge car. He had a head the shape of a shoe box, sitting on three or four folds of fat in the place where there used to be a chin, and a flap of thick hair dyed the color of oiled teak was plastered sideways across his flat skull. His eyes were small and gleamed merrily. He wore a double-breasted suit cut from many yards of lavender-colored silk and a fluffed-up crimson tie with a pearl pin stuck in it. For a hoodlum, he sure was a fancy dresser. I wouldn't have been surprised to glance down and see that he was wearing spats. Lovely Lou, they called him, behind his back. He owned a casino out in the desert. He was one of the big boys in Vegas, along with Randy Starr and a couple of other tough nuts in the gambling racket. They said he ran plenty of things besides the Paramount Palace: prostitutes, drugs, things like that. He was quite a boy, our Lou.

"I'm reliably informed," he said, "that you're looking for someone I'd be interested to hear something of myself."

"Oh? Who would that be?"

"A man called Peterson. Nico Peterson. Ring a sonorous bell, does it, that name?"

"I think I hear a tinkle, all right," I said. "Who's your reliable informant?"

His smile turned roguish. "Ah, now, Mr. Marlowe—you wouldn't reveal a source, why should you expect it of me?"

"You have a point there." I got out my case, took out a cigarette, but didn't light it. "I'm sure you know," I said, "that Nico Peterson is dead."

He nodded, making those supplementary chins wobble. "So we all thought," he said. "But now it seems we may all have been wrong."

I played with the unlit cigarette, turning it in my fingers and so on. I was trying to figure out how he knew Peterson had been spotted when he was supposed to be dead. Hendricks didn't seem the type who would be acquainted with Clare Cavendish. Who else had I talked to about Peterson? Joe Green and Bernie Ohls, and Travis the bartender, and the old guy who lived opposite the house on Napier Street. Who else? But maybe that was enough. The world is porous; things trickle through all by themselves, or so it always seems.

"You think he's alive?" I asked, still playing for time. He did his gloating, merry smile, wrinkling up the corners of his bright little eyes.

"Oh, come on, Mr. Marlowe," he said. "I'm a busy man, and I'm sure you are, too. We started out so briskly, but now you're positively dragging your feet." He heaved himself about, beached-whale fashion, and got a large white handkerchief from his pocket and blew his nose with a honk. "The smog in this city," he said, putting the handkerchief away and shaking his head. "It plays havoc with my air passages." He peered at me. "Does it trouble you?"

"Some," I said. "But I've got trouble in that department already."

"Oh, yes?"

Suddenly he didn't seem to mind wasting time.

"Smashed septum," I said, tapping a finger to the bridge of my nose.

"Tut tut, that must have been painful. How did it happen?"

"College days, football tackle, then a joke doctor who broke the nose again, worse, trying to fix it."

"Dear me." Hendricks shuddered. "I can hardly bear to think of it." All the same, I could see him wanting to hear more. I recalled his reputation as a hypochondriac. How is it that the life of crime breeds so many genuine oddballs?

"You know Peterson's sister got killed," I said.

"Yes, indeed. Came in contact with a couple of truculent persons from the south, so I hear."

"You're very well informed, Mr. Hendricks. The papers didn't say where the killers were from."

He simpered, as if I'd paid him a big compliment. "Oh, I keep an ear to the ground," he said modestly. "You know how it is." He picked an invisible speck of something from the sleeve of his suit. "You think those southern gentlemen were also after her brother? You did run across them, didn't you?" He tut-tutted again. "Or, rather, I think, they ran across you—that bruise on your cheek speaks volumes."

He looked at me with sympathy. He was a man who would know about pain—the kind that gets inflicted on others, that is. Then he turned businesslike. "Anyway, back to the matter in hand—I really would appreciate a word with our friend Nico, if indeed he is still with us. You see, he used to run regular errands for me down in the land of the sombrero and the mule—nothing serious, just some little items hard to come by up here, where the laws are so unnecessarily strict. At the time of his supposed death, he had something of mine that's since gone missing."

"A suitcase?" I said.

Hendricks gave me a long, careful look, his eyes glittering. Then he relaxed, letting his square, lavender-draped frame sink back against the soft leather of the seat. "Shall we have a drive?" he said, then spoke to the black man in the front. "Cedric, take us for a spin around the park, will you?"

Cedric met my eye again in the rearview mirror. It seemed a little less unfriendly this time. I guess by now he knew there was nothing about me he needed to be resentful of. He steered the car away from the curb. The engine must have been idling all the time, but I hadn't heard a sound. The British sure know how to build cars. Turning back, I caught a glimpse of the kid in the pork-pie hat snapping away from the wall and lifting an urgent arm, but neither Cedric nor his employer took any notice. Muscle like that are a dime a dozen.

We whispered out into the traffic on Cahuenga, heading south at a steady twenty-five. It was strange to be moving in such a big car so quietly. Car rides in dreams are like that. Hendricks opened a walnut cabinet built into the door beside him and took out a tube of something, unscrewed the top, squeezed out an inch of thick white unguent, and began working it into his hands. The perfume that the stuff gave off seemed familiar. I glanced at the label: "Lily of the Valley Hand Lotion," by Langrishe. It might have been an interesting coincidence, except that most of the folks in this town who lived above the breadline used Langrishe products. That was how it seemed to me, anyway—ever since I'd met Clare Cavendish, that damned perfume was everywhere.

"Tell me," Hendricks said, "how did you know it was a suit-case I was interested in?"

I looked away from him, out at the houses and the storefronts we were passing by along Cahuenga. What could I say to him? I didn't know where the word had come from; it had just popped out, surprising even me. In fact, it wasn't *suitcase* that had come to my mind but the Spanish word *maleta*, and I had automatically translated it.

Maleta. Who had I heard saying that? It could only have been the Mexicans. I must have been still hearing in some sort of way even after Gómez had whacked me on the bean with his burly silver gun in Nico's house and sent me in a heap to the floor. They must have begun grilling Lynn Peterson as I lay at their feet with stars and twittering birds circling my head, like Sylvester the Cat after he's been socked by Tweety Pie.

Hendricks had begun drumming his sausage-shaped fingers

on the leather armrest beside him. "I'm waiting for you to answer me, Mr. Marlowe," he said, still sounding pleasant and nice. "How did you know it was a suitcase? Did you speak with Nico, maybe? Did you catch sight of the article in question?"

"I took a guess," I said lamely and looked away again.

"Then you must be clairvoyant. That's a useful gift to have."

Cedric had steered us off Cahuenga, and we were traveling westward now along Chandler Boulevard. Nice street, Chandler, nothing mean about it: it's broad and clean and well lighted at night. It wasn't the park, though; that had just been one of Hendricks's little fancies. He was a playful fellow, I could see that.

"Look, Hendricks," I said, "will you please tell me what this is about? Say Peterson had your suitcase, say he died and you lost it, or he didn't die and he took it. What's that got to do with me?"

He gave me a mournful look, seeming sadly offended. "I told you," he said. "Peterson gets himself dead, then suddenly he's not dead, and next I hear you're on his trail. That interests me. When I have an inquisitive itch, I have to scratch it—if you'll forgive the indelicacy."

"What was in the suitcase?"

"I told you that, too."

"No, you didn't."

"You want a detailed inventory, is that it?"

"Doesn't have to be detailed."

His face had turned ugly, and suddenly he reminded me of a fat boy I knew at college, name of Markson, if I recall. Markson was a rich man's son, spoiled and of a testy temperament. He colored easily, just like Hendricks, especially when he was annoyed or was told he couldn't have something he wanted. He moved on after a couple of semesters—kicked out, some said, for smuggling a girl into his room and beating her up. I don't like the Marksons of this world; in fact, they're one of the reasons I'm in the business I'm in.

"Are you going to tell me what I want to know?" Hendricks said.

"Tell me what it is and maybe I will. Or maybe I won't."

He was looking at me and shaking his head. "You're a stubborn man, Mr. Marlowe."

"So I'm told."

"I could get seriously irritated by you—by your manner, if nothing else. I'm thinking perhaps I should tell Cedric here to turn back and go pick up Jimmy—Jimmy is the young man in the unfortunate hat who invited you into the car. Jimmy carries out for me the more—what shall we say?—the more messy chores."

"That gunsel lays a finger on me I'll break his back," I said.

Hendricks widened his piggy little eyes. "Oh-ho!" he said. "How very tough we are all of a sudden."

"I don't know about us," I said, "but I am, when I need to be."

Now Hendricks chuckled. It made him wobble all over, like Jell-O dressed up in a suit. "You're a two-bit snooper," he said, without raising his voice. "Have you any idea of the things I could have my people do to you? Young Jimmy may not impress you much, but I assure you, Marlowe, there are more Jimmys where he came from, and each one is bigger and nastier than the last."

I tapped the Negro on the shoulder. "You can drop me here, Cedric. Like to stretch my legs."

He ignored me, of course, and drove blithely on.

Hendricks sat back in the seat and kneaded his hands—without lotion, this time. "Let's not fall out, Mr. Marlowe," he said. "When we picked you up outside your office, you didn't have the look of a man bent on urgent business, so why the hurry now? Stay a while, enjoy the ride. We can speak of other things, if you like. What topics interest you?"

It occurred to me he'd fit in well at the Cahuilla Club, with his phony British voice and his prissy manners. I wondered if maybe he was already a member there. Then it came to me:

Floyd Hanson must have told him about me. How could I have forgotten my visit to the Cahuilla Club and my talk there with the manager? I still had that cigarette in my fingers, and now I lit it. Hendricks frowned, pressed a button on the armrest, and cracked open the window beside him. I blew some smoke in his direction, as if by accident.

"Maybe we can do a swap," I said. "You tell me what you know about Peterson's death, and I'll tell you what I know about him coming back to life." It was a long shot, especially since what I knew about Peterson, dead or alive, amounted to a very small hill of beans—in fact, it wasn't even that; there was no hill, and the few beans I had were dry and tasteless. Still, you've got to try.

Hendricks was watching me, watching and thinking. I guess he was counting his beans, too. "All I know about it," he said, "or what I was told, at least, is that the poor chap was run over one dark night in Pacific Palisades by a very irresponsible driver who didn't stop."

"Did you go up there and have a look at where it happened?"

He frowned again. "Why?" he said. "Should I have?" His frown this time was prompted by worry and not disapproval of my cigarette. I decided he must really think there were a whole lot of things I knew that I wasn't telling him. How much further could I string him along?

"Well," I said, trying to sound smug and in the know, "if he wasn't killed, what did happen that night? There was a body, it was brought to the morgue and identified as Peterson's, and then it was cremated. That would've taken some organizing."

To be honest, I hadn't given much thought myself to this particular aspect of things. There *was* a body, someone *did* die, and whoever it was, Lynn Peterson had said it was her brother. But if Peterson hadn't died, then who had? Maybe it was time to go and talk to Floyd Hanson again.

Or maybe it wasn't. Maybe it was time I forgot about Nico
Peterson, and his sister, and the Cahuilla Club, and Clare
Cavendish—but hold up there. Clare? The rest would be easy to
put out of my mind, but not the black-eyed blonde. I've said it
before, and I know I'll have cause to say it again: women are nothing but trouble, whatever you say, whatever you do. I thought of
the painted roses on the lamp beside my bed. That shade, like
Oscar's wallpaper, would definitely have to go.

Hendricks was thinking again. For all his silver-tongued
smoothness, he wasn't the quickest when it came to brainwork.
"Nico must have organized it all himself," he said at last. "The accident, the hit-and-run car, the cremation. That's obvious, isn't it?"

"He would have needed help. Plus, he would have needed a
body. I don't imagine he found a volunteer—nobody has friends that
accommodating."

Hendricks was silent again for a time; then he shook his head
as if there were flies around it. "None of that matters," he said. "I
don't care about any of that. All I want to know is whether he's
alive and, if so, where he is. He has that suitcase, and I want it."

"Okay, Hendricks," I said, "I'll level with you. And don't get
mad at me when I do—I didn't get in this car of my own free will,
remember."

"All right." He scowled. "Start leveling."

I tapped my cigarette on the edge of the ashtray in the armrest
on my side. It had a little lid with a spring in it. Someone—Cedric,
I supposed—had forgotten to clean it out, and an acrid smell came
up out of it. Probably it was the smell my lungs would give off if
my chest cavity were to be opened up. Sometimes I think I should
lay off cigarettes for good, but if I did that, I'd have no hobbies
except chess, and I keep beating myself at chess.

I took a good deep breath, one without smoke in it. "The truth
is," I said, "I don't know any more than you do, about Peterson or

anything else. I was hired to look into his death, because there was a question as to whether it had in fact occurred. I talked to a few people, including his sister—"

"You talked to her?"

"For about five minutes, mostly to say what I'd like her to put in the drink she was mixing for me. Then the two men from the south burst in, and that was that."

"Lynn Peterson told you nothing?" He was sitting very still now and watching me very closely.

"Nothing," I said. "I swear it. There wasn't time."

"She say anything to you about the suitcase?"

"No."

He thought that over. "Who else did you talk to?"

"Nobody much. An old guy who lived opposite Peterson. Bartender in Barney's Beanery, where Peterson used to drop in for a drink once in a while. The manager of the Cahuilla Club"—now it was me who was giving him the searching look—"name of Hanson, Floyd Hanson." The name didn't have the desired effect—in fact, it had no effect at all, and I wasn't even sure he recognized it. "Know him?" I asked, as casually as I could.

"What?" He hadn't been listening. "Yes, yes, I know him. I go there sometimes, to the club, for dinner or whatever." He blinked. "What's Hanson got to do with anything?"

"Peterson was killed outside the Cahuilla Club."

"I know that—I knew that."

"Hanson was one of the first people on the scene of the accident that night."

"So he was." He paused, biting at the side of his mouth. "Did he have anything to say—anything to tell you?"

"No."

Now Hendricks got out Ma Langrishe's lily of the valley lotion again and gave his hands another tender treatment. Maybe it soothed his nerves or helped him think. In that department, he

could use all the help available. "Look, Marlowe," he said, "I like
you. I like the way you conduct yourself. You've got a brain, that's
apparent. Plus, you know how to keep your mouth shut. I could
use a man like you."

I laughed. "Don't even bother asking," I said. He held up a hand
the size of a small side of pork. Why do fat men insist on wearing
rings? A ring on fingers like those always makes me think of prize
hogs.

"I'm not offering you a job," he said. "I know I'd be wasting my
time. But I'd like to hire you to look for Nico Peterson."

I laughed again, and put a bit of mirth in it this time. "Don't
you listen? I'm already looking for Peterson, on behalf of someone
else."

He closed his eyes and shook his head. "I mean really look for
him. You obviously haven't put your heart into it so far."

"Why do you think that?"

He opened his eyes and bored them into me. "Because you
haven't found him! I know you, Marlowe, I know what you're
like. You put your mind to something, you're going to get it done."
By now his British accent had slipped badly. "What are you being
paid, couple of hundred? I'll give you a thousand. Cedric!" He held
out his hand. In the front seat the black man leaned sideways, not
taking his eye off the road, clicked open the glove compartment,
and brought out a tall black leather wallet and passed it back over
his shoulder. Hendricks took it from him and flipped the clasp and
extracted from a pocket inside it five C-notes in mint condition and
fanned them in front of me like a hand of cards. "Half now, half
on discovery. What do you say?"

"I say phooey," I said. I stubbed out the cigarette in the ashtray
and let the spring lid snap shut. "I've already been hired to find
Peterson—if he's alive, which he's probably not. But if he is, and I
find him, it won't be for you I do it. You got that? I have standards.
They're not very high, they're not very noble, but on the other

hand, they're not for sale. Now if you don't mind, I'll get back to my job. Cedric, stop the car—and do it this time or I'll twist your head off."

Cedric glanced into the mirror, in Hendricks's direction, and Hendricks gave a curt nod, and we drifted to the right and stopped. Hendricks still had the money in his hand, but now he heaved a sigh and tucked the bills away into the wallet and snapped the clasp. "It doesn't matter," he said, pursing his lips so that he looked like a baby—a baby hippo, say. "If you find him, I'll know. Then I'll come get him. And when that happens, I hope you won't try to stand in the way, Mr. Marlowe."

I opened the door—it felt like it had as much steel in it as a ship's bulkhead—and put a foot to the pavement. Then I turned back. "You know, Hendricks," I said, "you're all the same, all you guys in the rackets. You think because you have limitless wads of dough and a team of heavies behind you, there's no one who'll say no to you. Well, someone just did say no, and he's going to keep on saying it, no matter how many Jimmys you send after him."

Hendricks was beaming at me with what seemed genuine delight. "Ah, Mr. Marlowe, you're a man of spirit, you are that, and I admire you for it." He nodded happily, once more every inch the picture of a proper British gent. "I hope our paths cross again. I have a fair notion they will."

"If they do, be careful you don't get tripped up. So long."

I climbed out and pushed the door shut behind me. As the car purred out into the traffic, I heard Hendricks blowing his nose again. It was like the sound of a distant foghorn.

17

The hour was long past midnight, and I was lying on my bed in my shirtsleeves, smoking a cigarette and staring at the ceiling. The bedside lamp was on, and those painted roses were throwing shadows up the walls—they looked like bloodstains someone had started to wash away and then given up on.

I was thinking about this and that, this being Clare Cavendish, and that being Clare Cavendish too. The side of the bed I was on was the side where she'd lain, and I could smell the fragrance of her hair on the pillow, or thought I could, anyway. I was telling myself how right I'd been to let her go. She was not only good-looking but loaded, and that kind of woman just wasn't for me. Linda Loring, over there in Paris, was another of the same type, which was why I wasn't too keen on marrying her, though she kept on asking. Linda and I went to bed together once, and I guess she did love me, but why she thought love should inevitably lead to marriage, I didn't know. Her sister had been married to Terry Lennox and ended up with a bullet in her brain and her face smashed in. Hardly an example of conjugal bliss. Besides, I wasn't young anymore, and maybe I wasn't going to marry anyone.

The phone rang, and I knew it was Clare. I didn't know how I knew, but I did. I have a thing with phones—I hate them, but I seem to be on their wavelength in some funny way.

"Is that you?" Clare said.

"Yes, it's me."

"It's late, I know. Were you asleep? I'm sorry if I woke you." She spoke very slowly, as if in a trance. "I couldn't think who else to call."

"What's wrong?"

"I wonder—I wonder if you could come to the house?"

"To your house? Now?"

"Yes. I need—I need someone to—" Her voice began to shake and she had to stop for a few seconds and get it under control. She sounded close to hysteria. "It's Rett," she said.

"Your brother?"

"Yes—Everett."

"What's the matter with him?"

She paused again. "I really would appreciate if you could come here. Do you think you could? Am I asking too much?"

"I'll come," I said.

Of course I'd come. I would have gone to her if she'd been calling from the dark side of the moon. It's strange, the sudden way things can change. A minute ago I'd been congratulating myself on getting rid of her, but now it was as if a door had been flung open inside me and I was running out through it with my hat in my hand and my coattails flying. Why had I driven her away, making dumb wisecracks and acting like a heel? What the hell was wrong with me, to send a gorgeous woman like that out into the night with her lips set like a vise and her forehead pale with anger? Did I think I was such a hotshot that I could afford to push her away like that, as if the world were crowded with Clare Cavendishes and all I had to do was snap my fingers and another one would come hurrying up the steps to my front door, with her head down, putting one foot neatly in front of the other in little figure eights?

Outside, the street was deserted, and a warm mist was wafting down from the hills. Across the way, the eucalyptus trees stood motionless in the light from the streetlamp. They were like a band of accusers staring at me silently as I got into the Olds. Hadn't they told me so? Hadn't they said I was a fool that other night when I'd stood on the redwood steps and watched Clare Cavendish hurrying down them and made no attempt to stop her?

I drove across the city, too fast, but luckily there were no patrol cars out. Ahead of me a quarter-moon was flying through the mist as I hit the coast and turned right. Ghostly waves were breaking in the moonlight, and farther out the night was an empty blackness, with no horizon. *I need someone,* she'd said. *I need someone.*

I turned in at the gates of Langrishe Lodge and cut the headlights, as Clare had asked me to. She hadn't wanted anyone to know I was coming; by "anyone" I presumed she meant her mother, maybe her husband, too. I drove around the side of the house and parked opposite the conservatory. There were lights in some of the windows, but it didn't look like there were people in any of the rooms.

I turned off the engine and sat with the window down, hearing the distant sound of the ocean and the odd seabird sleepily crying. I needed a cigarette but didn't want to strike a light. The misted air was warmly damp against my face. I couldn't be sure that Clare would know I had arrived. She'd told me where to stop and said she'd find me. I settled down to wait. It's part of the story of my life, sitting in cars late at night with stale cigarette smoke in my nostrils and the night birds crying.

I didn't have to wait long. No more than a couple of minutes had passed when I spotted a figure coming toward me through the mist. It was Clare. She had on a long, dark coat that was tightly fastened at her throat. I got out of the car.

"Thank you for coming," she said in an agitated whisper. I wanted to take her in my arms but didn't. She closed her fingers on my wrist for a second, then turned back toward the house.

I followed her. The French doors were standing open, and we went inside. She didn't switch on the light. She knew her way through the darkened house, but I had to go cautiously among the dim shapes of the furniture. She led me up a long, curving staircase and down a carpeted corridor. There were wall lights burning here, the bulbs turned low. She had taken off the dark coat downstairs. Underneath she wore a cream-colored dress. Her white shoes were wet from the garden, and her ankles were slim and shapely, with deep scoops at the back, smooth and pale, like the inside of a seashell, between the bone and the tendon.

"In here," she said and again fixed her fingers urgently on my wrist.

The room had the look of a stage set, I'm not sure why. Maybe it was the way it was lit. There were two lamps, a small one on a dressing table and a big one beside the bed, with a tan shade that must have been two feet in diameter. The bed was the size of a raft, and Everett Edwards the Third looked very small lying on it, passed out cold under a tangle of sheets. He was on his back, with his hands clasped over his breast, like the corpse of a martyr in a painting by an old master. His face was the same color as the sheets; his hair hung lank, soaked with sweat. He was wearing an undershirt with dried vomit on the front of it, and there were flecks of dried foam at the corners of his mouth.

"What's the matter with him?" I asked, though I could pretty well guess.

"He's sick," Clare said. She was standing beside the bed, gazing down at her brother. She looked like the mother of the martyr. "He—he took something."

I lifted his left arm and turned it over and saw the puncture marks, some old and some new, stretching in a ragged line from the wrist to the inner side of the elbow. "Where's the needle?" I asked.

She made a jerking motion with her hand. "I threw it away."

"How long has he been like this?"

"I don't know. An hour, maybe. I found him on the stairs. He'd been wandering through the house, I suppose, and must have passed out. I got him in here, somehow—this is my room, not his. I didn't know what else to do. That's when I called you."

"Has he been like this before?"

"Never like this, no, never this bad." She turned to me with a stricken look. "Do you think he's dying?"

"I don't know," I said. "His breathing's not too bad. Have you called a doctor?"

"No. I didn't dare."

"He needs medical attention," I said. "Have you got a phone in here?"

She led me to the dressing table. The phone was custom-made, black and shiny with silver trimmings. I picked up the receiver and dialed. How the hell I had the number in my head I don't know—it was as if my fingers remembered, not me. It rang for a long time; then a crisp, cold voice said, "Yes?"

"Dr. Loring," I said. "It's Marlowe, Philip Marlowe."

I thought I heard a quick intake of breath. There was a humming silence for some seconds; then Loring spoke again. "Marlowe," he said, making it sound like a curse word. "Why are you calling me at this hour of the night? Why are you calling me at all?"

"I need your help."

"You have the nerve to—?"

"Listen," I said, "it has nothing to do with me—I'm acting for a friend. There's a man passed out here, and he needs help."

"And you call *me*?"

"I wouldn't have, if I'd been able to think of someone else."

"I'm going to hang up now."

"Wait. What about that oath you guys take? This man may die if he doesn't get help."

There was a silence. Clare had been standing close beside me all this while, watching me as if she could read in my face Loring's side of the exchange.

"What's wrong with this person?" Loring asked.

"He took an overdose."

"He tried to kill himself?"

"No. He was shooting up."

" 'Shooting up'?" I could picture him grimacing in distaste.

"Yeah," I said, "he's an addict. That make a difference? Addicts are people too."

"How dare you lecture me!"

"I'm not lecturing you, Doc," I said. "It's late, I'm tired, you were the only name I could come up with—"

"Doesn't this person have a family? Don't they have a doctor of their own?"

Clare was still watching me, hanging on every word. I turned away from her and cupped my hand around the mouthpiece. "The name here is Cavendish," I said quietly. "Also Langrishe. That mean anything to you?"

There was another pause. One good thing about Loring was that he was a snob—a good thing in the present circumstances, I mean. "Is this Dorothea Langrishe you're talking about?" he asked. I could hear the change of tone in his voice, the little reverent hush that had come into it.

"That's right," I said. "So you realize how much discretion is required."

He hesitated for no more than a moment, then said, "Give me the address. I'll come over right away."

I told him how to get to Langrishe Lodge and about dousing the car lights and parking by the conservatory, as I had. Then I hung up and turned to Clare. "You know who that was?"

"Linda Loring's ex?"

"That's right. You know him?"

"No. I never met him."

"He's a martinet and in love with himself," I said, "but he also happens to be a good doctor—and discreet."

Clare nodded. "Thank you."

I shut my eyes and massaged the lids with my fingertips. Then I looked at her and asked, "You think you could rustle up a drink?"

She seemed helpless for a second. "There's Richard's whiskey," she said. "I'll go and see what I can find."

"Where is Richard, by the way?" I said.

She shrugged. "Oh, you know—out."

"What happens if he comes back and finds your brother in this state?"

"What will happen? Dick will laugh, probably, and go to bed. He doesn't take much notice of what goes on between Rett and me."

"And your mother?"

A flicker of alarm crossed her face. "Mother mustn't know. She *mustn't.*"

"Shouldn't she be told? He is her son, after all."

"It would break her heart. She doesn't know about the drugs. When Richard gets angry at me, he threatens to tell her. It's another way he holds power over me. Another of the many ways."

"I get the picture," I said. I rubbed my eyes again; they felt like they'd been lightly toasted in front of an open fire. "About that drink?"

She went away, and I returned to the bed and sat down on the edge of it and looked at the unconscious young man with the vomit on his shirt and his hair in a mess. I didn't think he was dying, but I'm no expert when it comes to dope and dope fiends. Everett the Third was obviously a veteran—some of those needle marks on his arm had been there a long time. Sooner or later his mother was going to find out what her darling son did when he wasn't at home having his hair stroked by her. I just hoped she wouldn't find out the hard way. Having lost her husband like she had, the last thing she needed, at this stage of her life, was another violent death in the family.

Clare came back with a bottle of Southern Comfort and a cut-glass tumbler. She poured a generous measure and handed it to me. I stood up and tipped the edge of the glass to her in a gesture of appreciation. I don't like Southern Comfort—too sickly sweet, for my taste—but it would do. I started to get out my cigarette case but changed my mind. It wouldn't have seemed right, some-how, smoking in Clare Cavendish's bedroom.

I glanced down at her brother again. "Where does he get the dope?" I asked.

"I don't know where he gets it now." She looked aside, biting her lip. Even in distress, she was beautiful. "Nico used to get him some, now and then," she said. "That's how I met him—Everett introduced us." She made a sad little smile. "Are you shocked?"

"Yes," I said, "a bit. I didn't realize you and Peterson had that kind of relationship."

"What do you mean? What kind of relationship?"

"The kind where you're sleeping with a drug peddler."

She flinched at that but made a quick recovery. She was getting her spirit back, now that she knew help was on the way and she could stop being responsible for everything. "You don't under-stand women at all, do you," she said.

I suddenly wondered if I'd ever heard her say my name, if she'd ever called me Philip. I didn't think she had, not even when we were in bed together, in the glow of those blood-red painted roses. "No," I said, "I don't suppose I do. Does any man?"

"Yes, I've known some men who do."

I drank my drink. It really was sickly sweet; they must put caramel or something in it. "Are you being straight with me?" I asked. "Did you really see Peterson on Market Street that day?"

Her eyes grew round. "Of course. Why would I lie?"

"I don't know. Like you say, I don't understand you."

She sat down on the bed and folded her hands together and set them on her knees. "You're right," she said quietly, "I should have had nothing to do with him. He's"—she searched for the word—"he's unworthy. Does that sound strange? I don't mean unworthy of *me*—God knows, I'm not worth all that much either. He's charming, and funny, and he has an elegant mind. He's even brave, in a way, but at the center there's only a hollow."

I watched her eyes. Inside them, she was far, far away. It came to me that it wasn't Peterson she was talking about, that she was only using him as a way of talking about someone else. It was true; I was sure it was. And that someone else was precious to her in a way that a man like Nico Peterson could never be—in a way that a man like me could never be, either. I suddenly wanted very much to kiss her. I couldn't think why that was, I mean why I wanted to kiss her now, while she was so far from me, thinking of someone she loved. Women are not the only thing I don't understand—I don't understand myself, either, not one little bit.

Suddenly she lifted her head, holding up a hand. "I hear a car," she said. "It must be Dr. Loring."

We went down through the dark house, the way we had come up, and out into the garden. Loring's car was there, stopped behind mine. As we arrived, Loring opened the door and got out.

Loring was thin, with a small goatee and arrogant eyes. We'd had some rough exchanges, the two of us. I didn't know if he knew that his ex-wife wanted to marry me. It probably wouldn't have made any difference; he couldn't loathe me any more than he did already. And he'd washed his hands of Linda some time ago. "Marlowe," he said coldly. "I've come, as you see."

I introduced him to Clare. He shook her hand briefly and said, "Where's the patient?"

We returned through the house to Clare's bedroom. I shut the door behind us, turned, and leaned my back against it. I figured Clare could handle it from here. Everett was her brother, and it was best that I stay out of Loring's way as much as possible.

He walked to the bed and set down his black bag on the bedspread. "What was it?" he said. "Heroin?"

"Yes," Clare said in a hushed voice. "I think so."

Loring felt Everett's pulse, lifted his eyelids and examined the pupils, put a hand on his chest and pressed gently a couple of times. He nodded and took a hypodermic syringe out of his bag. "I'll give him a shot of adrenaline," he said. "He'll come around in a while."

"You mean it's not—it's not serious?" Clare asked.

He gave her a baleful glance. His eyes had a way of seeming to shrink in their sockets when he was angry or outraged, which was pretty often. "My dear woman," he said, "your brother's heart rate is less than fifty, and his respiratory rate is less than twelve. I should guess that for a period tonight he was on the point of death. Luckily, he's young and relatively healthy. However"—he held an ampoule of clear liquid upside down and pierced the rubber cap with the tip of the hypodermic—"if he continues to indulge this habit, it will almost certainly kill him, sooner rather than later. There are people who can live with a heroin habit— they don't live well, but they live—but your brother, I can clearly see, is not of that type."

He plunged the needle into Everett's arm and glanced up at Clare. "He's weak. He has weakness written all over him. You should get him into a clinic. I can give you some names, people to call, places to go and see. Otherwise, without the slightest doubt, you'll lose him." He extracted the needle and put it away in his bag, along with the empty vial. He turned to Clare again. "Here is my card. Call me tomorrow."

Clare sat down on the side of the bed again with her hands clasped in her lap. She looked as if someone had punched her. Her brother stirred and groaned.

Loring turned away brusquely. "I'll walk out with you," I said. He gave me a cold stare.

We went down through the shadowy house. Loring was one of those men whose silence was more eloquent than his conversation. I could feel contempt and hatred coming off him like waves of heat. It wasn't my fault his wife had left him and now wanted to marry me.

We walked through the dark conservatory and out into the night. The mist clung to my face like a wet scarf. Out at sea a light was winking on the mast of someone's anchored boat. Loring opened the door of his car, threw his bag inside, and turned to me. "I don't know why you keep turning up in my life, Marlowe," he said. "I don't like it."

"I don't enjoy it much myself," I said. "But I'm grateful to you for coming out here tonight. You think he might have died?"

He shrugged. "As I said, he's young, and young men tend to survive all manner of self-pollution." He was about to get into the car but paused. "What's your connection with this family? You're hardly at their social level, I'd have thought."

"I'm doing some work for Mrs. Cavendish."

He made a sound that from someone else might have been a laugh. "She must be in very deep trouble, if she had to call on you."

"She's not in trouble at all. She hired me to trace someone—a friend of hers."

"Why doesn't she go to the police?"

"It's a private matter."

"Yes, you're good at poking into people's private lives, aren't you."

"Look, Doc," I said, "I've never knowingly done you harm. I'm sorry your wife left you—"

I could feel him stiffen in the darkness. "How dare you speak of my marriage."

"I don't know how I dare," I said wearily. "But I want you to know I mean you no ill."

"You think that matters to me? You think anything about you is of the slightest interest to me?"

"No, I guess not."

"What happened to your face, by the way?"

"A fellow hit me with the barrel of a gun."

He did that cold laugh again. "Nice people you deal with."

I stepped back. "Anyway, thanks for coming. It can't be a bad thing, if you saved a life."

He seemed about to say more, but instead he got into the car and slammed the door and started up the engine and did a quick reverse, then skidded forward over the gravel and was gone.

I stood in the damp darkness for a minute, my damaged face lifted to the sky, breathing in the night's salty air. I thought of going back into the house, then decided not to. I didn't have anything more to say to Clare, not tonight, anyway. But she was back in my life. Oh, yes, she was back.

≡ 18 ≡

When I was young, a couple of millennia ago, I used to think I knew what I was doing. I was aware of the world's caprices—the goat dances it likes to do with our hopes and desires—but where my own actions were concerned, I was pretty confident that I was sitting square in the driver's seat, with the wheel held firmly in my own two hands. Now I know different. Now I know that decisions we think we make are in fact made only in hindsight, and that at the time things are actually happening, all we do is drift. It doesn't trouble me much, this awareness of how little control I have over my affairs. Most of the time I'm content to slide along with the current, paddling my fingers in the water and tickling the odd fish out of its element. There are occasions, though, when I wish I'd made at least some effort to look ahead and calculate the consequences of what I was doing. I'm thinking here of my second visit to the Cahuilla Club, which was, I can safely say, a hell of a lot different from the first . . .

———

It was afternoon, and the place was busy. Some kind of convention was going on, and there were a lot of guys, most of them old, in colored shirts and tartan Bermuda shorts milling about among the bougainvillea with tall glasses in their hands, not all of them entirely steady on their pins. They were all wearing red fezzes, like upended flowerpots with tassels. Marvin the twitching gatekeeper had called ahead to the manager's office and then waved me on. I left the Olds under a shady tree and walked up to the clubhouse. Halfway there I met the young-old guy who had accosted me last time. He was raking leaves off the pathway. He didn't seem to recognize me. I greeted him anyway.

"Captain Hook about?" I asked. He gave me a nervous glance and went on with his raking. I tried again: "How are the Lost Boys today?"

He shook his head stubbornly. "I'm not s'posed to be talking to you," he muttered.

"Is that so? Who says?"

"You know."

"The captain?"

He looked warily this way and that. "You didn't ought to mention him," he said. "You gonna get me in trouble."

"Well now, I wouldn't want to do that. Only—"

A voice behind us spoke. "Lamarr? Didn't I tell you about annoying the visitors?"

Lamarr gave a start, making a ducking motion with his shoulders, as if expecting a blow. Floyd Hanson strolled up, as usual with a hand in the pocket of his fresh-pressed slacks. Today he wore a light blue linen jacket and a white shirt and a shoelace tie fastened with the head of a bull carved from some shiny black stone.

"Hello, Mr. Hanson," I said. "Lamarr wasn't being annoying."

Hanson nodded to me, with his crooked little smile, and laid a hand on Lamarr's khaki-clad shoulder and spoke to him softly: "You run along now, Lamarr."

"Sure thing, Mr. Hanson," Lamarr said, stammering. He threw a glance at me that was half resentful and half scared. Then he shuffled off with his rake in tow. Hanson watched him go with an indulgent expression.

"Lamarr has a good heart," he said, "only he fantasizes."

"He thinks you're Captain Hook," I said.

He nodded, smiling. "I don't know how he knows about Peter Pan. I guess someone must have read the story to him once, or maybe he was taken to see it performed. Even the Lamarrs of this world had mothers, after all." He turned to me. "What can I do for you, Mr. Marlowe?"

"You heard about Lynn Peterson?" I said.

He frowned. "Yes, of course. A tragic thing. Did I see your name somewhere in the newspaper reports of her death?"

"You probably did. I was with her when the killers took her."

"I see. That must have been upsetting."

"Yeah," I said. "*Upsetting*, that's the word."

"Why did they 'take her,' as you put it?"

"They were looking for her brother."

"Even though he's dead?"

"Is he?"

Hanson said nothing to that, only gave me a long, reflective look, holding his head to one side. "Have you come to ask me more questions about Nico?" he said. "There's really nothing further I can tell you."

"You know a guy named Lou Hendricks?" I asked.

He thought about it. "The man who runs that casino out in the desert? I've met him. He's been here at the club once or twice."

"He's not a member?"

"No. He came as a guest."

Off across the lawn, the conventioneers sent up a ragged cheer. Hanson glanced in their direction, shading his eyes with a hand. "We have the Shriners in today," he said, "as you see. They're holding a charity golf tournament. They tend to get a little rowdy. Would you care for a drink?"

"I guess it wouldn't do any harm. Just so long as it's not tea."

He smiled. "Come this way."

We went in through the front door, past the ornate desk and the pert receptionist with the blue spectacles. There were groups of old fellows in fezzes loitering about the corridors and in the bar and the dining room. "Let's go to my office," Hanson said. "It's quieter there."

His office was a big high handsome room discreetly fitted with choice pieces of blond furniture and some nice native Indian rugs on the floor. The walls were paneled in cherrywood, and there was a desk just like the one in the reception area, only bigger and more ornate. Hanson sure didn't stint himself when it came to his creature comforts. What I did miss were any signs of a personal life—no framed photos of a wife and kiddies or a glamour shot of a lady love with a cigarette and a Veronica Lake wave that guys like Hanson usually have in a prominent position on their desks. Maybe he didn't go in for ladies, or maybe the club frowned on the personal touch—what did it matter? All the same, there was something almost uncanny in the clipped neatness of the place.

"Take a seat, Mr. Marlowe," Hanson said. He crossed to a sideboard on which an array of bottles was set out. "What can I get you?" he asked.

"Whiskey is fine."

He searched through the bottles. "I've got some Old Crow here—will that do? I'm a martini man myself."

He poured me a stiff one, added some cubes of ice, and came and handed me the glass. I was sitting on a neat little sofa with beveled wooden legs and a high back. "You not joining me?" I asked.

"Not while I'm working. Mr. Canning has strong views on the perils of the bottle." He did his twinkling smile.

"Mind if I smoke? Mr. Canning got views on the weed, too?"

"Go ahead, please." He watched me light up. I offered him my case, but he shook his head. He went to his desk and sat back against the front of it with his arms and ankles crossed. "You're a persistent man, Mr. Marlowe," he said lightly.

"You mean, I'm a pain in the rear."

"That's not what I said. I admire persistence."

I sipped my drink and smoked my smoke and glanced about the room. "What exactly do you do, Mr. Hanson?" I asked. "I know you're the manager, but what does that require of you?"

"There's a lot of administration involved in running a club like this—you'd be surprised."

"Mr. Canning give you a free hand?"

His eyes narrowed a fraction. "More or less. We have, you might say, an understanding."

"Which is?" I seemed to know a lot of people who had understandings with each other.

"He leaves me alone to manage the place, and I don't trouble him when difficulties arise. Unless the difficulties are—how shall we say?—hard for me to deal with alone."

"Then what happens?"

He smiled, the corners of his eyes crinkling. "Then Mr. Canning takes charge," he said softly.

I found myself blinking, as if there were dust in my eyes. The bourbon seemed to be working its magic awful fast. "I can see," I said, "you have a healthy respect for your employer."

"He's a person who commands respect. How's your drink, by the way?"

"My drink is very fine. It tastes of hickory fires on fall afternoons in the far backwoods of Kentucky."

"Why, I do believe you're something of a poet, Mr. Marlowe."

"I've read a line or two of Keats in my time. Shelley, too." What the hell was I talking about? My tongue seemed suddenly to have a mind of its own. "But I didn't come here to talk poetry," I said. I felt myself sliding down on the sofa and struggled to sit up straight. I looked at the glass in my hand. The liquor in it trembled and the ice cubes knocked together with a gentle sound, as if they were discussing me among themselves. I peered around the room again, blinking some more. The sun was very bright in the window, cutting like sword blades through the slats of the wooden blind.

Hanson was watching me with close attention. "What did you come here for, Mr. Marlowe?" he asked.

"Came to talk to you some more about Peterson, didn't I," I said. "Nico Peterson, that is." I was having trouble with my tongue again; it seemed to have swollen to about twice its normal size and sat in my mouth like a hot, soft potato with a bristly skin. "Not to mention his sister." I frowned. "Even though I have mentioned her. Haven't I? Lynn, her name is. Was. Good-looking woman. Nice eyes. Nice green eyes. Of course, you know her."

"Do I?"

"Sure you do." I was having difficulty now with my *s*'s; they kept getting caught on my front teeth, like knotted-up lengths of dental floss. "She was here, that day I came to see you. When was that? Anyway, doesn't matter. We met her coming out of the—out of the whaddyacallit, the swi—the swim—the *swimming* pool." I leaned forward to put the tumbler down on a low glass table in front of the sofa but miscalculated and let go of it when it still had a couple of inches to go and it landed on the glass with a sharp crack. "You know what," I said, "I think I'm—"

Then my voice finally gave out. I was sliding forward on the sofa again. Hanson seemed very far away and high above me and was wavering somehow, as if I were sunk underwater and looking up at him through the swaying surface.

"Are you all right, Mr. Marlowe?" he asked in a voice that boomed in my ears. He was still leaning back against the desk, still with his arms folded. I could see he was smiling.

With a big effort, I got my voice to work again. "What did you put in the drink?"

"What's that? You seem to be slurring your words. I would have thought you'd be a man who could hold his liquor, Mr. Marlowe. It seems I was wrong."

I reached out a hand in a crazy attempt to get hold of him, but he was way too far off, and besides I don't think my fingers would have had the strength to fix on anything. Abruptly I lost control and felt myself tumbling to the floor heavily, like a sack of grain. Then the light slowly went out.

≡ 19 ≡

It wasn't the first time in my life I'd been slipped a Mickey Finn, and it probably won't be the last. As in everything else, you learn to cope with it, or at least with the aftermath. Like now, for instance, when I came around and knew better than to open my eyes straight off. For one thing, when you're in that state, even the most muted shaft of daylight can hit your eyes like a splash of acid. For another, it's always better to let whoever it was that slipped you the dose think you're still out cold—that way you get a while to mull things over and maybe figure out your next move, while your body readjusts itself to whatever surroundings and circumstances it finds itself in.

The first thing I realized was that I was tied up. I was sitting on a straight-backed chair and lashed to it with loops of rope. My hands were bound too, behind my back. I didn't make a move, just stayed slumped there with my chin on my chest and my eyes shut. The air around me had a warm, woolly feel to it, and I seemed to hear water lapping gently with a hollow, echoing sound. Was I in a bathroom? No, the place was bigger than that. Then I noticed the chlorine smell. A swimming pool, then.

My head felt as if it had been jammed full of cotton wool, and the bruise at the back that López had given me had taken on a whole new lease on life.

Someone groaned nearby. The groan had a rattle in it that told me the groaner was in a lot of distress, maybe even dying. For a second I wondered if it was myself I had heard. Then a voice spoke a few yards away: "Give him some water, bring him around."

I didn't recognize the voice. It was the voice of a man, not young. There was a harsh edge to it. Whoever he was, he was used to giving orders and being obeyed.

There were gagging sounds then, and a hoarse cough, and the sound of water splashing on stone. "He's almost done for, Mr. C.," another voice said. This one I seemed to know, or to have heard before, at least. The accent was familiar but not the tone.

"Don't let him go yet," the first voice said. "He has to pay some more, before he gets his release." There was a pause, and I heard footsteps approaching, with sharp, echoing clicks of shoe leather on what had to be a marble floor, and stop in front of me. "What about this one? He should be awake by now."

A hand suddenly grasped my hair at the back and jerked my head upright, so that my eyes snapped open like a doll's. The light didn't hit me too hard, but for the first few seconds all I could see in front of me was a burning whitish mist with some blurred figures moving in it. "He's awake, all right," the first voice said. "That's good."

The mist began to clear. I was in the swimming pool room. The space was large and long and had a high, domed glass roof through which the sunlight streamed. The walls and floor were covered with big tiles of veined white marble. The pool must have been fifty feet long. I couldn't see who was behind me, still holding on to a handful of my hair. In front of me and off a little to one side was Hanson, pale and sick-looking in his light blue jacket and his string tie with the bull's-head fastener.

Next to Hanson was a short, thickset, elderly man, entirely bald, with a pointed skull and heavy black eyebrows that looked as if they'd been painted on. He wore knee-high brown boots as shiny as new-shucked chestnuts, twill pants, and a black shirt with an open collar. Around his neck he had a set of wolf's teeth threaded on a string, along with an Indian amulet made of some kind of bone with a big, slanted blue eye painted in the middle of it. In his right hand he was holding a malacca cane, what the British call a swagger stick, I believe. He looked like a scaled-down version of Cecil B. DeMille crossed with a retired lion tamer.

Now he approached me, peering at me with his bald head held to one side and slapping himself lightly on the thigh with his bamboo stick. He stopped and leaned down and put his face close to mine, his flinty blue eyes seeming to look into my very soul. "I'm Wilberforce Canning," he said.

I had to do some work unscrambling my lips and tongue before I could get my voice in operation again. "I guessed that," I said.

"Did you, now. Good for you." Hanson was hovering at his shoulder anxiously, as if he thought I might break free of my bonds and go for the little guy. Fat chance of that. Aside from the ropes holding me fast to the chair, I had about as much strength in me as a cat with the mange. "How did you get that scar on your cheek?" Canning asked.

"Mosquito bit me."

"Mosquitoes don't bite, they sting."

"Well, this one had teeth."

I squinted past Canning to the swimming pool. The blue water looked painfully inviting. I pictured myself floating on its cool, silken surface, calmed and soothed.

"Floyd here tells me you're a very inquisitive man, Mr. Marlowe," Canning said, still leaning forward and gazing into my face.

He touched the end of his stick almost caressingly against my cheek and the scar there. "That can be an awkward thing, inquisitiveness." There was another groan; it came from somewhere off to my right. I tried to look in that direction, but Canning pressed the swagger stick hard against my cheek and would not let me turn my head. "You just pay attention to me, now," he said. "Just concentrate on the matter in hand. Why are you asking all these questions about Nico Peterson?"

"All what questions?" I said. "There's only one, so far as I can see."

"And what's that?"

"Whether he's dead or just pretending to be."

Canning nodded and took a step back, and the one behind me at last let go of my hair. Free to look now, I turned my head. Gómez and López were there, a dozen feet away down the right-hand side of the pool and facing the water, seated side by side on straight-backed chairs to which, like me, they'd been tied with lengths of slender, tightly braided rope. López, I could see, was already dead. His head was a mass of gashes and bruises, and there was a cascade of half-dried, glistening blood down the front of his Hawaiian shirt. His right eye was swollen shut, while the left one bulged out of its socket, bloodshot and wildly staring. Someone had hit him very hard on the side of the head, hard enough to pop out that eyeball. His harelip was split in a dozen places now.

Gómez too was a mess, his powder-blue suit ripped and spattered all over with blood. At least one of them had soiled himself, and the smell wasn't pleasant. It was Gómez who was doing the groaning. He sounded half-conscious and terrified, like a man dreaming that he was falling from the roof of a high building. It looked to me as if it was only a matter of time before he joined his *compañero* in the happier hereafter. A man beaten to death and another one on the way there is a terrible sight, but I wasn't about to go into mourning for this pair. I recalled Lynn Peterson laid out on the pine needles in the clearing by the side of the road that night with her throat cut and Bernie Ohls telling me what had been done to her before she died.

Now the one who had been holding on to my hair stepped out where I could see him. It was Bartlett the butler, the old guy who had served tea to Hanson and me that first time I came to the club. He was wearing his striped vest and black morning pants under a long white apron, the strings of which were tied in a neat bow at the back, and his shirt sleeves had been rolled up. He didn't look any younger than he had before, and his skin was still gray and slack-looking, but otherwise he was a different man. How had I missed how tough he was, hard and muscular, with short thick arms and a chest like a barrel? A onetime boxer, I guessed. There were spills of blood down the front of his apron. In his right hand he was holding a blackjack, as neat a little number as you've ever seen, polished and gleaming from frequent use. Well, I guess butlers get called on to perform all kinds of duties in the course of their work. I wondered if he had taken the blackjack from López, the one López had used on me.

"You remember these gentlemen, I'm sure." Canning gestured toward the Mexicans. "Mr. Bartlett here has been in serious consultation with them, as you see. It's just as well you were in so deep a sleep, for it was a noisy exchange and at times painful to witness." He turned to the butler. "Get them out of here, will you, Clarence? Floyd will help you."

Hanson stared at him in horror but was ignored.

"Right-oh, Mr. Canning," Bartlett said. He turned to Hanson briskly. "I'll take this gentleman, you bring the other."

He went behind Gómez's chair and grasped the back of it and tilted it on two legs and began dragging it toward the door at the other side of the pool, the door Lynn Peterson had come through the day I'd glimpsed her here, with the towel wrapped around her head. Hanson, with a look of deep distaste, took López's chair and tilted it back and followed after Bartlett. The chair legs made a noise on the marble tiles like fingernails being dragged down a blackboard. Lopez's head fell sideways, that eyeball dangling.

Canning turned to me again, and again gave himself a light slap on the thigh with his swagger stick. "They weren't very forthcoming," he said, jerking his head in the direction of the departing Mexicans.

"Forthcoming about what?" I asked. I had a sudden, sharp craving for a cigarette. I wondered if I would end up like the Mexicans, beaten to a pulp and dragged out of here still strapped to this damned chair. What a lousy, undignified way to go.

Canning was shaking his bald head from side to side. "To tell you the truth, I didn't expect to get much out of them in the first place," he said.

"That must have been a relief to them."

"I wasn't in the business of offering them relief."

"No, I can see that."

"You feel sympathy for them, Mr. Marlowe? They were just a pair of animals. No, not animals—animals don't kill for fun."

He began to pace up and down in front of me, three tight steps this way, three tight steps that, his heels clicking on the tiles. He was one of those coiled, restless little guys, and right now he looked awfully agitated. I had that familiar metallic taste at the back of my tongue, as if I had been sucking on a penny. It was the taste of fear.

"You think I could have a cigarette?" I said. "I promise not to use it to burn through these ropes, or anything like that."

"I don't smoke," Canning said. "Filthy habit."

"You're right, it is."

"Have you got cigarettes? Where are they?"

I pointed with my chin toward the breast pocket of my suit jacket. "In there. Matches, too."

He reached inside my jacket and brought out my silver case

with the monogram, as well as a matchbook I'd forgotten I'd
picked up in Barney's Beanery. He took a cigarette from the case
and fitted it between my lips, lit a match, applied the flame. I drew
a long, deep lungful of hot smoke.

Canning dropped the case back in my pocket and resumed his
pacing. "The Latin races," he said, "I haven't much respect for
them. Singing, bullfighting, squabbling over women, that's about
their limit. You agree?"

"Mr. Canning," I said, working the cigarette to one side of my
mouth, "I'm not exactly in a position to disagree with anything
you say."

He laughed, making a thin, piping sound. "That's true," he
said, "you're not." He paced again. It seemed he had to keep moving, like a shark. I wondered how he had made his money. Oil, I
guessed, or maybe water, which was almost as precious in this
dry gulch the early Angelenos chose to build a city in. "There are
only two worthwhile races, in my opinion," he said. "Not even
races, in fact—specimens, rather. Know what they are?" I shook
my head, and immediately the pain made me regret it. A flurry of
cigarette ash tumbled silently down the front of my shirt and
landed in my lap. "The American Indian," he said, "and the English
gentleman." He glanced at me with a merry eye. "A strange pair-
ing, you suppose?"

"Oh, I don't know," I said. "I can see things they would have in
common."

"Such as?" Canning had stopped pacing and turned to me with
one of those thick black eyebrows lifted.

"Devotion to the land?" I said. "Fondness for tradition? Enthu-
siasm for the hunt—?"

"That's right, you're right!"

"—plus a tendency to slaughter anyone who gets in their way."

He shook his head and waved a reproving finger at me. "Now
you're being naughty, Mr. Marlowe. And I don't like naughtiness,

any more than I like inquisitiveness." He paced again, turning and turning about. I was keeping an eye on that swagger stick; a slash across the face from that would be a thing I wouldn't forget in a hurry.

"Killing is sometimes necessary," he said. "Or, rather, call it elimination." His expression darkened. "Some people don't deserve to live—that's a simple fact." He approached nearer again and squatted down on his heels beside the chair I was tied to. I had the uneasy feeling that he was going to make a confession. "You knew Lynn Peterson, didn't you," he said.

"I didn't know her, no. I met her—"

He nodded dismissively. "You were the last human being to see her alive. That's not counting"—he nodded toward the door— "those two pieces of crud."

"I suppose I was," I said. "I liked her. I mean I liked what I saw of her."

He looked into my face from the side. "Did you?" A muscle was twitching in his left temple.

"Yes. She seemed a decent sort."

He nodded absently. A strange, tense expression had come into his eyes. "She was my daughter," he said.

That took a while to absorb. I couldn't think of anything to say, so I said nothing. Canning was still watching me. There was a far, deep sorrow in his face; it came and went in a matter of moments. He rose to his feet and walked to the edge of the pool and stood there in silence for a while with his back to me, looking down into the water. Then he turned. "Don't pretend you're not surprised, Mr. Marlowe."

"I'm not pretending," I said. "I am surprised. Only I don't know what to say to you."

I had smoked my cigarette to the end, and now Canning came and with an expression of disgust extracted the butt from my mouth and carried it to a table in the corner, holding it in front of him nipped between a finger and thumb, as if it were the corpse of a cockroach, and dropped it in an ashtray there. Then he came back.

"How is it your daughter's name was Peterson?" I asked.

"She took her mother's name, who knows why. My wife was not an admirable woman, Mr. Marlowe. She was part Mexican, so maybe I should have known. She married me for my money, and when she'd spent enough of it—or, I should say, when I put a stop to her spending—she ran off with a fellow who turned out to be a con man. Not an attractive history, I know. I can't say I'm proud of that particular passage of my life. All I can offer in my defense is that I was young and, I suppose, bewitched." He grinned suddenly, showing his teeth. "Or is that what all cuckolds say?"

"I wouldn't know."

"Then you're a lucky man."

"There's luck and there's luck, Mr. Canning." I glanced down at the ropes. "Mine doesn't seem to be much in operation just now."

My mind was foggy again, probably due to a drop in circulation because of the ropes. But my strength was coming back, I could feel it, unless it was just the effect of the nicotine. I wondered how long all this was likely to go on for. I wondered too—again—how it might be going to end. I thought of López's bulging eye and the blood on his shirtfront. Wilber Canning was playing the part of the soft old boy, but I knew there was nothing soft about him, except maybe in his regard for his dead daughter.

"Listen," I said, "can I take it that if Lynn was your daughter, then Nico is your son?"

"They were both my offspring, yes," he said, not looking at me.

"Then I'm sorry," I said. "Your son I never met, but like I said, Lynn seemed all right to me. How come you weren't at her funeral?"

He shrugged. "She was a tramp." He spoke without emphasis. "And Nico was a gigolo, when he wasn't being worse. They both

had a lot of their mother in them." Now he did look in my direction. "You're shocked by my attitude toward my son and daughter, Mr. Marlowe, even though I've lost them both?"

"I'm hard to shock."

He wasn't listening. He had started pacing again, and it made
me feel dizzy, watching him. "I can't complain," he said. "I wasn't
exactly a perfect father. First they ran wild, then they ran off. I
didn't try to find them. Afterward, it was too late to make it up to
them. Lynn hated me. Nico probably did, too, only there were
things he needed from me."

"What sort of things?" He didn't bother to answer that. "Maybe
you weren't as bad as you thought," I said. "Fathers often judge
themselves too harshly."

"You have children, Marlowe?" I shook my head, and again
what felt like a set of big wooden dice rattled together inside my
skull. "Then you don't know what you're talking about," he said,
sounding more sad than anything else.

Though the day must have been waning, the heat in the big,
high-ceilinged room was rising. It felt a little like an August afternoon in Savannah. Plus the dampness in the air seemed to have a
tightening effect on the ropes around my chest and my wrists. I
wasn't sure I'd ever get the feeling back in my upper arms.

"Look, Mr. Canning," I said, "either tell me what you want
from me or let me go. I don't care a damn about the Mexicans—
they deserved all they got from your man Jeeves. Rough justice is
enough justice, in their case. But you've got no reason to keep me
trussed up here like a Sunday chicken. I've done nothing to you,
or to your son or daughter. I'm just a gumshoe bent on making a
living, and not doing too well at it."

If nothing else, my words had the effect of getting Canning to
stop pacing, which was a relief. He walked up and stood in front
of me with his hands on his hips and his swagger stick clamped

under his arm. "The thing is, Marlowe," he said, "I know who you're working for."

"You do?"

"Come on—what do you take me for?"

"I don't take you for anything, Mr. Canning. But I have to say, I very much doubt you know the identity of my client."

He leaned forward and held out to me the amulet that was hanging on the string around his neck. "Know what this is? It's the eye of a Cahuilla god. Very interesting tribe, the Cahuilla. They have powers of divination that are scientifically attested to. No point in lying to these folks—they see right through you. I was privileged to be inducted as an honorary brave. Part of the ceremony was the presentation of this precious image, this all-seeing eye. So don't try telling me lies or try to sidetrack me by playing the innocent. Talk."

"I don't know what you want me to talk about."

He shook his head sadly. "My man Jeeves, as you call him, is going to be back here shortly. You saw what he did to the Mexicans. I wouldn't want to be forced to have him do the same to you. Despite the circumstances, I have a certain respect for you. I like a man who keeps a cool head."

"The problem is, Mr. Canning," I said, "I don't know what you want from me."

"No?"

"Really, I don't. I was hired to find Nico Peterson. My client thought, like everybody else, that Nico was dead but then saw him on the street and came to me and asked me to track him down. It's a private matter."

"Where is he supposed to have seen Nico, your client, as you call him?"

Him. So he didn't know what he thought he knew. It was a relief. I wouldn't have wanted to think of Clare Cavendish here, tied to a chair with this murderous little madman strutting up and down in front of her.

"In San Francisco," I said.

"So he's up here, is he?"

"Who?"

"You know who. What was he doing in San Francisco? Was he looking for Nico? What made him suspect Nico wasn't dead?"

"Mr. Canning," I said, as patiently and gently as I could, "none of what you're saying makes sense to me. You've got it wrong. It was a chance sighting of Nico—if it *was* Nico."

Canning was again standing in front of me with his fists planted on his hips. He gazed at me in silence for a long time. "What do you think?" he said finally. "Do you think it was Nico?"

"I don't know—I can't say."

There was another silence. "Floyd tells me you mentioned Lou Hendricks. Why did you?"

"Hendricks picked me up on the street and took me for a drive in his fancy car."

"And?"

"He's looking for Nico too. Popular boy, your son."

"Hendricks thinks Nico is alive?"

"He didn't seem to know one way or the other. Like you, he'd heard I was sniffing around, trying to pick up Nico's trail." I didn't mention the suitcase, which to my regret I had mentioned to Hendricks. "There was nothing I could tell him, either."

Canning sighed. "All right, Marlowe, have it your way."

The door at the other end of the pool opened then, right on cue, and Bartlett and Floyd Hanson came back in. Hanson was looking more troubled than ever. His face was gray with tinges of green. He had bloodstains on his nice linen jacket and on his previously spotless white pants, too. Disposing of a couple of badly roughed-up corpses—I thought it a pretty fair assumption that the second Mexican was dead by the time he got to wherever it

was he was taken—would be hell on your clothes, especially if
you were as natty a dresser as Floyd Hanson. Clearly he wasn't
used to the sight of gore, at least not in the quantities shed by the
two Mexicans. But hadn't he said he had fought in the Ardennes? I
should have known to take that with a shovelful of salt.

Bartlett came forward. "That's all fixed then, Mr. Canning," he
said in his Cockney voice.

Canning nodded. "Two down," he said, "one to go. Mr. Marlowe here isn't being cooperative. Maybe a good soaking would
clear his head. Floyd, give Mr. Bartlett a hand, will you?"

Bartlett went behind me again and began untying the ropes.
When he got them off, he had to help me stand since my legs were
too numb to support me. He had released my hands, too, and I
flexed my arms to get the blood flowing in them. Now he walked
me to the edge of the pool and put a hand on my shoulder and made
me kneel on the marble tiles. The water level was only an inch or
two below the edge. Bartlett held one of my arms, and Hanson
came forward and took the other. I thought they were going to
tip me into the pool, but instead they yanked my arms behind
my back and Bartlett grabbed my hair again and pushed my head
forward and plunged it into the water. I hadn't taken a deep enough
breath, and right away I began to experience the panic of a drowning man. I tried to get my face turned sideways so I could snatch
some air, but Bartlett's fingers were as strong as a pit bull's jaws,
and I couldn't move. Very soon I felt as if my lungs were about to
burst. Then at last I was hauled upright again, with water streaming in under my collar. Canning came and stood beside me, leaning
down with his hands braced on his knees and his face close to
mine. "Now," he said, "are you ready to tell us what you know?"

"You're making a mistake, Canning," I said between gasps. "I
don't know anything."

He sighed again and nodded to Bartlett, and once more I
was underwater. Funny the things you notice, even in the most

desperate circumstances. I had my eyes open and could see, far down, on the pale blue bottom of the pool, a small ring, a plain gold band, that must have slipped off some woman bather's finger without her noticing. At least this time I had been smart enough to fill my lungs, but it didn't make much difference, and after a minute or so I was a drowning man all over again. I'd never gone in the water much and certainly had never learned to hold my breath the way champion swimmers do. I wondered if maybe that ring down there would be the last thing I'd ever see. I could think of worse sights to have your eye fixed on while you were breathing—or, in my case, not breathing—your last.

Bartlett could feel when I began to panic and was close to opening my mouth and letting my lungs fill up, and he wasn't ready to let me die, not yet. He and Hanson pulled me up again. Canning leaned down, peering into my face. "You ready to talk, Marlowe? You know what they say about going down for the third time. You don't want to join those two spics on the rubbish heap, now do you?"

I said nothing, only hung my dripping head. Hanson was on my right, holding my arm twisted behind me; I could see his nifty loafers and the cuffs of his white linen pants. Bartlett was on the other side, grasping my left arm and with his right hand still clutching the back of my head. I reckoned they would probably drown me this time. I had to do something. I thought I'd rather be beaten to death than die underwater. But what could I do?

I've never been much of a fighter—when you're past forty, you're past it. I've been in fights, quite a few, but only when I was forced. There's a big difference between defending yourself against an assault and launching an assault yourself. One thing I have learned, though, is the importance of balance. Even the hardest of cases—and Bartlett, despite his age and his low stature, was as hard as they come—can be knocked off their feet if you get them at just the right moment, in just the right position. Bartlett, as he prepared to push me under again, was concentrating his strength in his right hand, the one that was grasping the back of my head, and for a second he relaxed his grip on my arm. Pushing me toward the water, he had to rise up on his toes. I whipped my arm free of his grasp and flexed my elbow and rammed it into his ribs. He gave a low grunt and let go of my head. Hanson still had hold of my right arm, but his heart wasn't in it, and I pulled away from him and he took a step back, afraid that I would do to him what I'd already done to Bartlett.

Behind me Canning shouted something, I don't know what. I was concentrating on Bartlett. Rising from my knees, I brought my left fist around in a wide arc and caught him square on the side of the neck, and with another muffled grunt he teetered on the side of the pool, waving his arms in a way that would have been funny if this were the movies, then toppled over backward, headfirst, into the water. The splash he made was amazing, the water rising up in a great transparent funnel and falling back again with strange slowness—my brain must still have been sluggish from the dope.

I turned. It had all taken no more than a couple of seconds. I knew I'd probably have even less time than that before Canning and Hanson recovered enough to throw themselves on me. But they didn't need to. Hanson, I saw, had a gun in his hand, a pistol, a big black job with a long barrel—a Webley, I thought. Where had it come from? It was probably Canning's; he'd favor a British-made weapon, the sort of gun employed by your superior English gentleman.

"Stop right where you are," Hanson said, just like all the baddies he'd seen in so many B pictures.

I studied him carefully. He didn't have the eyes of a killer. I stepped forward. The gun barrel wavered.

"Shoot him!" Canning yelled. "Go on, pull the damned trigger!" He could shout, all right, but still he held back.

"You're not going to kill me, Hanson," I said. "We both know it."

I could see the sweat glistening on his forehead and on his upper lip. It doesn't make you a coward that you won't shoot a man. Killing is never easy. Out of the corner of my eye, I could see Bartlett hauling himself out of the pool. I took another step. The gun was pointing at my breastbone. I grabbed the barrel and wrenched it sideways. Maybe Hanson was too surprised to resist, or maybe he just wanted to be rid of the weapon, but he let go of it and stepped back, lifting his hands and extending them toward me as if they would ward off a bullet. That crazy gun weighed about as much as an anvil, and I had to hold it in both hands. It wasn't a Webley, and it wasn't British. In fact, it was German-made, a Weihrauch .38. An ugly weapon, but awfully effective.

I turned and shot Bartlett in the right knee. I don't know if it was his knee I was aiming at, but that was what I hit. He made a strange mewling noise and toppled over on his side and lay there hunched over and squirming. A big bloodstain was spreading down the leg of his sodden trousers. There was a sound behind me. I stepped quickly to one side and Canning stumbled past, cursing, his arms reaching out helplessly in front of him. He stopped and spun around and seemed about to lunge at me again. I thought of shooting him, too, but didn't. "I don't want to kill you, Canning," I said, "but I will if I have to." I waved the gun in Hanson's direction. "Get over here, Floyd," I said.

He came and stood beside his boss. "You lousy milksop!" Canning hissed at him.

I laughed. I didn't think I'd ever heard anyone actually say the word *milksop* before, in real life. Then I kept on laughing. I suppose I was in some sort of shock. All the same, the events of the past half minute or so, seen from a certain angle, would have looked as comical, and as grotesque, as a Charlie Chaplin routine.

Bartlett was clutching his leg just below his shattered knee and moving the other leg in a circle around and around on the tiles, like a slow-motion cyclist. He was still making those mewling sounds. No matter how tough you are, a smashed kneecap can only hurt like hell. It would be quite a while, I thought, before he got back to serving afternoon tea.

My arms, still tingling with pins and needles, ached from holding up the weight of that kraut cannon and keeping the barrel in a more or less horizontal plane. Canning was watching me with a nasty gleam of contempt. "Well, Marlowe," he said, "what are you going to do now? I guess you'll have to kill me, after all. Not to mention my loyal majordomo here." Hanson threw him a look of rancid hatred.

"Get in the pool," I said to the two of them. They both stared at me. "Now," I said, gesturing with the gun. "Get in the water."

"I—I can't swim," Hanson said.

"Here's your chance to learn," I said, and laughed again. It was more of a giggle. I wasn't myself. Hanson swallowed hard and began to ease off his shiny shoes. "No," I said, "leave them on— leave everything on."

Canning was still glaring at me. His little mad eyes were icy with rage, yet there was something fixed and almost dreamy in his look. I suppose he was lovingly picturing the things he would have Bartlett—or, more likely, Bartlett's successor—do to me if he ever got the chance.

"Come on, Canning," I said, "into the water, unless you want me to do to you what I did to jolly old Jeeves here. And drop the cane, by the way."

Canning threw the swagger stick on the marble, like a kid throwing down someone else's toy he's been told to give back, and turned and set off walking toward the other, shallow end of the pool. I hadn't noticed before how bowlegged he was. He had his fists clenched at his sides. Fellows like him don't quite know how to behave, how to carry themselves, when suddenly they're the ones being told what to do and are powerless not to do it.

Hanson gave me a pleading look and started to say something. I waved the gun barrel in his face to shut him up—I was tired of listening to his voice, so jaded and cool before, so thin and whiny now. "Go on in, Floyd," I said, "the water's lovely." He nodded miserably and turned away and followed Canning. "Atta boy," I said to his back.

When Canning got to the far end of the pool, he turned and looked at me along the length of it. I could almost hear him asking himself if there might still be a way to get the jump on me. "I can shoot you just as well from here," I called to him, my voice making watery echoes under the high glass dome of the roof. He hesitated another moment, then stepped into the pool, stumping with his bandy gait down the white steps that led under the water. "Now keep going," I said, "right out into the middle." Floyd Hanson had reached the end of the pool now, and after hanging back for a few seconds, he too descended gingerly into the water. "Keep walking till you're in it up to your chin," I said to him, "then you can stop. We wouldn't want you to drown."

Canning waded toward me until the water had reached his chest, then breaststroked forward and swam the rest of the way to the center of the pool, where he stopped and bobbed up and down, moving his arms and treading water. Hanson too waded out, halting when his shoulders were covered. "Come on, Floyd," I called. "Like I said, till it's up to your chin." He advanced another agonized step. Even at that distance I could see the panic in his eyes. At least he hadn't claimed it was the navy he'd been in. "That's right," I said. "Now stop." It looked eerie, the way his bodiless head seemed to float there on the water. I thought of John the Baptist.

There are moments in life that you know you'll never forget,

that you'll remember ever afterward in bright, hard-edged, hallu-
cinatory detail.

"All right," I said. "I'm going to step outside the door here and
wait for a certain time—you won't know for how long—and in
that time if I hear one of you climbing out of the pool, I'll come
back in and shoot whichever of you it is. You got that?" I pointed
the gun at Canning. "*You* got that, old man?"

"You think you'll get away with this?" he said. "Wherever you
run, I'll hunt you down."

"You're not going to be doing any hunting for a while, Mr.
Canning," I said. "Not when you're in the slammer wearing a suit
with stripes on it and making your own bed at night."

"To hell with you, Marlowe," he said. He was breathing hard
already, floating and kicking there. If he had to stay in for much
longer, he might drown. I didn't really care if he did.

Of course, once I was out the door, I didn't hang around. Canning probably hadn't believed that I would, anyway. I decided not
to risk leaving by the front door—there might be a button the
receptionist could push that would summon a whole pack of
goons—so I looked for a side exit instead. I found one straight off,
and one that I knew, at that. I had opened a couple of doors and
hurried through a couple of rooms when I turned into a corridor
that looked familiar and pushed open another door—at random, I
thought—and there I was in the drawing room with the chintz
armchairs and the head-high fireplace, where that other time Hanson had brought me after our walk and where Bartlett, in his role
as venerable retainer, had served us tea. I crossed the room and
opened the glass-paneled door and stumbled out into sunlight and
the delicate perfume of orange trees.

The Shriners were still staggering around the grounds. Half of
them were drunk and the other half were well on the way. Their
fezzes sat askew now, and their voices sounded more raucous. In

my drug-heightened state, I thought for a minute I'd barged into a scene from *Ali Baba and the Forty Thieves*. I set off along the path beside the hanging bougainvillea in all its exaggerated glory.

I had a vague notion of how to get to where I had parked my car, and I was headed in that direction when, at a bend in the path, I found my way blocked by a redheaded, red-faced fellow in a slightly battered fez, who was built on the scale of a family-sized refrigerator. He was wearing a lime-green shirt and purple shorts and clutching a highball glass in his big pink paw. He looked at me with a broad, happy grin, then frowned in mock disapproval and pointed at my head. "You're bare up there, brother," he said. "That's not allowed. Where's your fez?"

"A monkey stole it and ran off with it into the trees," I said.

This caused the fat man to laugh heartily, and his belly shook under his blindingly bright green shirt. I realized I was still carrying the Weihrauch, and now he spotted it. "Why, lookee here!" he said. "Ain't that a dandy weapon you're packing. Where'd you get it from?"

"They're handing them out at the clubhouse," I said. "The manager embezzled the club funds, and there's a posse being formed to go after him. Hurry up and you might get to join."

He looked at me open-mouthed; then a sly grin spread over his face, which was the color and glistening texture of a Christmas ham. He wagged a roguish finger at me. "You're teasing me, brother," he said. "Ain't you? I know you are."

"You're right," I said and hefted the gun in my hand. "This thing is just a model of the real item. The big chief here, man by the name of Canning, collects 'em—model guns, that is. You should ask him to let you see his gun room. It's quite something."

The fat man put his head back and squinted at me. "Why," he said broadly, "I might just do that. Where can I find him?"

"He's in the swimming pool," I said.

"He's where?"

"In the pool. Cooling off. Go along that way"—I jerked a thumb over my shoulder—"and you'll find him. He'll be happy to see you."

"Well, thank you, brother. That's mighty friendly of you."

And he waddled off happily in the direction of the clubhouse.

When he had rounded the bend and was out of sight, I looked about—a bit wildly, I imagine. I was wondering what to do with the gun. My brain still wasn't working so well, given all the insults it had suffered in the past few days and hours. I was standing beside a high wall with heavy hangings of the official flower of San Clemente, and now I just heaved the weapon away from me. I heard it strike the wall and fall into the dirt at the base of it with a soft thud. Later, it would take Bernie Ohls's men nearly two days to find it.

The sun was shining full on the car, of course, and inside it was as hot as a steam oven. I didn't care—the steering wheel could sear my palms to the bone and I'd hardly feel it. I drove in the direction of the front gate. On one of the turns in the roadway I felt suddenly woozy, and the car nearly slammed into a tree. My arms still ached from those ropes. Marvin the gatekeeper gave me a leery look and pulled a gargoyle face, but he raised the barrier without a challenge. I stopped at the first phone booth I spotted and called Bernie. My voice wasn't working so well, and at first he couldn't make out what I was saying. Then he did.

What followed was kind of downbeat, or so it seemed to me, given all the colorful and exciting events that had taken place earlier. Bernie and his cohorts raided the Cahuilla Club and found Bartlett still there by the pool, passed out from loss of blood. They'd had some trouble making their way through the crowd of drunken Shriners wandering about the grounds. Floyd Hanson they nabbed at his apartment down by the ocean in Bay City. He had been in the middle of packing his bags. Bernie said that if Hanson hadn't tried to take so many of his things with him, there might have been just enough time for him to have made the skip.

"Jeez, you should have seen his place," Bernie said. "These big framed photos of musclemen on the walls and purple silk dressing gowns in the closets." He flapped a limp-wristed hand and whistled softly. "Whoo-whoo!"

I wanted to know about Canning, of course. Why wasn't I surprised to hear that he, unlike Hanson, had gotten away? That evening Bernie had led a squad over to Canning's house in Hancock Park, but the bird had already flown. The help couldn't say where he'd gone; all they knew was that he'd arrived home in a great hurry, his clothes looking as if he'd been caught in a flash flood, and ordered for a bag to be packed and the car to be brought around immediately to take him to the airport. The Sheriff's office set to work on combing through the passenger lists for departing flights, while Bernie's men went out to the airport and showed Canning's picture around among the airline staff. One check-in girl thought she recognized him, but the name he had given hadn't been Canning. As to what he had called himself, she couldn't remember. The flight he had taken was a direct shot to Toronto, with an onward leg to London, England, but she didn't know which destination had been on his ticket. Bernie called the office and told his men to concentrate on the passenger manifest for the Air Canada night flight to Toronto and see what they came up with.

Bernie and I took ourselves out for a drink. I suggested Victor's, and Bernie drove us over there. I ordered us both a gimlet. Victor's is the only bar I know where they make a proper gimlet—that is, half gin and half Rose's Lime Juice tossed in some crushed ice. Other places put in sugar and bitters and stuff like that, but that's all wrong. It was Terry Lennox who introduced me to Victor's, and every so often I go over there and lift a glass to the memory of an old friendship. Bernie had known about Terry, but not in the way I did.

I asked where Floyd Hanson was now, and Bernie told me they'd taken him downtown, where the boys in the back room had got to work on him right away. They didn't have to work hard. When they asked where the blood by the swimming pool had come from, he told them all about the Mexicans and how Bartlett, on Canning's orders, had tortured them for information and then finished them off. Hanson even offered to take them to the Cahuilla Club and show them the lime pit, off in a far corner of the club grounds, where he and Bartlett had dumped the two bodies. "Seems the soil is real acid out there," Bernie said.

"Hence the lime? Handy, having a pit full of it, when you need to get rid of a couple of stiffs."

Bernie made no comment on that. "This is a good drink," he said, taking a sip of his gimlet and smacking his lips. "Refreshing." He wasn't looking at me; even with his eyes wide open, Bernie has a way of seeming not to look at anything at all. "I can guess what Canning wanted information about, from you and the Mexicans," he said. "Our old pal Peterson, right? Talk about a bad penny."

I got out my cigarette case and offered it to him. He shook his head. "You still off them?" I asked.

"It ain't easy."

I put the case and my matchbook down on the bar. Bernie is not the type who should give up smoking; it just made him more irritable. I lit up and blew three smoke rings, all three of them perfectly formed—I hadn't thought I was that good.

Bernie was scowling. He really wanted a cigarette. His face darkened and he gave me his spill-the-beans-or-else look. "All right, Marlowe," he said, "let's hear it."

"Bernie," I said, "would it kill you to call me by my first name once in a while?"

"Why?"

"Because all day, people have been calling me Marlowe, followed by menaces and threats and then a lot of violence. I'm sick of it."

"So you want me to call you Phil—"

" 'Philip' would do."

"—and then we'd be pals and all, that right?"

I turned away from him. "Forget it," I said.

The barkeep was passing by and raised an inquiring eyebrow, but I waved him on. With gimlets you have to pace yourself, unless you want to wake up the next morning with a head like a cageful of cockatoos. I could hear Bernie beside me breathing heavily. You always know it's getting dangerous when Bernie starts snorting down his trunk like that.

"Let me lay it out for you, *Marlowe*," he said and started ticking off items on his big, meaty fingers. "First, this guy Peterson gets dead, then maybe he's not dead. Someone hires you to look into it. In the course of your investigations, you run into Peterson's sister. Next thing, Peterson's sister is dead, and in this case there's no doubt at all, since we saw her with her throat slit from ear to ear. I invite you to the scene of the crime and ask you, nicely, to let me know what you know. You tell me where to go and what I can do with myself—"

"Come on!" I protested. "I was perfectly polite!"

"—and then I get another call from you, and this time there's two corpses, and some kind of flunky lying beside a swimming pool with a slug in his leg, and a rich guy on the lam, and another guy attempting to be. I say to myself, *Bernie, this is one hell of a business*. The kind of business, *Marlowe*, that the Sheriff, when he hears about it any minute now, is going to expect me to clear up double quick. This Canning guy, you know who he is?"

"No, not really. But you're going to tell me."

"He's one of the biggest real estate investors in these parts. He owns department stores, factories, housing tracts—you name it."

"He's also the Petersons' father," I said. "Lynn and Nico, that is."

That shut him up for a second or two. He thrust his head forward and drew his eyebrows together so that he looked like a bull about to charge a particularly annoying matador. "You're kidding," he said.

"Would I kid you, Bernie?"

He sat there thinking. It was an awesome thing, the sight of Bernie deep in thought. Suddenly he reached out and grabbed my cigarette case, extracted a cigarette, stuck it in his mouth, and lit a match. He held the flame suspended for a second or two, with the look in his eye, sorrowing but defiant, of a sinner about to give in to his sin, Then he applied the light to the business end of the pill and took a long, slow drag. "Ah," he sighed, expelling smoke. "Jesus, that tastes good."

I caught the barkeep's eye and held up two fingers. He nodded. His name was Jake. It was here, at Victor's, that I first met Linda Loring, and Jake still remembers her. It's not surprising. Linda is the kind of woman you remember. Maybe I should marry her, if she's still interested, which maybe she's not. Did I mention that she's Terry Lennox's sister-in-law? Sylvia Lennox, Terry's missus, was the one who was murdered, which Terry took the rap for. In fact, Sylvia was killed by a woman crazy with jealousy—her husband and Sylvia had been lovers—and also just plain crazy. Terry wanted to disappear anyway, which is why he faked his suicide down in a flyblown nowhere town in Mexico called Otatoclán—though not many people know it was a fake, including Bernie. Why should I tell him? Terry was a heel, but I liked him anyway. He was a heel with style, and style is something I appreciate.

Jake brought the two fresh gimlets. Bernie was now thinking and smoking at the same time, and breathing hard between drags. I needed this drink, and maybe even another one after it.

"Listen, Bernie," I said, "before you get going again and start counting things off on your fingers and so on, let me repeat what I already told you: my involvement in the Peterson business is accidental. It has nothing to do with Canning and the Mexicans and Lynn Peterson's murder and—"

"Whoa there, smart guy!" Bernie said, holding up a hand that would have stopped the traffic on Bay City Boulevard. "Just back up a bit. You're telling me Canning is this guy Peterson's old man?"

"That's what I'm telling you."

"But how—?"

"Because Canning told me. He'd heard I was on the trail of his son—that's why he hauled me round and had his man dunk me in the swimming pool."

"And what about the two Mexes that he had 'his man' stomp to death? Where the hell do they come in?"

"They come in because they killed his daughter—they killed Lynn Peterson."

"I know that—but why?"

"Why what?"

"Why did they kill her? Why did they snatch her at Nico Peterson's house? Why were they at Peterson's house in the first place?" He stopped, and sighed, and leaned his forehead on his hand. "Tell me I'm stupid, Marlowe, tell me my brain is fried after all these years of being a cop, but I just don't get it."

"Drink your drink, Bernie," I said. "Have another cigarette. Relax."

He snapped his head up and glowered at me. "I'll relax," he said, "when you quit stonewalling and tell me what the hell is going on."

"I can't tell you that," I said. "I can't tell you, because I don't know. I got caught up in the works of this thing by accident. Let me say it again: I was hired to look for a guy who was supposed to be dead. Next thing I know I'm up to my knees in corpses, and I damn near became a corpse myself. But listen to me, Bernie, please, listen when I say it once more. I don't know, just as you don't, what's going on here. I feel like I stepped out one fine morning to take a little stroll and at the first street corner found myself involved in a ten-car pileup. Blood and bodies everywhere, burning vehicles, ambulance sirens wailing, the whole schlamozzle. And I'm standing in the middle of it, scratching my head like Stan Laurel. It's a fine mess, all right, Bernie—*but it ain't my mess*. Will you please believe me?"

Bernie swore and, in his agitation, picked up his nearly new drink and knocked it back in one short gulp. I winced. You don't do that to a gimlet, one of the world's most sophisticated drinks—simple, but sophisticated. Also, one of the world's most sophisticated drinks has to be sipped nice and slow or it will hit you like a depth charge.

Bernie blinked a few times as the gin sank and found its target; then he got at my cigarette case again and lit up another cancer stick. I watched him and thought how I wouldn't want to be Bernie's wife, later on, or Bernie's cat, since there was likely to be a lot of shouting and kicking going on in the Ohls residence tonight. "You got to tell me," he said, in a voice made raspy by cigarette smoke and the liquor he had just flushed over his vocal cords, "you got to tell me who it was that hired you to find Peterson." I had taken out my pipe, but he clamped a hand on my wrist. "And don't start playing with that goddamned thing!"

"All right, Bernie," I said soothingly, "all right." I put the pipe back in my pocket and took a cigarette instead, figuring I might as well get one before Bernie smoked them all. I was searching around for another diversionary tactic. "Tell me what Hanson had to say," I said.

"What do you mean, what he had to say?"

"I mean, what did he tell your boys when they went at him with the thumbscrews? What goods did he cough up?"

Bernie turned aside as if to spit, then turned back again. "Nothing worthwhile," he said disgustedly. "He didn't have anything. My guess is Canning didn't trust him, not with the sensitive stuff, anyway. He said Canning wanted to find out what you knew about Nico Peterson, whether he might be alive and, if so, where he could be found. That was hardly news. As for the Mexicans, Canning knew they'd killed the girl, and took his revenge."

"How did Canning get hold of the Mexicans? Did Hanson say?"

"He has associates south of the border. They nabbed the Mexes and shipped them up here. Pays to have influential friends, eh?" He picked up his empty glass and looked into it mournfully. "What a mess," he said. "What an all-time, rip-roaring, Empire State Building of a mess." He lifted his sad gaze and fixed it on me. "You know why I'm here, Marlowe? You know why I'm here, drinking with you and smoking? Because when I go home, my boss will have been on the telephone half a dozen times already, wanting to know if I've apprehended the miscreants yet, and if I've got you safely locked up in the sneezer, and how he's going to explain to Canning's fancy pals in city hall and elsewhere, who are *his* associates, too, most of them, how come we conducted a raid on this club of his—what's it called?"

"The Cahuilla."

"—how come we conducted a full-scale raid on the Cahuilla Club, where they're all members, before I consulted him and got his permission."

"What?" I said. "You went out there without telling the big man?"

Sheriff Donnelly had been elected just recently, beating his predecessor by a couple thousand votes in an election upset that had surprised everyone, including Donnelly himself, I imagine. The guy he'd ousted had been in the job since before World War I, or so it felt like, and Donnelly had a lot to prove. The Sheriff's chair was still warm when he put his backside on it, and from day one he'd been throwing his considerable weight around and leaning heavily on Bernie and the other officers in his command. Maybe they deserved it—they'd probably gotten soft under the old regime.

"It seemed urgent," Bernie said, "from the way you described the shenanigans out there at the club. If I'd involved Donnelly, there'd have been so many hoops to jump through before we moved that everyone in the joint, including the bar staff and the gardeners, would have vamoosed long before we got there." He stopped and looked at me. "What's the matter now?"

I must have given what they call an involuntary start. A thought had struck me, a big, dirty, nasty, obvious thought.

"Is there a list of the people who work out there, at the club?" I asked.

"A list? Whaddya mean?"

"There must be some kind of record of who's on the staff," I said, talking more to myself than to Bernie, "a personnel or a payroll list, something like that."

"What are you talking about?"

I took a little of my drink, noticing yet again how the lime juice perfectly complemented the juniper-berry tang of the gin. Good old Terry—if he'd done nothing else, he'd certainly introduced me to a great cocktail. "When I was out there, at the club," I said, "this guy, his name is Lamarr, came up and started talking to me. He's a bit, you know"—I touched a finger to my temple—"but not crazy crazy, and harmless, I'd guess. He said he'd seen me talking to Captain Hook and that he was one of the Lost Boys."

"Captain Hook," Bernie repeated in a flat voice, nodding. "The Lost Boys. What's this, for Christ's sake?"

"Floyd Hanson told me that the club has a policy of hiring the likes of Lamarr, loners, drifters, people with no past and not much future. Kind of a philanthropic thing, though I can't see Wilber Canning as a philanthropist—that would have been his father."

I stopped. Bernie waited, then said impatiently, "So? What's the deal?"

"If Nico Peterson is alive and his death was faked, there had to be a body—Lynn Peterson was shown a stiff in the morgue and identified him as her brother. Maybe she was lying, to cover up the fact that Nico was alive and the whole thing was a setup."

Bernie thought it over. "You're saying the body in the morgue could have been one of the hobos working at the club? That Nico killed someone there, changed clothes with him, ran over the body enough times to make it unrecognizable, then dumped it at the roadside and hightailed it?"

I nodded slowly. I was still thinking it out myself. "'The Lost Boys,' Lamarr said. 'We're the Lost Boys.'"

"Who the hell are the Lost Boys? And who's Captain Hook?"

"He's a character in *Peter Pan*. You know—by J. M. Barrie?"

"Crazy but well-read, then, this Lamarr."

"He was talking about Floyd Hanson. Hanson was Captain Hook. And the night Nico Peterson is supposed to have died, Hanson was one of the first on the scene and gave a preliminary identification. You bring Hanson back in and sweat him properly this time, I'll bet you'll get the whole story out of him."

Bernie was silent for a while, playing with my matchbook, turning it in his fingers edge over edge on the bar. "You still saying you know nothing about all this except what the rest of us know?"

"I am saying that, Bernie, yes. You might notice I've said it a few times. It give you the idea that maybe I'm telling the truth?"

"It all started with you, Marlowe," Bernie said with his eyes downcast, watching the matchbook, his tone almost gentle. "You're the key to it all, somehow, I know that."

"How could I—?"

"Shut up. Peterson I don't care about, or even his sister. The Mexes, too—what's a couple of dead wetbacks? That fairy Hanson I can live without, also Canning's pin-striped blackjack artist. But Canning—Canning's a different matter. He's the name that's going to be splashed all over the papers tomorrow, unless someone steps in and applies a gag."

"Oh?" I said. "Who might that someone be?" I was asking, but I had a sudden idea what the answer was, and my heart began to sink in anticipation.

"I guess one of the many things you didn't know," Bernie said, in that half-angry, half-smug way of his, "is that Wilber Canning is a close business associate of Harlan Potter's."

He'd been saving that one up. I looked into my glass. I wondered who invented the gimlet. And how had he thought up the name? The world is full of little questions like that, and only Ripley knows the answers to them all.

"Ah," I said.

"What does that mean?"

"It means 'Ah.'"

Harlan Potter owned a large chunk of this strip of the California coast, along with about a dozen major newspapers, last count. He also happened to be the father of Linda Loring and of the late Mrs. Sylvia Lennox, which of course made him Terry Lennox's father-in-law. At every turn in my life, it seemed, there was Terry, smiling his rueful smile and twirling a gimlet glass in his bone-white fingers. Funny—most people thought he was dead, like they thought Nico Peterson was dead, but he wasn't, though he kept haunting me as if he were.

If I marry Linda Loring, I thought, Harlan Potter will be *my* father-in-law. That was a three-gimlet prospect. I gave the sign to Jake the barkeep, and he replied with his nod that was so understated it was hardly a nod at all.

"So," I said, releasing a slow breath. "Harlan Potter. Well, well. Citizen Kane himself."

"Have some respect!" Bernie said, trying not to snigger. "You're almost one of the family—I hear Potter's daughter is still carrying a torch for you. You going to let her light up your gray little life?"

"Don't push it, Bernie," I said evenly.

He lifted his hands in the sign of peace. "Hey, calm down. You're losing your sense of humor, Marlowe."

I swiveled on the bar stool so I was facing him. His eyes moved away from mine. He knew he'd overstepped the mark, but I kept going anyway. "Listen, Bernie, you can pummel me all you like about stuff that's of legitimate interest to you, but stay out of my private life."

"All right, all right," he mumbled, looking sheepish and still frowning at the floor. "I'm sorry."

"Thanks."

I turned back to the bar, not wanting him to see the shadow of a smirk I couldn't keep off my face. I didn't often get the chance to make Bernie blush, and when I did, I milked it for all it was worth.

Jake brought our drinks. I could see that Bernie didn't really want another one, but given the fact that his size eleven foot was still in his mouth, he couldn't very well refuse.

"Anyway, you're probably right," I said, cutting him some slack.

"About what?"

"About Potter making sure that his pal Canning doesn't get completely roasted in tomorrow's editions."

"Uh-huh." He took a sip of his drink and replaced the glass on the bar with a worried grimace. He was probably going to have to see Donnelly before long, and it wouldn't go down too well if he stank of gin, which he would now anyway, since he'd put away two gimlets already. "This town," he said, clicking his tongue. "I've about had it up to here with it." He put a hand horizontally under his chin. "You know I been on the force nearly a quarter century? Think of that. It's a meat grinder, and I'm not even prime chuck steak."

"Come on, Bernie," I said, "you'll have me weeping in a minute."

He looked at me morosely. "And what about you?" he said. "You going to pretend your world is any cleaner than the one I'm stuck in?"

"It's the same all around," I said. "But look at it this way. With guys like you and me on one side of the scale, it's not going to go down the whole way on the other side, where the Cannings and the Potters sit with their bags of gold in their laps."

"Yeah, sure," Bernie said. "You're a regular Pollyanna this evening, ain't you."

I shut up then, not because of Bernie's taunt but because I had a misgiving over putting Harlan Potter in the same league as Wilber Canning. Potter was tough, and you didn't make his kind of money—they say he's worth a hundred million—without cutting a few corners, and maybe a few throats, too. But a man who'd fathered a girl like Linda Loring couldn't be all bad. I'd had a talk with him once. He started off by threatening me, went on to give me a lecture about what a dismal lot the rest of us were, then threatened me again, and ended up with the casual suggestion that he might think of putting some business my way, if I kept my nose clean. I said thanks but no thanks. At least, I thought I did.

Bernie looked at his watch. It was the size of a potato, but it still looked small on that arm of his. "I gotta blow," he said and began shifting off the stool.

"You haven't finished your drink," I said. "Cocktails don't come cheap, you know."

"Listen, I'm officially on duty. Here"—he brought out his billfold and threw a five-spot on the bar—"have it on me."

I gave him a look, then picked up the bill, folded it, and stuffed it in the top pocket of his blue serge suit. "Don't insult me, Bernie," I said. "I ask you to come for a drink, I pay. That's part of what they call the social contract."

"Yeah. I'm not so good on society rules." He smiled, and I smiled back. "I'll be seeing you, Phil," he said.

"Do you have to?"

"It's my job." He put on his hat, adjusted it, and flicked the brim with a fingertip in a sort of salute. "So long, for now."

I finished my drink and thought of finishing the one Bernie had left undrunk, but there are some limits us Marlowes just won't cross. Instead I paid the bill and took up my own hat. I could see Jake getting ready to ask me how my lady friend was doing these days, meaning Linda Loring. To cut him off, I pretended to remember an urgent appointment elsewhere and made my escape.

It was a clear, cool night, and one big star was hanging low in the sky and throwing a long stiletto of light down into the heart of the Hollywood Hills. Bats were out too, squeaking and flickering like scraps of charred paper from a fire. I looked for a moon but couldn't see one. Just as well—the moon always makes me feel melancholy. I had nowhere to go and nothing to do. I remembered that I didn't have the car with me and flagged a taxi and told the driver to take me home. He was an Italian, as big as Bernie Ohls and about as good-humored. Every time a light turned red, he swore under his breath. The swear words were Italian, but I didn't need a translation to know what they meant.

In the house the air was stuffy, as if a gang of people had been squatting in here all day with the windows sealed. I set up a chess game out of a book, Lasker vs. Capablanca, in which Capablanca demolished the German master with one of his sweetest and most deadly endgames. Chess doesn't come any better. All the same, I wasn't in the mood. I still had a buzz on from all the gin I'd put away, and I didn't want it to fade. There are times when you wish your mind would stop working, and tonight mine was being much too busy for comfort. Some thoughts you try to keep out, but they get in anyway.

I hopped in the Olds and drove over to Barney's Beanery, where I drank six straight bourbons and would have kept going only good old Travis, my guardian angel behind the bar, refused to serve me any more. Instead he made me give him my car keys and helped me out to the street and poured me into a cab. After that I don't remember much. Somehow I got myself up the redwood steps and through the front door and even made it into the bedroom, where I woke around midnight, sprawled diagonally across the bed, on my face, with all my clothes on. I smelled like a raccoon and was as thirsty as a camel.

I stumbled into the kitchen and leaned over the sink and drank a quart or so of water straight from the faucet, then straightaway I stumbled into the bathroom and leaned over the toilet and threw up a couple of quarts. The first quart was water, followed by another quart of pale green liquid composed, I figured, half of gimlet and half of bile. It had been a long day.

And it wasn't over yet. In the middle of the night, the phone woke me. At first I thought it was a fire alarm, and I would have run out into the night except that, for some reason, I couldn't get the front door to open. I picked up the receiver as if it were the head of a rattlesnake. It was Bernie, calling to tell me that Floyd Hanson had just been found in his cell, hanging from one of the bars in the window. He had torn the bedsheet into strips and wound them together into a makeshift rope. The window hadn't been high enough, and he'd had to let himself hang there with his feet on the floor and his knees flexed. It would have taken him a long time to die.

"So that's one canary that won't be singing," Bernie said. I told him he was all heart. He laughed, without enjoying it. "What's the matter with you?" he asked. "You sound like you're wearing a gag."

"I'm drunk," I told him.

"You're what? I can't make out what you're saying."

"I said I'm *drunk*. Iced. Soused. Spifflicated."

He laughed again, with conviction this time. I supposed it must have been funny, hearing someone as far gone as I was trying to pronounce those words, especially the last one.

I took a deep breath, which made me feel dizzy, but then my head cleared enough for me to ask about Bartlett.

"Who's Bartlett?" Bernie said.

"Jesus, Bernie, don't shout," I said, holding the receiver away from my ear. "Bartlett is the butler—the old guy with the black-jack, the one I shot in the knee."

"Oh, him. He's not so good. In a coma, last I heard. Lost a barrel of blood. They're giving him transfusions. Maybe he'll pull through, maybe not. You proud of yourself, Wild Bill?"

"He damn near drowned me," I growled.

"That old guy? You're losing it, Marlowe."

"There you go, calling me Marlowe again."

"Yeah, well, there's a lot worse things I could call you. And just because you buy me a couple of drinks don't mean I got to be your best friend and playmate. And the booze wore off as soon as I got into the office—Donnelly had been at some fancy fund-raiser, and he came in in a tuxedo and black tie, stinking of cologne and high-toned women. You ever notice how the smell of women is everywhere on that kind of evening?"

"Have I ever been to that kind of evening?"

"Makes your head swim. Has effects lower down, too. Any-way, Donnelly was pretty sore at being dragged away from the ball, but that was nothing compared to what he was like when he heard what had happened out at the Cahuilla Club, what with you shooting butlers and Canning doing the Indian rope trick and vanishing into thin air."

"Bernie," I said, in the voice of some infinitely gentle, infinitely suffering thing, as the poet writes, "Bernie, I'm drunk and I'm sick and there's a guy with a jackhammer hard at work on the back of my skull. I was almost drowned today. I also shot a guy who's maybe not going to make it and probably doesn't deserve to, but still, even popping bad guys takes it out of you. So can I please go back to bed?"

"Yeah, you go and sleep it off, Marlowe, while the rest of us stay up all night trying to sort out a mess that, as far as I can see, *you* started."

"I'm sorry you're in the wrong job, Bernie. What did you want to be, a kindergarten teacher?"

He exploded then into the kind of language the likes of which you wouldn't find in one of those books you buy in a plain brown wrapper from a shop where the shades are always pulled and there's no sign over the door. I let him rant, and eventually he ran out of steam and shut up, though I could hear him breathing angrily into the mouthpiece. Then he asked what I'd done with the gun.

"What gun?"

"*What gun?* The gun you shot Bartleby with."

"Bartlett. I threw it away."

"Where?"

"Into the bougainvillea."

"Into the *what*?"

"The bushes. At the Cahuilla Club."

"You dumb bastard. What were you thinking of?"

"I wasn't thinking of anything," I said. "I was operating on instinct. You remember what instinct is, Bernie? It's what mostly guides the behavior of ordinary human beings, people who haven't been on the police force for a quarter of a century."

Then I hung up on him.

== 21 ==

I slept till noon. What did I feel like like when I woke up? There was a stray cat in the neighborhood that kept cozying up to me in the hope that I'd take her in and let her run my life for me. She was a moth-eaten Siamese, but of course she thought she was the reincarnation of an Egyptian princess. The other day I opened my back door and there was Pharaoh's daughter, sitting on the stoop holding in her mouth the remains of what had been some kind of bird. She gave me a winsome look and delicately laid the corpse down at my feet. I guess it was meant as a present for me, sort of a down payment prior to her moving in.

Well, that bird was me, glazed of eye and feeling chewed all over, as I lay there in a tangle of sweat-soaked sheets and watched the light fixture in the ceiling, which seemed to be spinning slowly around and around in an elliptical orbit. Take my advice: never drink six bourbons on top of a trio of gimlets. When I had unsealed my lips sufficiently to open my mouth, I was surprised that heavy green smoke didn't come pouring out of it.

I got up and dragged myself into the kitchen, moving very

carefully, like a very old man, brittle and frail. I spooned some coffee into the percolator and put it on the stove and set a flame going under it. Then I stood for a long time leaning on the edge of the sink and gazing vacantly into the backyard. The sunlight out there was as acid as lemon juice. The recent rain had livened things up greatly, though. Most of the blossoms on Mrs. Paloosa's potato vine were starting to turn to berries by now, but the oleander bush behind the garbage can was a mass of pink flowers, where half a dozen tiny hummingbirds were busy about their work of pollination. Ah, nature, and hungover me the only blot on the landscape.

The percolator began to rumble, sounding just like my stomach.

I put on a robe and went out and picked up the paper the delivery boy had lobbed onto the porch. I stood in the cool shadow and scanned the front page. There was a report in column seven of "an incident" at the Cahuilla Club. A couple of unidentified intruders had broken into the club and had been tackled by the security staff—Bartlett wasn't named—and two deaths had resulted. It appeared that the manager of the club, Floyd Henson (*sic,* as they say), had been complicit in the raid and later had accidentally died while in police custody. The owner of the club, Wilberforce Canning, had left late last night for an undisclosed destination abroad. I whistled, shaking my head. You had to hand it to Harlan Potter. When he killed a story, he did it with impressive thoroughness.

I went back into the house and poured a cup of coffee from the percolator and drank it. It was too strong and had a bitter taste. Or maybe the bitterness was already in my mouth, from what I'd just been reading.

A little while later, I took my pajama top off in the bathroom and was impressed by the bruises Bartlett's ropes had left on my arms and across my chest and rib cage. They ranged in color from putty gray through livid crimson to a sickly, sulfurous shade of yellow. My lungs were sore, from the pressure of my being trussed up for so long and then from having to work so hard not to burst when my head was underwater, not to mention the cigarettes I'd smoked last night in the Beanery as I sank deeper and deeper into that bourbon bottle.

Bad as I felt, it was better than being dead, but only just.

When I had shaved and showered and buffed myself up as best I could, I put on a gray suit, a white shirt, and a dark tie. It's always best to dress soberly after a drunken night. I poured another cup of the muddy coffee, which was lukewarm by now, and took it into the living room and sat with it on the sofa and lit up an experimental cigarette. It tasted like wormwood, or what I imagined something that was called wormwood tasted like. I have a suspicion that the worst thing you can do when you have a hangover is drink coffee and partake of nicotine, but you've got to do something.

When the mailman dropped the day's second delivery of mail through the mail slot and it fell on the tiles in the hall, I jumped about a foot at the noise it made. I was in that kind of state. I went out and gathered up the sheaf of envelopes. Utility bills. An offer from a company in Nebraska to supply me with prime rib-eye steaks packed in salt and dispatched by air. A notice from PG&E that my electricity account was overdue. And a cream-colored envelope with my name and address written in violet ink in a neat, looping hand. I sniffed it. Langrishe Lace, faint but by now unmistakable.

I carried the letter back to the sofa, sat down, and held it up between a finger and thumb and gazed at it. I recalled Clare Cavendish at her little wrought-iron table in the conservatory that day, a day that now seemed an awful long time ago, writing in her notebook with her fancy fountain pen. I put the envelope down on the coffee table and looked at it some more, finishing my cigarette. What would it be, a Dear John letter, delivering me the final brush-off, the coup de grâce? A note accusing me of having engaged in improper relations with a client? Was I about to be given the sack? Or maybe it was a check, settling the account and saying a curt bye-bye.

There was only one way to find out. I picked up the envelope and slipped a finger under the flap, and as I did so I thought of Clare licking it, the sharp little crimson tip of her tongue sliding swiftly along it and moistening the gum.

> I wish to know if you have made any progress in the matter which
> I engaged you to investigate. I would have expected significant
> developments by now. Please let me know soonest.
>
> CC

That was it. No sender's address, no greeting, and no name, only the initials. She wasn't taking any chances. It was the hand-written version of a kick in the guts. I started to get mad but then told myself not to be so dumb. Getting mad puts a strain on the liver and doesn't do a damned bit of good.

I put Clare Cavendish's cold little note aside, sat back on the sofa, lit another cigarette, and, since there was no avoiding it, set myself to thinking. The Nico Peterson affair hadn't made much sense from the start, but by now it was making no sense at all. I came across a nice word recently: *palimpsest*. The dictionary said it was a manuscript with the original text partly erased and a new one written over it. What I was dealing with here was some-thing like that. I was convinced that behind everything that had happened there was another version of things that I couldn't read. All the same, I knew it was there. You don't do my kind of work for as long as I have without developing a nose for the missing facts.

I went over it all again, sitting there on my sofa in the quiet of noontime—the nice thing about living on a dead-end street is that there's not much traffic and consequently the noise level stays low. But the text was the same as before and I got nowhere, or nowhere new, anyway. The thing I was certain of, the *only* thing I was certain of, was that Clare Cavendish was the one piece of the puzzle that didn't fit. Nico Peterson I sort of understood. He was a rich man's son whose aim in life was to get rich himself and spit in his father's eye, only he didn't have his old man's brains, or daring, or ruthlessness, or whatever it is you need to make a million bucks. He'd gotten nowhere in the agenting business—even Mandy Rogers could see he was useless—and he'd probably fallen in with the wrong crowd.

I also suspected that whatever contraband Nico had been shipping up in a suitcase from Mexico for delivery to Lou Hendricks was worth a lot of dough: you don't fake your own death for nickels and dimes. And I was pretty certain Floyd Hanson had been in cahoots with Nico and had supplied one of his Lost Boys as a substitute corpse. My guess was that Wilber Canning didn't know what Hanson and Nico had cooked up between them and had believed that Nico was dead until I stuck my beak into the tent. As for Gómez and López, I presumed they were the original owners of whatever was in the suitcase Nico had made off with and they had come up here to find Nico and reclaim their goods.

That left Clare Cavendish. She'd hired me to find a boyfriend who had two-timed her in a spectacular fashion, first pretending to be dead and then turning up alive, but I didn't buy that version of things. From the start I'd been unable to believe that a woman like her would have gotten involved with a man like Peterson. Sure, there are women who like to dabble in the dirt—it excites them to risk their reputations and maybe even their health. But Clare Cavendish wasn't the type. I could see her throwing herself into the arms of a cad, but he would have to be her kind of cad, with class and style and money. All right, she'd gone to bed with me, a guy who wouldn't know how to work the gears in a fancy foreign sports car. I couldn't account for that. How could I be expected to, when every time I thought of it I could see nothing but her in my bed that night, leaning above me in the lamplight, touching my lips with her fingertips and letting her blond hair fall around my face? Maybe I reminded her of someone she once knew—once loved, even. Or maybe she was just keeping me sweet, so she could go on using me for whatever the hell it was she was up to. That was a possibility I'd rather not have entertained. But once you think a thing, it stays thought.

I had the phone in my hand and was dialing her number before I knew what I was doing. There are times when you find yourself following your instincts like a well-trained dog trotting behind the heels of its master. A maid answered and told me to hold on. I could hear her footsteps as she walked off down an echoing hallway. A house has to be awful big to produce echoes that loud. I remembered Dorothea Langrishe's look of wonderment when she'd remarked how she'd made a fortune from the crushed petals of a flower. It's a funny world.

"Yes?" Clare Cavendish said, in a voice that would have put a skim of ice on the surface of Lake Tahoe. I told her I wanted to see her. "Oh, yes?" she said. "You have something to report?"

"I have something to ask you," I said.

"Can't you ask it over the phone?"

"No."

There was a silence. I didn't know why she was being so cold. We hadn't parted on good terms at my house that night, but I'd come when she'd called me to help her when her brother had overdosed. That hadn't made me Sir Galahad, but I didn't think I deserved such a chilly tone, or that nasty little note she'd sent me, either.

"What do you suggest?" she said. "It's not a good idea to come to the house."

"How about lunch?"

Again she let the seconds pass. "All right. Where?"

"The Ritz-Beverly," I said. It was the first place that came to mind. "It's where I met your mother when we had our talk."

"Yes, I know. Mother is out of town today. I'll be there in a half hour."

I went into the bedroom and took a look at myself in the wardrobe mirror. The gray suit looked shabby, and besides, it was about the same shade as my face. I changed into a dark blue number and took off the tie I was wearing and put on a red one. I even thought of shining my shoes, but in my delicate state I didn't fancy the prospect of bending over to do it.

When I stepped out the front door and saw the empty space at the curb, I thought at first the Olds had been stolen. Then I remembered how Travis had taken the keys from me last night and sent me home in a taxi. I walked down the street toward Laurel Canyon. The sun was on the eucalyptus trees and the air was fresh with their scent. I told myself I didn't feel so bad, and I almost believed it. A cab cruised past me and I whistled after it and it stopped. The driver was the size of a moose, and when I looked at him I did a double take: he was the same Italian I'd flagged last night outside Victor's. This town seems to get smaller every day. His mood hadn't improved any, and sure enough he swore at every traffic light that was against us, as if someone in control of them was switching to red every time he approached.

It was turning out to be a day of coincidences. At the Beverly, I was led to the same table where I'd sat with Ma Langrishe. It was the same waiter, too. He remembered me and asked in a worried tone if Mrs. Langrishe would be joining me. I said no, and he smiled like he'd just thought of Christmas. I ordered a vodka martini— what the hell—and told him to make it as dry as Salt Lake City. "I understand, sir," he said softly, and I wouldn't have been surprised if he'd winked. He was an experienced fellow, and no doubt he could spot a hangover at a hundred paces.

I looked around while I waited for my drink to come. Even the shapely fronts and rears of the Nefertiti statues couldn't interest me much today. A few tables had the usual lunching ladies in hats and white gloves, and there were some sober-suited deal makers being businesslike and forceful. A young couple sat side by side on a banquette under a leaning palm. Honeymooners—he had that unmistakable goofy grin smeared over his face, and there was a hickey on the side of her neck the size and color of a mussel shell. I silently wished them happiness and good fortune. Why not? Even a man with a head as thick as a turnip couldn't help smiling benignly upon such a tender display of young love.

My martini arrived on a gleaming tray. It was cold and just a little oily, and it tripped happily over my teeth with a silvery tinkle.

She wasn't very late. The waiter led her to my table. She wore a white wool suit with a sort of bodice jacket and a slim skirt. Her hat was of cream straw with a black band and a big, swooping brim. My mouth had gone dry. She was staring at me with a shocked expression—I could imagine what I looked like—and when I leaned my face down to her, she kissed the air quickly a couple of inches short of my cheek and murmured, "My God, what happened?"

The waiter was hovering, and I turned to him. "The lady will join me in a martini," I said.

Clare began to protest, but I pretended not to notice; this was going to be a liquid lunch. She put her patent leather purse on the table and sat down slowly, still staring. "You look terrible," she said.

"And you look like your mother's bank balance."

She didn't smile. This wasn't a good start. "What happened?" she asked again.

"Yesterday was what you'd probably describe as 'trying.' You saw the story in this morning's *Chronicle*?"

"What story?"

I smiled at her with my teeth. "Those frightful incidents at the Cahuilla Club," I said. "Can't think what that establishment is coming to, what with dead Mexicans about the place and the manager turning out to be a creep. You knew Floyd Hanson, of course."

"I wouldn't say I *knew* him."

The waiter came with her drink and set the glass almost reverently in front of her. I could see him giving her that swift, all-over appraisal waiters are experts at. Probably his mouth had gone dry too. She bestowed on him a faint smile of thanks and he backed away, bowing.

"I imagine what appeared in the paper wasn't what really happened, was it," Clare said. She was looking at me with one eye from under the sloping brim of her hat.

"It rarely is."

"Were you at the club? I suppose that's why your day was—what was the word you used?—trying." I said nothing, only kept looking at that single, searching eye and maintaining my steely smile. "How is it you weren't named?" she asked.

"I have friends in high places," I said.

"Do you mean Linda's father?"

"Harlan Potter probably lifted the phone, yes," I said. "Has Linda told you how well she and I know each other?"

Now she did smile at me, but barely. "She didn't *tell* me, but from the way she speaks of you I can guess. Is the feeling mutual?"

I lit a cigarette. "I didn't come here to talk about Linda Loring," I said, more harshly than I'd meant to. She flinched a little, but I think it was only because she thought she should.

"I'm sorry," she said. "I didn't mean to pry."

She opened her purse and took out her cigarettes—so it was a Black Russian day—and fitted one into her ebony holder. I leaned across the table and offered her a lit match. "All right," she said, blowing smoke toward the ceiling, "what *did* you come here to talk about?"

"Well," I said, "I guess there's only one subject between you and me, Mrs. Cavendish."

She was silent for a moment, absorbing the tone in which I'd said her name. "It's a bit late, don't you think," she said quietly, "to revert to formalities?"

"I think it's better," I said, "if we keep things strictly businesslike."

She gave me another flicker of a smile. "Do you?"

"Well, that note you sent me certainly meant business."

She colored just a little. "Yes, I suppose it was rather brusque."

"Listen, Mrs. Cavendish," I repeated, "we've had some misunderstandings, you and I."

"What kind of misunderstandings?"

I told myself this wasn't the time to indulge in the luxury of getting angry. "Misunderstandings," I said, "that I'd like to clear up."

"And how would we do that?"

"It's up to you. You could start by leveling with me about Nico Peterson."

"'Leveling' with you? I'm not sure I know what you mean."

My glass was empty—I'd even eaten the olive. I caught the waiter's attention and he nodded and veered off in the direction of the bar. I felt tired suddenly. My chest and my upper arms still hurt like hell, and there was the dull, distant pounding in my head that it seemed by now had been going on in there all my life. I needed to lie down in some cool, shaded spot and rest for a long time.

"What I'm talking about isn't difficult or puzzling, Mrs. Cavendish," I said, "although I *am* having difficulty, I *am* puzzled. Look at it from my point of view. At first it seemed simple. You come to my office and ask me to find your boyfriend who's disappeared. It wasn't the first time a woman had sat in that chair you were sitting in and asked me to do the same thing. Men tend to be weak and cowardly, and often, when love wanes, they prefer to scram rather than face their lover and tell her that as far as they're concerned she's history. I listened to you, and although I had some reservations at the back of my mind—"

"Which were?"

She was leaning forward intently, the cigarette holder tilted at a sharp angle and the smoke from her cigarette streaming upward in a thin, swift line.

"Like I said already, I couldn't quite put you together with the kind of man I took Nico Peterson to be, from your description of him."

"And what kind was that?"

"Not your kind." She started to say something more, but I cut her off. "Stop," I said. "Let me go on." She wasn't the only one who could be brusque.

The waiter came with my new martini. I was glad of the interruption. The sound of my own voice was becoming a scraping ground bass alongside that drumming in my head. I took a cooling sip of my drink and thought of the line in the Bible about the hart that panteth after water. Good thing the psalmist didn't know about vodka.

I lit another cigarette and went on: "Anyway, despite my misgivings, I say to you, all right, sure, I'll find him. Then I discover he's passed on to the Happy Hunting Ground, then it turns out not, since you've spotted him trotting along Market Street in the cool and fashionable city of San Francisco. This is interesting, I think to myself, in fact, this is a three-pipe problem, and I put on my deerstalker and set off again on the chase. Next thing I know, people start getting killed all around me. Plus, I almost get killed myself, more than once. This gives me pause. I look back along the tangled way I've come and I see you off there in the distance behind me, at the point where I started, wearing that inscrutable expression I've come to know so well. I ask myself, Can this be as simple as at first it seemed? Surely not."

I too leaned forward now, until our faces across the table were no more than a foot apart. "So, Mrs. Cavendish, I'm asking you, *is* it as simple as it seemed? That's what I mean when I say I want you to level with me. You once asked me to do like Pascal and make a wager. I did. I think I lost. And by the way, you haven't touched your drink."

I sat back in my chair. Clare Cavendish glanced to her right and left and then frowned. "I've just realized," she said, "this is my mother's favorite table."

"Yes," I said. "It's a coincidence."

"Of course, you met here, didn't you."

"In this very spot."

She nodded distractedly. She seemed to be thinking of many things, sifting, calculating, deciding. She took off her hat and put it on the table, beside her purse. "Is my hair awful?" she said.

"It's lovely," I said. "Your hair."

I meant it. I was still in love with her, in some sort of painful, hopeless way. What a chump I was.

"What were we saying?" she said.

I think she really had lost the thread. It crossed my mind that maybe she didn't know any more than I did, that maybe her hiring me to look for Nico Peterson really had no connection with the rest of the stuff that followed. It was possible, after all. Life is far more messy and disconnected than we let ourselves admit. Wanting things to make sense and be nice and orderly, we keep making up plots and forcing them on the way things really are. It's one of our weaknesses, but we cling to it for dear life, since without it there'd be no life at all, dear or otherwise.

"We were saying," I said, "or, that is, *I* was saying, I was *asking,* if you can explain to me how your hiring me to go after Nico Peterson ties up with Peterson's sister being kidnapped and murdered, and then her killers themselves getting killed, and Floyd Hanson killing himself, and Wilber Canning fleeing the country, and me ending up feeling like all these people rushing around have been rushing around over me, like a herd of buffalo."

She lifted her head quickly and stared at me. "What did you say about Floyd Hanson? The newspaper said—"

"I know what the newspaper said. But Hanson didn't die by accident—he tore up a sheet and made a rope of it and put it around his neck like a noose and tied the other end to a bar in the window and let himself drop. Only the window wasn't high enough off the ground, so he had to make his legs go limp and dangle there until he had no more breath left. Think how much effort and determination that took."

Her face had gone ashen, which made those black eyes of hers seem to start from her face, huge and moist and glossy. "Dear God," she whispered. "The poor man."

I watched her carefully. I can always tell when a man is acting, but with women I'm never sure. "This is a dirty affair," I said, keeping my voice low and as gentle as I could make it. "Lynn Peterson died in a cruel, painful fashion. So did Floyd Hanson, though maybe he deserved to. A pair of Mexicans were beaten to death, and even if no one should feel sorry for them, it was brutal and ugly. Maybe you don't understand the full extent of what you're involved in. I hope you don't, or I hope you didn't, at least. Now you can't pretend anymore. So are you ready to tell me what you know? Are you ready to let me in on the things I'm convinced you've been keeping from me all along?"

She was staring before her, seeing horrors, and maybe she was really seeing them for the first time. "I can't—" she said, then faltered. "I don't—" She made a fist and pressed the whitened knuckles against her lips. A woman at a nearby table was watching her and spoke now to the man opposite, who turned his head and looked too.

"Drink some of your drink," I said. "It's strong, it will do you good."

She shook her head quickly, still with her fist pressed hard against her mouth.

"Mrs. Cavendish—Clare," I said, leaning forward over the table again and speaking in an urgent whisper, "I've kept your name out of this all along. A very tough policeman—in fact, two policemen—have leaned on me pretty hard to tell them who hired me to look for Nico Peterson. I gave them nothing. I told them my search for Peterson had nothing to do with all the other things that happened, that it was just a coincidence that I was involved. Cops don't like coincidences—it offends their sense of how things are in the world as they know it. As it happens, in this case it suits them to take my word for it, however much they grouse. If it turns out I'm mistaken, they won't believe it's a mistake, and they'll come down on me like the vengeance of Jehovah. I don't mind—I've been through things like this before, and worse. But if they turn me over, it means they'll get to you. And you won't like how that feels, take it from me. Even if for some reason you're not concerned for yourself, think of what a scandal like that would do to your mother. Long ago she saw enough violence and suffered enough grief to last a lifetime. Don't put her through that wringer again."

I stopped. By now I was sick to death of the sound of my own voice, and the lone drummer in my head had been joined by an entire percussion section, a bunch of amateurs who made up for in energy what they lacked in proficiency. I hadn't eaten anything yet today, and the vodka was burning like acid through my defenseless innards. Clare Cavendish, sitting hunched in front of me and still staring before her, suddenly looked ugly to me, and I wanted to be away somewhere, anywhere that wasn't here.

"Give me time," she said. "I need time to think, to—"

I waited. I could see she wasn't going to go on. "To do what?" I said. "Is there someone you have to consult?"

She looked up at me quickly. "No. Why do you say that?"

"I don't know," I said. "You just look to me like you're calculating what someone else will say when you report back on what we've talked about here today."

It was true: she did seem to be thinking of someone else, the same someone she had been thinking of that night in her bedroom, though I didn't know how I had guessed it. The mind has doors that it insists on leaning against and keeping firmly shut, until a day comes when what's outside can be resisted no longer, and the hinges give way and the thing bursts open and all kinds of stuff comes tumbling in.

"Give me time," she said again. She had made fists of both hands now and was pressing them down hard, side by side, on the table. "Try to understand."

"That's exactly what I'm doing," I said, "trying to understand."

"I know. And I appreciate it"—she glanced up at me again, in a sort of beseeching way—"really, I do."

Suddenly she became very busy, gathering up her cigarettes and the ebony holder and putting them away in her purse. She picked up her hat, too, and put it on. The brim leaned down lazily over her forehead, as if a breeze had caught it in its caress. How could I have thought her ugly, even for a second? How could I have thought her anything but the most lovely creature I had ever seen, or would ever see again? My diaphragm gave a heave, like a roadway rippling in an earthquake. I was losing her, I was losing this precious woman, even if I had never really had her in the first place, and the thought filled me with a sorrow the like of which I didn't think a person could experience and still survive.

"Don't go," I said.

She looked at me and blinked rapidly, as if she had forgotten I was there or no longer knew who I was. She stood up. She was trembling a little. "It's late," she said. "I have—I have an appointment."

She was lying, of course. It didn't matter. She had been trained from a young age to tell such lies, the mild, social ones, the lies that everyone takes for granted, or everyone in her world, anyway. I got to my feet, my ribs creaking under their casing of bruised flesh. "Will you call me?" I said.

"Yes, of course."

I didn't think she'd heard me; that didn't matter, either.

She turned to go. I wanted to put out a hand to stop her, to hold her there, to keep her with me. I saw myself reaching out and taking her by the elbow, but it was only in my imagination, and with a murmured word that I didn't catch she turned from me fully and walked away, weaving among the tables, ignoring the many male eyes that were lifted to watch her go.

I sat down again, though it felt more like a collapse. On the table stood her untouched drink, with a solitary olive submerged in it. Her crushed cigarette in the ashtray had a smear of lipstick. I looked at my own glass, half empty, at a crumpled paper napkin, at a flake or two of ash on the table that a breath would have blown away. These are the things that get left behind; these are the things we remember.

I took a cab over to Barney's Beanery to collect my car. There were three parking tickets clipped to the windshield. I tore them up and dropped them down a storm drain. It wasn't raining; it only seemed to be, to my eyes.

22

That was the second time I came close to giving up. I was sore in body and spirit and could see no way forward along the path I'd been following for what seemed a very long time, although it had been no more than a week or so. The heat showed no sign of lifting, and in the mornings a pall of brownish-blue smog hung above the streets, the sun trying its best to strike through it, with not much success. The city felt like one vast, congested lung.

I sat for hours in my office with my feet on the desk, my jacket off, and my shirt collar open, gazing listlessly into space or watching a small squadron of flies circling endlessly around the light fixture dangling from the ceiling. More than once I was tempted to get the bottle out of the drawer in my desk, but I knew what would happen if I did.

A few would-be clients dropped in, but none of them stayed. One was a woman who was convinced that her next-door neighbor was trying to poison her cat. There was something familiar about her, and then I realized she had come to me before, a few years back, with the same complaint, and I'd given her the same brush-off. I guess she'd worked her way through all the private investigators in the phone directory and was now going down the list a second time. I should have bawled her out, I suppose, but I felt sorry for her. Awash in sadness myself, I was feeling sorry for everything, even the bonsai tree, a Japanese maple, that I had bought one day on a whim, to brighten up the office and keep me company in the long hours when nothing was happening and no one called, and that was dying despite all my efforts to save it, or because of them, maybe.

One particularly slow morning when even the flies seemed jaded, I called Bernie Ohls, to ask him how things were going in what the newspapers, during the day or two that Harlan Potter had allowed them to stay interested, had dubbed the Cahuilla Club Case. There was nothing new, Bernie said. He sounded as listless as I felt. There was a rasp in his voice, and I guessed he had kept on smoking after he'd fallen off the wagon that night at Victor's. I had helped him fall and felt guilty now.

"No trace of Canning," he said. "Bartlett is still not talking, because he can't—you certainly fixed him, Marlowe, with that quick draw of yours. Seems the cap you put in his knee blasted a hole in an artery. They're not holding out much hope for him. And the Mexes remain unidentified."

"You talk to your friends in the Tijuana border patrol again?" I asked.

"What for? They know nothing, those guys, and care less. I figure that pair were after something of theirs your pal Peterson had run off with, and then they made the mistake of tangling with Canning and that so-called butler of his."

He stopped to cough. He sounded like an old Nash sedan with real bad carburetor trouble. "What about you?" he said. "You still in touch with the mystery man who hired you to find Peterson?"

"We have off-and-on contact," I said. "I haven't been paid yet."

"That so? And to think of all the trouble you went to on his behalf."

"Go easy there, Bernie," I said. "I don't want you getting all choked up with sympathy."

He chuckled, but that made him cough again. "Hold out for your dough," he croaked when the fit had passed. "Booze and smokes ain't getting any cheaper."

"Thanks for that advice. I'll try to keep it in mind."

He laughed again. "So long, sucker," he said, and I could hear him wheezing as he hung up.

I'd hardly put the receiver back in its cradle when the thing rang, making me jump, as usual. I thought it was Bernie calling me back with some further amusing crack. But it wasn't.

"Marlowe?" a man's voice said, low and guarded.

"This is Marlowe."

"Philip Marlowe?"

"That's right."

"The private investigator?"

"How long is this questionnaire going to be, bud?" I asked.

There was a pause. "This is Peterson. Nico Peterson."

It was commuter hour at Union Station. The main terminus always looks to me like a giant adobe church. I parked on Alameda Street and joined the hurrying crowd. It was like diving into a swollen, surging river, except for the heat and the mingled smells of sweat and hot dogs and trains. The public address system was squawking stuff that no one could understand. A redcap, crossing in front of me, ran over my foot with the back wheel of his trolley and didn't even say he was sorry.

I was a little early, and to use up time I stopped at a paper stand and bought a pack of chewing gum. I don't chew gum, but I couldn't think what else to ask for—I'd seen enough newspapers to last me for a long time. The guy who ran the stand was fat, and his face was greased with sweat. We sympathized with each other about the heat, and he gave me a free copy of the *Chronicle,* which I was too polite to refuse. As soon as I was out of his sight, I dumped it in a trash bin.

I felt as keyed up as a bobby-soxer on her way to her first Sinatra concert.

I was still a long way off when I glimpsed Peterson through a parting in the crowd. I knew straight off it was him. There was no mistaking that pencil mustache, the oiled, wavy hair, the too-bright blue jacket and the pale slacks. He was sitting on a bench under the big departures board, which was where he'd said he'd be waiting. He looked scared all over. There was a suitcase standing beside him, and he was holding on to the handle of it as if he thought the thing might suddenly sprout legs and scuttle away.

I hung back, struggling with a surge of surprise and confusion that hit me like a sucker punch. The shock was that I recognized the suitcase. It was made of pigskin bleached from age and had battered fittings of gold metal. I hadn't seen it in quite a while, but there was no mistaking it.

I moved sideways through the crowd and stopped in front of him. "Hello, Mr. Peterson," I said. He looked up at me with suspicion and hostility in his eyes. He was everything I'd expected, and more. He was deeply tanned, and a single, glistening black curl hung down on his forehead, real cute, as if it had been arranged there, which it probably had. The collar of his shirt was open, the two flaps of it folded back nicely over the lapels of his jacket. He wore a fine gold chain around his neck, with a crucifix almost hidden in a nest of wiry black chest hair. "I'm Marlowe," I said.

"Oh, yeah?"

He looked past me, to see if I'd brought backup, I suppose. "I came alone," I told him, "like you said I should."

"How about flashing some ID?" He hadn't got to his feet; he just sat there looking up at me narrowly. He was trying to seem unconcerned and insolent, but he was gripping the handle of the suitcase so tightly his knuckles were white under the suntan. He had his sister's green eyes. It was uncanny, looking into them and seeing hers.

When I put my hand inside my jacket, he couldn't stop himself from flinching. I brought out my license slowly and showed it to him. "All right," he said. "Let's go somewhere and talk." He stood up and flexed his shoulders to make his suit jacket sit right. I could see he was a man blissfully in love with himself.

We were about to move away when the numbers on the departure board above us changed with a loud rattle, and he flinched again. When you're in the state he was in, the crackle from a bowl of breakfast cereal will sound like a firing squad cocking its rifles. He was one worried fellow.

He picked up the suitcase. "That looks heavy," I said. "Why don't you let a redcap take it for you?"

"Don't make jokes, Marlowe," he said through clenched teeth. "I'm not in the mood for humor. You packing a gun?"

"No."

"No? What kind of private eye are you?"

"The kind who doesn't carry a gun with him everywhere he goes. Besides, a couple of Mexicans helped themselves to my weapon."

But he didn't react to that the way I thought he would. He didn't react at all.

We found a coffee shop away from the main concourse and sat down at a table in the corner, facing the door. The place wasn't too busy. Customers kept looking at their watches and jumping up and rushing out, but then others came in, more slowly, to replace them. Peterson shoved the suitcase against the wall behind his chair.

"Nice bag," I said.

"What?"

"The suitcase. A handsome piece, with the gold fittings and all."

"It's not mine." He was watching the door. His green eyes were sharp and bulged a little, like a hare's.

"So," I said, "you're not dead."

"You're real perceptive," he said, with a nasty snicker.

The waitress came and we ordered coffee. Peterson had his eye on a tough-looking type standing at the counter, wearing a gray fedora and a tie with a dragon painted on it.

"How come you called me?" I asked.

"Say what?"

"Why me?"

"I'd heard your name, then I saw you mentioned in the paper when they were running stories on Lynn."

"So you knew I was after you."

"What do you mean, after me?"

"I've been looking into the circumstances of your sad demise."

"That so? On behalf of who?"

"Can't you guess?"

His face took on a bitter twist. "Sure, I can guess."

The fellow at the counter in the fedora drank the last of his coffee and sauntered out, whistling. I could feel Peterson relaxing a notch or two.

"I talked to Mandy Rogers," I said.

"Oh, yeah?" he said indifferently. "Nice kid." It was obvious Mandy wasn't a significant part of his landscape anymore. If she ever had been.

"I'm sorry about your sister," I said.

He as good as shrugged. "Yeah, she was always unlucky."

I felt like hitting him, but instead I said, "What do you want with me, Peterson?"

He scratched his jaw with a fingernail, making a rasping

sound. "I need you to run an errand for me," he said. "Pays a hundred bucks."

"What kind of errand?"

He was watching the door again. "An easy one," he said. "I need the suitcase delivered to a certain party."

"Oh, yes? Why can't you do it yourself?"

"Too busy," he said. He snickered again. It was the kind of noise that would make me very irritated if I had to hear it very often. "You want the job or not?"

"Let's hear some details," I said.

Our coffee came, in those big, off-white cups you see only in railway stations and the less greasy of greasy spoons. I tasted the coffee and was sorry I had.

"Okay," Peterson said, lowering his voice, "here's the deal. I stand up and walk out of here, leaving the suitcase against the wall there. You wait, say, half an hour, then take it and bring it to a guy called—"

"Lou Hendricks?" I said.

He gave me that hare-eyed stare again. "How did you know—?"

"Because," I said, "Mr. Hendricks invited me for a ride in his big black car and issued threats, assuring me he'd break my legs if I didn't tell him where you were."

He frowned. "He's not the one that hired you to find me?"

"Nope."

"He just picked you up off the street?"

"That's right."

He scowled and chewed on a knuckle for a bit. "So what did you say to him?" he asked at last.

"I said I didn't know your whereabouts and that even if I did, I wouldn't tell him. I said so far as I knew, you were dead. He didn't buy that. Someone had put him straight."

Peterson nodded, thinking hard. There was a light film of sweat on his forehead. He fingered his mustache, which had tiny beads of moisture sprinkled through it. I didn't like looking at it. The worst thing about it was the little gap down the middle of it, a pale nick that seemed too intimate a part of him to be on public show.

I pushed the coffee aside and lit a cigarette. "You want to tell me what happened, Nico?"

He flew straight into a bluster. "I don't need to tell you anything! I'm offering you a hundred dollars for a job, and that's it. You ready to do it?"

I pretended to consider. "If you mean the money, I can live without it. As for the job, let's see."

He took a silver pillbox from his jacket pocket and extracted a small white pill and slipped it under his tongue.

"Got a headache?" I asked.

He didn't seem to think that worth replying to. "Listen, Marlowe," he said, "I'm in something of a hurry here. You going to take the suitcase and deliver it to the person we mentioned or not?"

"I don't know yet," I said. "And you may as well slow down. You're scared, you're on the run, and if I'm the only one you could think to turn to, then obviously you're in serious trouble. I've been on your trail for some time, and there are a few things I want cleared up. Now, are you ready to talk?"

He pouted, and I could see him as a sulky kid. "What do you want to know?" he mumbled.

"Everything, pretty much. Let's start with the suitcase. What's in it that Lou Hendricks is so eager to get his hands on?"

"Just some stuff."

"What kind of stuff?"

"Look, Marlowe—"

I grabbed his wrist where it had been resting on the table and squeezed until the bones inside it creaked. He tried to pull away, but I held on.

"You're hurting me!" he snarled.

"Yeah, and I'll hurt you a lot more if you don't start talking. What's in the suitcase?"

He tried again to free himself, but I squeezed harder. "Let go," he whined. "I'll tell you, for Christ's sake!"

I loosened my fingers, and he slumped back on his chair as if all the air had suddenly gone out of him. "It has a false bottom," he said in a sullen undertone. "Underneath there's ten keys of horse, in twenty cellophane bags."

"Heroin?"

"Keep your voice down!" He threw a quick look around the room. No one was taking any notice of us. "Heroin, yeah, that's what I said."

"For delivery to Lou Hendricks. Who from?"

He shrugged. "Just a guy." He was massaging his wrist with the fingers of his other hand. His eyes were full of rage. I told myself to remember never to let him get the drop on me.

"What guy?" I asked.

"A guy down south."

"Give me the name."

He took a white handkerchief from the breast pocket of his jacket and wiped his mouth with it. "You know Mendy Menendez?"

I paused. That wasn't the name I had expected. Menendez was a hoodlum, used to be very big in these parts—one of the biggest, in fact. But he'd moved to Mexico, and the last I'd heard of him, he was operating out of Acapulco. Nice work if you can get it, if you choose to call it work. "Yeah, I know him," I said.

"He and Hendricks have a business going between them. Menendez sends up a consignment every couple months or so and Hendricks handles the distribution."

"And you're the courier."

"I did it a few times. Easy money."

"You bring that much junk every time?"

"More or less."

"What's ten kilos of heroin worth?"

"On the street?" He pursed his lips, then grinned. "Depending on demand, about as much as a flatfoot like you will earn in a lifetime."

Those lips of his were pink and almost as shapely as a woman's. This wasn't the man Clare Cavendish was in love with, the one she had spoken of with such passion that night in her bedroom, sitting on the bed beside her unconscious brother; I had only to look at Peterson, to see those mean eyes and hear his whining tone, to know she wouldn't have touched him with an ebony cigarette holder. No, there was someone else, and now I knew who it was. I'd known for some time, I suppose, but you can know something and at the same time not know it. It's one of the things that help us put up with our lot in life and not go crazy.

"You know how many lives that much dope would destroy?" I asked.

He sneered. "You think the life of a junkie is worth saving?"

I studied the tip of my cigarette. I hoped that at some point before we parted I might get the opportunity to smash my fist into Peterson's pretty, suntanned face. "So what did you do," I said, "decide to keep the stuff for yourself and make a deal of your own with someone else?"

"There's a guy I knew in Frisco, he said that for a cut he could take whatever I had and sell it to the mob, no questions asked."

"But it didn't work out."

Peterson swallowed; I heard him do it. I thought maybe he was going to cry. It must have seemed so simple, the old switcheroo. He'd hang on to the suitcase and let his pal sell the dope to a client that even Lou Hendricks, if he got to hear about the deal, wouldn't dare challenge. In the meantime, Peterson would be on his way to somewhere far off and safe, his pockets bulging with more dough than he'd ever dreamed could be his.

"The guy I knew," Peterson said, "he met with a fatal accident—

his old lady caught him two-timing and shot him in the face, before blowing her own brains out."

"A tragic tale," I said.

"Yeah. Sure. Tragic. And there I was, stuck with twenty bags of horse and no one to sell it to."

"Couldn't you have gone to the mob yourself?"

"I didn't have the contacts. Plus"—he gave a sad little laugh—"I was too scared. Then I heard about Lynn, and that made me even more scared. Things seemed to be—they seemed to be closing in around me. I knew what would happen if Hendricks got his hands on me."

"Why didn't you just surrender, call up Hendricks and say you were sorry and hand over the suitcase?"

"Oh, sure. Hendricks would say thanks, relieve me of the goods, and then have one of his boys pull out my fingernails with a pair of pliers. And that would be just for starters. You don't know these people."

He was wrong there, but it wasn't worth contradicting him. The coffee in my cup had developed a shiny skin, like a miniature oil spill. The smoke of my cigarette tasted acrid in my mouth. You can feel tainted just by being in the vicinity of a two-bit swindler like Peterson.

"Let's back up a bit," I said. "Tell me how you faked your death."

He gave an angry sigh. "How long you going to keep me here, Marlowe," he demanded, "answering your damn fool questions?"

"As long as it takes. I'm a man prone to curiosity. Humor me."

He had begun distractedly massaging his wrist again. It was beginning to show bruise marks already. I didn't think I had such steely talons.

"I knew Floyd Hanson," he said in his sulky way. "He used to let me in the club when the old man was away."

"What do you mean?"

He twisted up his face again in that way that made it no longer pretty. "My father had disowned me, banned from coming anywhere near him or his precious Cahuilla Club. I liked going in there and getting drunk and throwing up on his Indian rugs."

"What did you have on Hanson?"

"Did I have to have something on him?"

"I'd say so. He was taking a big risk, letting you come in there. I've met your father. He didn't seem to me a tolerant man. Were you paying Hanson?"

He laughed; it was the first genuine laugh I'd heard from him. "Naw," he said. "I didn't need to pay him. There were things I knew about him. He made a pass at me once, when I was young. He said afterward he didn't know what had come over him and begged me to swear not to tell the old man. I said sure, I wouldn't tell. But I let Hanson know that from then on we had a deal." He smiled to himself, proud of his own smartness.

"The body you dressed up in your clothes that night and left at the side of the road," I asked, "where did it come from—who was it?"

"Some roustabout working at the club," he said.

"Did you kill him?"

He reared back from me, staring. "What, are you kidding?"

"Then Hanson must have done it." I paused. "Funny, I didn't take him for a killer. I didn't think he had it in him."

Peterson was thinking it over. "I didn't ask him about the body," he said petulantly. "I guess I thought whoever it was had died from natural causes. I didn't see any marks on him. Floyd and I put him into my suit out back of the clubhouse, then brought him in a wheelbarrow out onto the road. I'd been playing drunk all evening, making sure everyone saw me—"

"Including Clare Cavendish."

"Yeah." He nodded. "Clare was there. Also, I'd fixed it with Lynn to identify the body and arrange for the cremation. Everything was set up, everything was in place. I had a car parked down the road, and as soon as Floyd and I had got the body dumped I hightailed it north, with the suitcase in the trunk. It should have worked." He smacked a fist into the palm of his other hand. *"It should have worked."*

"Your father know about any of this?"

"I don't think so. How would he? Floyd wouldn't have said anything." He picked a matchstick from the ashtray and rolled it between two fingers and a thumb. "How come you met him?"

"Who? Your father? I went out to the club to ask about you. I spoke to Hanson, who was less than helpful. Then, later, two Mexicans turned up, the ones who'd killed your sister, also looking for you, and your father and Bartlett the butler got ahold of them and squeezed them till their pips popped. I made the mistake of paying a return visit while this was going on, and next thing I knew I was being dunked in the swimming pool, to encourage me to tell all I knew about you and your supposed whereabouts. Impressive man, your father. Forceful. I can see why you and he wouldn't get along so well."

I was watching the waitress at her station by the counter, sneaking a break. She was a washed-out blonde with sad eyes and an unhappy mouth. She kept pushing out her lower lip and blowing upward, so that the fringe of damp hair at her forehead lifted and fell back again. I felt a sudden stab of pity for her, for the mean life she'd been condemned to, running around here all day, amid the noise and the smells and the endless rush of hurrying, impatient, ill-tempered people. Then I thought, who am I to pity her? What do I know about her and her life? What do I know about anyone?

"I hate the old bastard," Peterson said, in a faraway tone. "He queered everything for me, from the start."

Oh, sure, I wanted to say, *it's all the old man's fault—it always is, with people like you.* But I didn't. "You know he's on the run," I said, "your father."

That cheered him up a bit. "He is? Why?"

"He killed those Mexicans, or had them killed."

"Yeah?" He seemed amused. "Where'd he go?"

"That's what a lot of people would like to know."

"He'll be in Europe somewhere. He has dough stashed there. He'll be operating under a false name." He chuckled, almost admiringly. "They'll never find him."

We were silent for a while, the two of us; then Peterson stirred himself. "I got to move, Marlowe," he said. "What's it to be? Will you take the stuff to Hendricks?"

"All right," I said, "I'll take the stuff."

"Good. But don't get any ideas yourself—I'm going to let Hendricks know you have the suitcase."

"Do what you like," I said.

He slid a hand inside his jacket and brought out a billfold and held it in his lap, under the level of the table, and began to count out a stack of sawbucks. There were a lot of them in there. I hoped he hadn't pulled any funny tricks with Mendy Menendez's dope, like taking a slice of it for himself and replacing it with a couple of bags of plaster of paris. Hendricks wouldn't be dumb enough to be fooled by that old trick.

"I don't want your money, Peterson," I said.

He gave me a sidelong look, suspicious and calculating. "How come?" he said. "You operating a charity?"

"Those bills have been through hands I wouldn't want to touch."

"Then why—?"

"I liked your sister," I said quietly. "She had spirit. Let's say I'm doing this for her." He would have laughed, if it hadn't been for the look in my eye. "What about you, what are your plans?" I asked. Not that I cared, only I wanted to be sure I was never going to see him again.

"I've got a pal," he said.

"Another one?"

"Works for a South American cruise line. He can get me a job.

Then when we get to Rio or Buenos Aires or someplace like that, I'll jump ship and start a new life."

"What kind of a job is your friend offering?"

He smirked. "Nothing very demanding. Being nice to the passengers, helping them with any little problems that might arise. That kind of thing."

"So your dad was right," I said. "It'll be official."

"What do you mean?"

"You'll be a bona fide, paid-up member of the honorable order of gigolos."

The smirk died. "That's rich," he said, "coming from a peeper. But think of this—you'll still be here pounding the pavement and spying on people's husbands to catch them shtupping their girlfriends, while I'm in a hammock basking in the southern sun."

He began to get to his feet, but I caught him by the wrist again and held him back. "I've got one last question," I said.

He licked those lovely pink lips of his, glanced longingly toward the door, then sat down again, slowly. "What's that?"

"Clare Cavendish," I said. "She says you and her were romantically involved."

He opened his eyes so wide they almost bulged out of their sockets. "She said that?" He breathed a laugh. "Really?"

"You're telling me it's not true?"

He shook his head, not in denial but a kind of amazement. "I'm not saying I would've turned her down—I mean, who would?—but she never had an eye for me. A dame like that, she was way out of my league."

I let go of his wrist. "That's all I wanted to know," I said. "Now you can leave."

But he stayed where he was, his eyes narrowing. "She's the one that hired you to go after me, right?" he said, and nodded. "Yeah, that figures."

He was looking at me the way I'd looked at the waitress, with pity in his eyes. "He sent her to you, didn't he? He used to talk about you—that's where I first heard your name mentioned. He knew you'd fall for her, for those eyes of hers, that hair, the ice maiden act. You'd be the type that couldn't resist her." He leaned back, a big broad smile spreading slowly over his face, like molasses. "Jeez, Marlowe, you poor sap." Then he stood up and was gone.

There was a phone booth beside the cash register. I squeezed myself into it and pushed the folding door shut behind me. The air inside smelled of sweat and warm Bakelite. Through the glass panel in the door I could see across the room to the suitcase under the table, by the wall. Maybe I was hoping someone would snatch it and run off with it, but I knew that wouldn't happen; things like that never happen, not when you want them to.

I dialed Langrishe Lodge. It was Clare who answered. "This is Marlowe," I said. "Tell him I want to see him."

I heard her catch her breath. "Who?"

"You know damned well who. Tell him to catch a plane, the next one out. It'll get him here by tonight. Phone me when he's in."

She began to say something more, but I hung up.

I went back to the table, and the waitress came over. She smiled at me, in her weary way, and gathered up the two cups. "You didn't drink your coffee," she said.

"It's all right. My doctor tells me I drink too much of the stuff anyway." I gave her a five-dollar bill and told her to keep the change. She stared at me, her smile growing uncertain.

"Buy yourself a hat," I said.

═ 23 ═

I should know how to wait, given the way I chose to make my living—if I did choose, and didn't just fall into it, like you'd fall down an open manhole—but I haven't got the right frame of mind. I can waste time, no problem. I can sit in the office for hours, in my swivel chair, gazing out my window at that secretary across the way, bent over her dictation machine, not even seeing her, half the time. I can dawdle over a King's Gambit until the pieces grow blurry and the checkerboard pattern sends my brain into a slow spin. I can sit nursing a beer in some musty saloon while the bartender tells me how dumb his wife is and how his kids have no respect for him, and not even yawn. A natural time-waster, that's me. But give me some specific thing that I have to wait for and within five minutes I begin to twitch.

That day I had an early lunch at Rudy's Bar-B-Q on La Cienega: spareribs glistening all over with what looked like dark red varnish—it tasted pretty much like varnish, too. I drank a Mexican beer; it seemed appropriate, in a gruesome sort of way. Mexico had been the theme tune all along, if only I'd been smart enough to hear it. Then I went back to the office for a while, hoping a client might drift in. I'd even have been glad to see the old dame whose neighbor was trying to poison her cat. But an hour passed, an hour that felt like three, and still I was on my own. I sneaked a nip or two from the office bottle. I smoked yet another cigarette. Miss Remington over the way had switched off the recorder and was putting the cover on her typewriter. Next thing she'd take out her compact and powder her nose, peering into the little mirror and puckering her lips, then run a comb through her hair, snap her purse shut, and go home. Yes, I'd gotten to know her habits pretty well.

I checked the movie listings. They were showing a revival of *Horse Feathers* at the Roxie. That sounded like just the thing— Groucho and the boys would pass a happy hour or two for me. So I strolled over and bought a ticket for the balcony and the usherette showed me to a seat. She was a redhead with bangs and a cute mouth and friendly eyes. Down in the stalls there was another nice-looking girl, posing in front of the screen with a tray of ice cream and candy and cigarettes. She wore a sort of chambermaid's outfit, with a short black skirt and a collar of white lace and a little white hat like an upturned paper boat. There weren't more than a dozen customers in the place, solitary souls like me, sitting as far apart from each other as they could get.

The crimson curtains swished open and the lights went down and on came a trailer for *Bride of the Gorilla*, starring Lon Chaney and Barbara Payton, with Raymond Burr as the manager of a plantation deep in the jungles of South America who is cursed by a native witch and every night turns into a you-know-what and causes beautiful women to scream and grown men to cower. There followed some advertisements, for Philip Morris and Clorox and things like that, and then the curtains were drawn shut again and a spotlight shone on the ice cream girl down in the stalls. She did her pose, flexing one knee and tilting her head and showing us her teeth in a come-hither smile, but all the same there were no takers, and after a minute the spotlight went off with a discouraged click, the curtains opened, and the movie came on.

I sat there waiting for the bouncing brothers to work their magic on me, but it was no good. I didn't laugh; nor did anyone else. Funny movies are funny only in a full house. When the place is nearly empty, you notice how after every joke there's a deliberate pause in the action to allow for a wave of laughter from the audience, and since this evening no one was laughing, the whole thing began to seem sad. Halfway through I got up and left. Outside the swing door, the redheaded usherette was sitting on a chair buffing her nails with an emery board. She asked if I was feeling unwell and I said no, I just wanted to get some air. She smiled her sweet smile, but that only made everything seem sadder still.

It was early twilight by now and the air was smoky and hot, like the air in a subway station. I strolled along the boulevard thinking of nothing much. I was in that state of suspension you get into when you're waiting to undergo a medical operation. What would come would come, what would happen would happen. Anyway, what the night would bring was going to feel for me pretty much like the aftermath to something that had already taken place. I thought there wasn't much more damage that could be done to me that hadn't already been done. You get hardened by life knocking away at you since you were old enough to feel heartsore, but then comes a knock that's bigger than anything you've experienced so far, and you realize just how soft you are, how soft you'll always be.

I stopped by a mailbox and checked the collection times and saw that it had just been emptied. I took an envelope from the inside breast pocket of my jacket and slid it into the slot and heard it fall to the floor inside.

The Cahuenga Building was empty except for the night watchman in his glass booth beside the elevator, and the janitor, a very tall Negro named Rufus. Rufus always had a friendly word for me. I gave him tips sometimes for the horses, but I don't know that he ever placed a bet. When I stepped out of the elevator he was there in the corridor, dragging a wet mop back and forth over the floor in his pensive way. He must have been at least six and a half feet tall, with a big handsome African head.

"You working late tonight, Mr. Marlowe?" he asked.

"There's a phone call I'm expecting," I said. "You all right, Rufus?"

He flashed a big smile. "You know me, Mr. Marlowe. Old Rufe is always right as rain."

"Sure thing," I said. "Sure thing."

In the office I didn't switch any lamps on. I sat down in the shadows and swiveled my chair so I could look out the window at the lights of the city and the moon suspended above the blue hills beyond. I got the bottle out of the drawer but put it away again. The last thing I needed tonight was a fuzzy head.

I phoned Bernie Ohls. He wasn't at the office, and I looked in my dog-eared address book and found his home number. He didn't like being called at home, but I didn't care. His missus answered, and when I said my name I thought she was going to hang up on me, but she didn't. I heard her calling to Bernie, and, more faintly, I heard Bernie bawling back at her, and then there was the noise of him coming down from upstairs. "It's your pal Marlowe," I heard Mrs. Ohls saying sourly, and then Bernie came on.

"What do you want, Marlowe?" he growled.

"Hello, Bernie. Hope I'm not disturbing you."

"Let's dispense with the small talk. What is it?"

I told him I'd seen Peterson. I could almost hear his ears pricking up.

"You saw him? Where?"

"Union Station. He phoned me and told me to come there. He chose the station because he had a suitcase with him and didn't want to look conspicuous."

There was a pause. "What sort of suitcase?"

"Just a suitcase. English-made, pigskin, gold fittings."

"And what's in it?"

"A gazillion bucks' worth of heroin. Property of a certain Mr. Menendez. You remember our old friend Mendy, now in residence south of the border?"

Again Bernie paused. I had the impression of a man screwing down the lid of a pressure cooker. Bernie's temper had been getting shorter and shorter with the years; I thought he really should do something about it. "All right, Marlowe," he said, in a voice as tight as Jack Benny's wallet, "start explaining."

I did. He listened in silence, except for an occasional snort of surprise or disgust. When I was done he took a deep breath. This caused him to start in with the coughing. I held the receiver away from my ear until he'd finished. "So let me get this straight," he said, gasping a bit. "Peterson was muling Menendez's dope up from Mexico and delivering it to Lou Hendricks, until he got the bright idea of keeping a shipment for himself and selling it to some gentlemen of Italian descent. But the deal got queered, and then the bodies started piling up, and Peterson lost his nerve and hired you—"

"Tried to hire me."

"—to deliver the suitcase to Hendricks."

"Yes, that's about it." There were some fumbling sounds on the line and then the scratch of a match. "Bernie, are you lighting a cigarette?" I asked. "Haven't you coughed enough?"

I heard him inhale, then exhale. "So where's the suitcase now?"

"It's in a locker at the railroad station. And the key to the locker is in an envelope in a mailbox on South Broadway. You'll have it by second delivery tomorrow. And before you ask, I did it because I promised Peterson I'd give him time to make himself scarce."

"And where is he?"

"He's gone on a cruise to South America."

"Very funny."

"He's not worth chasing, Bernie," I said. "Don't waste your energy and make yourself even more annoyed than you are."

"What about Hendricks?"

"What about him?"

"I should bring him in for a little chat."

"And what will you get him on? The dope wasn't delivered—you have it instead, or you will have, when that locker key drops on your doormat tomorrow noon. There's nothing to connect Hendricks to any of this."

Bernie took another deep drag on his cigarette. Nobody enjoys a cigarette like a man who's supposed to have given them up. "You realize," he said, "after all this thing, with—what is it?—four people dead, including Canning's enforcer, by the way—what's his name?"

"Bartlett."

"Including him—he died this afternoon."

"Too bad," I said, as if I might mean it.

"Anyway, after all that murder and mayhem, I haven't brought a single charge or got even one suspect in the slammer."

"You could do me for plugging Bartlett," I said, "if that would make you happy. Wouldn't be much of a case, though."

Bernie sighed. He was a weary man. I thought of suggesting that he start considering retirement, but didn't. After a pause he asked, "You watch the fights, Marlowe?"

"On television, you mean?"

"Yeah."

"Sometimes I do."

"I was upstairs watching one tonight. When you called, Sugar Ray was wiping the floor with Joey Maxim. I just heard, just now, from up there in my hideaway, where I have my own set, the sound of a bell and a big cheer. That probably means Joey's on the floor, dribbling blood and broken teeth on the canvas. I'd like to have seen him go down for the last time. I've got nothing against big Joey—he's a handsome guy and a plucky fighter. And I bet he put on quite a show before the lights went out for him. It's just a pity I didn't get to see the end of the fight. You know what I mean?"

"I'm sorry, Bernie," I said. "I wouldn't have kept you from your pleasure for the world, only I thought you might want to know about Peterson and the rest of it."

"You're right, Marlowe. I'm grateful to you for filling me in on what was going on, I really am. Only you know what you can do now? You want to know what you can do?"

"Not really, but I'm guessing you're going to tell me anyway."

I was right. He did. His suggestions were loud and graphic and for the most part anatomically impracticable.

When he'd finished, I said a polite good night and hung up the receiver. He's not a bad fellow, Bernie. Like I said, he has a short fuse, and it's getting shorter all the time.

I put my feet up on the desk. I could still see out the window. Why do the lights of the city, seen from a distance, appear to twinkle? When you look at them up close, they have a steady shine. It must have something to with the intervening air, with the millions of minute specks of dust swirling in it, maybe. Everything looks fixed, but it's not; it's moving. The desk I was resting my feet on, for instance, wasn't solid at all but a swarm of particles so small that no human eye will ever be able to see one. The world, when you come down to it, is a scary place. And that's not even counting the people.

I used to think Clare Cavendish could break my heart. I didn't realize it was already broken. Live and learn, Marlowe, live and learn.

24

It was a shade after ten o'clock when she phoned. I had weakened and got out the bottle again from its deep lair in the desk drawer and poured myself a modest two fingers of bourbon. Somehow liquor doesn't seem so serious a thing when you drink it from a paper cup. The whiskey stung my mouth, which was already raw from all the cigarettes I'd smoked in the course of this long day. I certainly wasn't the one to be telling Bernie Ohls he should kick the habit.

I knew the phone was going to ring a second before it rang. Her voice was hushed, almost a whisper. "He's here," she said. "Come by the usual way, through the conservatory. And don't forget to turn off your headlights."

I can't remember what I said in reply. Maybe I said nothing. I was still in that strangely dreamy state of suspension, seeming to float outside myself, watching my own actions but somehow not taking part in them. I suppose it was the effect of all the waiting and the time wasting.

Rufus had gone home, and the floor he had been mopping had

long since dried, though the soles of my shoes squeaked on it as if it were still wet. The night outside was cool now, and the day's smoke had cleared from the air at last. I had parked the car on Vine, under a streetlamp. It looked like a big dark animal, crouching there at the sidewalk, and the headlights seemed to be giving me a baleful glare. It took a while to start, too, coughing and sputtering before it rattled into life. It was probably due for an oil change, or something like that.

I drove slowly, but all the same it wasn't long before I came in sight of the sea. I turned right along the highway, with the waves a ghostly, turbulent white line out in the darkness on my left. I flicked on the radio. It was a thing I rarely did, and in fact I forgot for long periods that it was there. The station it was tuned to was playing an old number by the Paul Whiteman band, hot music made safely cool for the masses. It beats me how a guy with the name Whiteman ever got up the nerve to play jazz.

A jackrabbit ran across the road in front of me, its tail unnaturally aglow in the headlights. There was some comparison I could have made between the animal and me, but I felt too detached to bother.

When I came to the gate I killed the lights and took my foot off the gas and let the car drift to a stop. The moon had gone in and there was blackness everywhere. Trees loomed like great blind brutes nosing their way out of the night. I sat there for a while, listening to the engine ticking. I felt like a traveler come to the end of a long and weary journey. I wanted to rest, but I knew I couldn't, not yet.

I got out of the car and stood beside it for a minute, sniffing the air. There was a scorched smell from the engine, but beyond that the night was fragrant with the scent of grass and roses and other things I didn't know the names of. I set off walking across the lawn. The house at the front was dark except for a few lighted windows on the first floor. I came to the gravel sweep below the front door and veered off to the left. The smell of roses was intense here, cloying and almost overpowering.

There was a flurry somewhere close by and I halted, but could see nothing in the darkness. Then I caught a flash of blue, a deep, shiny blue, and there was a swishing sound that quickly faded. It must have been the peacock. I hoped it wouldn't do its scream, my nerves couldn't have borne it.

As I rounded the corner of the house and approached the conservatory, I heard the sound of a piano and stopped to listen. Chopin, I guessed, but I was probably wrong—to me everything on the piano sounds like Chopin. The music, tiny from this distance, seemed heartrendingly lovely, and, well, just heartrending. Imagine, I thought to myself, imagine being able to make a noise like that on a big black box made out of wood and ivory and stretched wires.

The French doors leading into the conservatory were locked, but I got that trusty gadget on my key ring into operation, and after a few seconds I was inside.

I followed the sound of the music. In the dimness I crossed what I remembered as the living room and walked along a short, carpeted corridor, at the end of which was a closed door to what I figured must be the music room. I crept forward, trying not to make a sound, but I was still a good five yards from the door when the music broke off in the middle of a phrase. I stopped too, and stood listening, but heard nothing, except a steady, low buzzing from a faulty bulb in a tall lamp beside me. What was I waiting for? Did I expect the door to burst open and a crowd of music lovers to come surging out and usher me inside and sit me down in the front row?

I didn't knock, just turned the knob and pushed open the door and stepped through.

Clare was seated at the piano. As I came in, she was closing the lid and turning sideways on the stool to look at me. She must have heard me in the corridor. Her face was expressionless; she didn't even seem surprised at my unannounced appearance. She was wearing a floor-length, midnight-blue gown with a high collar. Her hair was pinned up, and she had on earrings and a necklace of small white diamonds. She looked as if she had dressed for a concert. Where was her audience?

"Hello, Clare," I said. "Don't let me interrupt the music."

The drapes were drawn in front of the two tall windows in the wall behind the piano. The only light in the room came from a big brass lamp that stood on the piano lid. It had a globe of white glass, and its base was molded in the shape of a lion's claw. It was the kind of thing Clare's mother would think was the last word in style. Around it were arranged a couple of dozen photographs in silver frames of varying sizes. In one of them I recognized Clare as a young girl, wearing a tiara of flowers in her short blond hair.

She stood up now, the silk stuff of her gown making a faint, brittle rustling; it was the kind of female sound that always sets a man's heart pitter-pattering, whatever the circumstances. Her face still showed nothing of what she was feeling.

"I didn't hear your car," she said. "Perhaps I was playing too loudly."

"I left it at the gate," I said.

"Yes, but usually I hear when a car stops anywhere about."

"It was the music, then."

"Yes. I was distracted."

We stood there, with fifteen feet or so of floor between us, gazing at each other in a helpless sort of way. I hadn't known how hard this was going to be. I was holding my hat in my hand.

"Where is he?" I asked.

She drew back her shoulders and lifted her head, her nostrils flaring, as if I had said something offensive. "Why have you come here?" she asked.

"You told me to. On the phone."

She frowned, her brow wrinkling. "Did I?"

"Yes, you did."

Her mind seemed somewhere else; she was distracted, all right. When she spoke again her voice had become unnaturally loud, as if she meant it to carry. "What do you want with us?"

"You know what?" I said. "Now that you ask, I'm not really sure. I suppose I thought I could get some things cleared up, but all of a sudden I can't seem to remember what they are, exactly."

"You sounded very angry, when you called."

"That's because I was. I still am."

Her mouth twitched in what might have been a smile. "You don't show it."

"It's what they teach you at detective school. I think it's called 'masking your emotions.' You're not bad at it yourself."

"Do you care to tell me what it is you're angry about?"

I laughed, or made a laughing noise, anyway, and shook my head. "Ah, sweetheart," I said, "where would I begin?"

There was a sound off to my left, a sort of strangulated gurgle, and when I turned to look where it had come from I was surprised to see Richard Cavendish sprawled on a sofa, asleep or passed out, I couldn't tell which. How had I not noticed him when I first came into the room? A body on a sofa—that's the kind of thing I'm not supposed to miss. He was lying back with his arms flung out to either side and his legs splayed. He was wearing jeans and shiny cowboy boots and a checked shirt. His face had a gray pallor, and his mouth was open.

"He came stumbling in here a while ago, very drunk," Clare said. "He'll sleep for hours and remember nothing in the morning. It often happens. He's drawn by the sound of the piano, I think, though music repels him, or so he likes to tell me." She did that tense little smile again. "It's like the moth and the flame, I suppose."

"Mind if I sit down?" I said. "I'm kind of tired."

She pointed to an ornate, lyre-backed chair upholstered in yellow silk. It looked too delicate to support my weight, but I sat on it anyway. Clare returned to the music stool and arranged herself there, one knee crossed over the other under her gown and an arm draped along the lid of the piano. She sat with her back held very straight. Somehow I hadn't noticed before how long and slender her neck was. The diamonds at her throat sparkled, reminding me of the lights of the city I had been watching earlier from my office window, while I waited for her to call.

"I saw Peterson," I said.

That got a response. She drew herself forward quickly as if to jump to her feet, and I saw the knuckles of her left hand tighten where it rested on the piano lid. Her black eyes were wide, and an almost feverish light came into them. When she spoke, her voice was choked. "Why didn't you tell me?"

"I just did," I said.

"I mean, before now. When did you see him?"

"Today, around noon."

"Where?"

"It doesn't matter where. He called me, said he wanted to meet, I met him."

"But—" She blinked rapidly and gave herself a tiny shake that ran all the way down to the tip of her shoe where it was peeping out from under the hem of her blue gown. "What did he say? Did he—did he give any explanation of why he pretended to be dead? He can't just have appeared like that, with a phone call and a request to meet you. Tell me. *Tell me.*"

I fetched out my cigarette case. I didn't ask if she minded if I smoked; I didn't feel like being that polite. "He was never your lover, was he," I said. "That was just a line you fed me, so there'd be a reason for you to hire me to go search for him." She began to say something, but I spoke over her. "Don't bother lying," I said.

"Look, the fact is, I don't care. I never really bought the please-find-my-lost-boyfriend line anyway—just from your description of him I knew Peterson was the kind of guy you wouldn't give the time of day to."

"Then why did you pretend to believe me?"

"I was curious. Plus, if I'm honest, I didn't like the prospect of you walking out of my office and my never seeing you again. Pathetic, right?"

She blushed. That threw me, and made me wonder if I should revise, even if only by a little, all the harsh conclusions I'd been coming to about her and her character since I'd talked to Peterson that morning. Maybe she was the kind of woman who gets wrapped easily around men's little fingers. Who was I to judge her? But then I thought about the lies she'd told me, if only by omission, thought of all the ways she'd deceived me from the start, and the anger surged up in me again.

She was sitting now with her face turned to the left, showing me her perfect profile. You can hate a woman and still know that all she has to do is beckon and you'd throw yourself at her feet and shower her shoes with kisses.

"Please," she said, "tell me what happened when you met him."

"He had a suitcase with him. He wanted me to deliver it to a man called Lou Hendricks. Know the name?"

She shrugged dismissively. "I suppose I've heard it."

"Damn right you have. He's the guy Peterson was supposed to bring the dope to."

"What dope?"

I chuckled. She was still looking away from me, still giving me the classic profile, the one that was so much better than Cleopatra's. "Come on," I said. "You can stop pretending now—the charade is over. You've got nothing to lose by being honest—or have you forgotten how to do that?"

"There's no need to be insulting."

"No, I agree, but it's kind of enjoyable."

I'd been tapping the cigarette into my cupped palm, and now Clare stood up and took a big glass ashtray from the lid of the piano and came and handed it to me, and I emptied the ash from my hand into it and then set it on the floor beside my chair. She turned with another swish of silk and walked back and sat down again on the piano stool. Even though I was mad at her, mad as hell, the knowledge ached in me that I had lost for good whatever small fragment of her she had briefly allowed me to think was mine.

"Tell me something," I said. "Was it all a pretense?"

I noticed the drapes at the window on the left stirring a little, though I couldn't feel the least draft.

"What do you mean, all?"

"You know what I mean."

She looked down at her hands where they were clasped together in her lap. I was thinking of the lamp beside my bed with the blood-red roses painted on it, and her moaning in my arms, and her eyelids fluttering, and her fingernails pressing into my shoulder.

"No," she said, in a voice so small and soft I could hardly hear it. "No, not everything."

She lifted her eyes to mine and with a begging look put a finger to her lips and gave her head a tiny, quick shake. I returned a blank stare. She needn't have worried; I wasn't going to say out loud the thing she was silently asking me not to say. What would be the point? Why add more damage to what had already been done? Besides, I was desperate to believe she had gone to bed with me because she'd wanted to, that it wasn't another thing she'd done for the man she really loved.

Those drapes stirred again. "You're asking a lot, Mrs. Cavendish," I said, loud enough for everyone in the room to hear. Clare nodded and lowered her head again. I stubbed my cigarette into the ashtray on the floor and stood up.

"All right, Terry," I called. "You may as well come out now. We're done playing."

At first nothing happened, except that Clare Cavendish gave a funny, stifled little squeak, as if something had stung her, and clapped a hand over her mouth. Then those mysteriously moving drapes parted and the man I knew as Terry Lennox stepped into the room, wearing that smile of his I remembered so well: boyish, embarrassed, a little rueful. He wore a double-breasted dark suit and a blue bow tie. He was tall and thin and elegant, the elegance made all the more pointed by his seeming unawareness of it. He had dark hair and a trim mustache.

It struck me that I'd never seen his real face. When I'd first known him, some years back, his hair was white and his right cheek and jaw were frozen, the dead skin lined with long, thin scars. In the war he'd been caught in a mortar blast and then captured by the Germans, who had patched him up any old how. That, at least, was the story he'd spun. Then, later, when his wife got murdered and it looked like he was going to take the rap for it, he'd fled to Mexico—with my help, I may as well say—where he'd faked his suicide and had a big piece of plastic surgery done, an expensively expert job this time, and changed himself into a Suramericano. I'd seen him once under his new identity; then he'd disappeared from my life. And now he was back.

"Hello, old sport," he said. "Think you could spare me a cigarette? I smelled the smoke of yours and developed a sudden craving."

I had to hand it to Terry—who else could have hidden behind a curtain for half an hour and come out as poised and self-mockingly smooth as Cary Grant? I stepped forward, taking out my cigarette case and flipping it open with my thumb and holding it out to him. "Help yourself," I said. "You give it up, or what?"

"Yes," he said, taking one of my cigarettes and rolling it appreciatively in his fingers. "It was affecting my health." He put a hand to his chest. "The dry air down there doesn't agree with me."

Strange, isn't it, how even at a time like that people plunge right away into small talk? Clare was still sitting on the piano stool with her hand over her mouth. She hadn't even turned to look at Terry. Well, she didn't need to.

I offered a match and Terry leaned down to the flame.

"How was the flight?" I asked. "You came up from Acapulco, right?"

"No," he said, "I was in Baja on a little vacation when Clare called. Luckily I was able to catch a local crop duster to Tijuana and then a Mexicana Airlines flight up here. The plane was a DC-3. I clutched the armrests so tightly my fingers are still numb."

He did that trick he always used to do, taking a big draw of smoke and letting it hang on his lower lip for a second before inhaling it. "Ah," he said with a sigh, "that tastes good." He put his head to one side and ran a critical eye over me. "You look pretty ropey, Phil," he said. "Been having a hard time with all this business with Nico and so on? I'm sorry—truly, I am."

He meant it, too. That was Terry—he'd rob you of your wallet, knock you down, and trample on you, then a second later help you up, dust you off, and offer you his deepest apologies. And you'd believe him. You'd even find yourself inquiring if he was all right and saying you hoped he hadn't strained his wrist or anything by having to keep that heavy-looking gun trained on you while he was going through your pockets. Am I being unfair? Maybe a little. In the old days, when I thought I knew him, he'd been pretty straight. Couldn't hold his drink or hold on to his money, and always had a woman problem, but I'd never known him to be seriously crooked. That last bit had changed now.

"How's Menendez?" I asked.

He smiled wryly. "Oh, you know Mendy. He's the cat that always falls on his feet."

"You see much of him?"

"He keeps in touch. I owe him a lot, as you know."

Yes, I knew. It was Menendez, along with Terry's other old wartime buddy, Randy Starr, who'd helped him disappear and find a new identity after his so-called suicide in Otatoclán. The three of them had been in a foxhole together somewhere in France when that mortar shell landed, and it was Terry who'd saved all their lives by grabbing the shell and running outside and heaving it into the air like a quarterback throwing a Hail Mary pass. Or that, at least, was how the continuing story went. I never knew how much to believe about Terry and his adventures, and I still don't. For instance, later on I'd discovered that he wasn't Terry Lennox from Salt Lake City, as he claimed, but Paul Marston, a Canadian, born in Montreal. But who else might he have been, before that? And who would he be, I wondered, the next time I saw him, if I ever should see him again? How many layers does an onion have?

"Mendy's based in Acapulco, right?" I said. "That where you are, too?"

"Yes. It's pleasant there, on the ocean."

"What is it you call yourself? I've forgotten."

"Maioranos," he said, and looked sheepish. "Cisco Maioranos."

"Another alias. Doesn't suit you, Terry. I'd have said—"

"For God's sake!" Clare cried out suddenly, rising in a flurry from the piano stool and turning on us with white-faced fury. "Are you going to stand there *chatting* all night? It's grotesque! You're like two awful little boys who've done something naughty and got away with it."

We turned and stared at her. I think we'd forgotten she was there. "Steady on, old girl," Terry said, with a less than successful attempt at lightness. "We're just two old friends doing a bit of catching up." He tipped me a quick wink. "Aren't we, Phil?"

Clare was going to say something more, since it was obvious there was a lot she had to say, but just then there was a gentle tapping on the door and it opened a little way and a weird apparition appeared there. It was a head, with a face as white as a Noh actor's mask and a lot of hair gathered up in a sort of close-fitting mesh. We stared at this thing, all three of us, and then it spoke. "I was looking for a book in the library and heard voices. Have yiz no bed to go to?"

It was Clare's mother. She came all the way into the room now. She was wearing a pink woolen dressing gown and pink slippers with pink bobbles on them. The white stuff on her face was some kind of beauty mask. Her eyes staring out of it were red-rimmed, like a drunk's, and her lips were the color of raw steak.

"Oh, Mother," Clare said in a tone of desperation, with a hand to her forehead, "please go back to bed."

Mrs. Langrishe ignored her and stepped into the room and shut the door behind her. She was looking at Terry and frowning. She said, "And who is this, may I ask?"

Terry didn't hesitate but moved toward her smoothly, smiling, with a slim hand extended. "Lennox is the name, Mrs. Langrishe," he said. "Terry Lennox. I don't think we've met."

Ma Langrishe peered at him for a moment, trying to fix him, then suddenly smiled. None of them, the young ones or the old, could resist Terry when he turned the charm on them, like a spray of mist from a perfume bottle. She took his hand in both of hers. "Are you a friend of Richard's?" she asked.

Terry hesitated. "Ehm—yes, I suppose I am."

His glance flickered in the direction of the sofa, and now Ma Langrishe looked there as well. "Why, there he is!" she said, and her smile broadened and grew softer still. "Ah, God, will you look at him, sleeping like a baby." She turned to Clare and the lurid gash of her mouth tightened. "And what are you all dressed up for?" she demanded. "It's the middle of the night."

"Please go back to bed, Mother," Clare said again. "You know we have that meeting with the Bloomingdale's people in the morning. You'll be exhausted."

"Ach, will you leave me alone!" her mother barked. She turned to Terry again with a roguish twinkle. "Have you and Richard been out on the tiles, is that it? The poor boy, he shouldn't drink—it goes straight to his head." She turned and again gazed indulgently at the figure sprawled on the sofa. "He's a terrible man, so he is." As if he'd heard her, Cavendish stirred in his sleep and gave a loud snort. The old woman cackled delightedly. "Listen to him! Isn't he a fierce rascal altogether."

At last she noticed me. She frowned. "I remember you," she said, pointing a finger at my chest. "You're what's-his-name, the detective fella." Her lips curved upward in a sly, malignant smile, and the white mask developed a mesh of tiny cracks at either side of her mouth, and for a second she looked uncannily like a clown. "Have you found her ladyship's pearls?" she asked, in a softly suggestive, crooning voice. "Is that why you're here?"

"No, I haven't found them yet," I said. "But I'm hot on their trail."

The clown's smile died instantly, and she pointed that finger again, and this time it had an angry tremor. "Don't you be making a mock of me, my bucko," she rasped.

"I think, Mrs. Langrishe," Terry said, cutting in smoothly, "I think Clare is right, I think you should go back to bed. You don't want to miss your beauty sleep."

She looked at him and her eyes narrowed. I guess she'd dealt with too many smooth talkers like Terry over the years to be taken in for long by his hazy charm.

Clare stepped forward and laid a hand lightly on the woman's arm. "Come along, Mother, please," she said. "Mr. Marlowe and

Terry are old friends. That's why I invited them over tonight—it's sort of a reunion."

I judged the shrewd old bird knew she was being lied to, but probably she was tired and was happy enough to accept the lie and bow out. She smiled sweetly at Terry again, threw me a scowl, then allowed herself to be led away, to the door. Clare, walking her along, glanced back at Terry and at me. I wondered if a day would come when she'd look like her mother looked now.

When the two women had gone, Terry blew air out through pursed lips and then laughed softly. "Quite a lady," he said. "She had me terrified."

"You didn't look too scared to me," I said.

"Oh, well, you know me—a master of disguise." He went to where I'd been sitting and leaned down and crushed out his cigarette in the ashtray on the floor, then slipped his hands into his pockets and strolled over to the sofa and stood looking down at Cavendish where he lay sprawled like a cartoon image of a drunkard. "Poor Dick," he said. "Clare's mother was right: he shouldn't drink."

"Did you know him?" I asked. "I mean, before now?"

"Oh, yes. He and Clare often came down to Mexico. We all knew each other—Nico, our friend Mendy, some others. There's a bar on the waterfront where we used to gather of an evening for cocktails. Nice place." He turned to look at me over his shoulder. "You should come visit, one day. You look like you could do with some sun and relaxation. You push yourself too hard, Phil, you always did."

On the day after his wife was murdered, I had driven Terry down to Tijuana, to the airport there, where he'd caught a flight south. When I got back, Joe Green was waiting for me. They knew Terry had skipped and took me in as an accessory. I got roughed up by Joe's boss, a bruiser called Gregorius, and spent a couple of nights in the cooler before they let me go, after hearing of Terry's oh-so-convenient suicide. It was a close one, for me and my so-called reputation. Yes, Terry owed me.

He walked back now and stood in front of me, his hands still in his pockets. He had on his most cajoling smile. "You bring the suitcase, by any chance?" he asked. "I'm guessing that's why Nico wanted to see you, to hand it over. Nico never had much tenacity. He scares too easily. I have to admit, I always despised him a little."

"Not enough to stop you using him as your mule."

He widened his eyes. "*My* mule? Oh, now, sport, you don't think *I'm* in this business, do you? Too dirty for me."

"I'd have agreed with you once," I said. "But you've changed, Terry. I can see it in your eyes."

"You're wrong, Phil." He shook his head slowly from side to side. "Sure, I've changed—I've had to. Life down there isn't all guitar bands and margaritas and chicken mole. I've had to do some things I'd never have dreamed of doing up here."

"You saying you ran through the money you inherited from Sylvia? That was Harlan Potter's money, left to her. There had to be a lot of it."

He pursed his lips again, I think to stop himself from smiling. "Let's say I made some ill-judged investments."

"With Mendy Menendez?"

He said nothing, but I could see I was right. "So you're in hock to Mendy, and owe him big-time. That's why you sent Clare to me—it was on behalf of Mendy. I'm right, yes?"

Terry turned and paced away from me stiff-legged, looking at the floor, then turned and paced back the way he had come and stopped in front of me again. "As I say, you know Mendy. He doesn't give much quarter when it comes to money, debts, things like that."

"I thought you were his buddy and his hero," I said, "on account of you having saved him and Randy Starr from a bloody death on the battlefield."

Terry chuckled. "Heroes get tarnished, after a while," he said. "And then, you know as well as I do what people are like—they tire of being grateful. They even start resenting that they have to feel beholden to you."

I thought that one over. He was right. It had always surprised me that Mendy had helped him in the first place. I had suspected that Terry must have had some kind of hold on him. I thought of asking now if that had been the case, but I couldn't work up the interest.

"Of course," he went on, "Clare would have been happy to help me out. She has a lot of money of her own, you know. She wanted to give me some to pay off Mendy, but"—he flashed that apologetic, self-excusing smile—"I have a few shreds of honor still intact."

"What about the two Mexicans?" I said.

"Yes," Terry said, and a wrinkle formed between his eyebrows, "that was a bad business. Nico's sister—I never met her, but I'm sure she didn't deserve to die."

"She was in it with Nico," I said. "She identified the body."

"Yes, but all the same, to be murdered like that—" He made a grimace. "I swear I didn't know Mendy was sending the Mexicans after Nico. I thought he would wait until Clare had—had talked to you, until you'd had time to find Nico, as I had no doubt you would have, if Mendy had waited a while longer. But Mendy is an unfortunate blend of impatience and distrust. So he sent those two heavies up here to begin their own search for Nico. A sad mistake."

"Thing is, of course," I said, "no one, not you or Mendy or anyone else, would have known about Nico's disappearing act if Clare hadn't spotted him on the street that day in San Francisco."

"Yes, that's true. You know"—he swiveled on his heel and did another bit of stiff-legged pacing, his hands clasped behind his back now—"I can't help but wish she hadn't seen him. Everything would have been so much simpler."

"That's probably true. But was it her fault? She didn't tell Mendy she'd seen him, did she. I'm guessing she told you, and *you* told Mendy. And that's how the machine got rolling. Am I right?"

"I can't lie to you." That made me laugh, and when I did, Terry looked hurt—he really did. "Anyway, I'm not lying now," he said, in an offended tone. "Yes, I told Mendy. I shouldn't have, I know. But like I said, I have reasons to be grateful to him—"

"And also you needed to make yourself look good with him, by bringing him the choice snippet of news that Peterson was only playing dead and was still at large, with Mendy's suitcase full of junk in his possession."

"Ah, yes," Terry said. "That suitcase."

"You gave it to me to keep for you, one day."

"That's right, so I did. Was that the night you drove me to Tijuana, after poor Sylvia had died? I can't remember. When you saw Peterson with it you recognized it, of course."

"It sure has had a life."

"English-made, you see. The English build to last."

He stopped pacing and sat down on the piano stool and crossed one knee over the other and put a hand to his chin, like Rodin's *Thinker*. Terry had the spindliest legs I'd ever seen on anybody. Like a stork, he was.

He started to say something, but just then Richard Cavendish sat upright on the sofa and looked at us, licking his lips and blinking. "Wha's going on?" he said thickly.

Terry hardly gave him a glance. "It's all right, Dick," he said. "You go back to sleep."

"Oh, all right," Cavendish muttered and flopped down the way he had been before, with his arms and legs thrown out to either side. After a second or two he began to snore softly.

Terry was patting his pockets. I don't know what he expected to find there. "I'd ask you for another cigarette," he said, "only I don't want to start up again full-time." He looked up at me sideways. "You going to tell me where the suitcase is?" he asked.

"Sure. It's in a locker at Union Station, and the key to the locker is in an envelope on the way to a pal of mine—well, sort of a pal— named Bernie Ohls. He's assistant chief of homicide, works out of the Sheriff's office."

The room was suddenly very still. Terry sat there, all twisted up on himself, with his knees crossed and that hand to his chin and the other supporting his elbow. I went to the window and stepped into the opening between the drapes and looked out. There was nothing to see, only darkness and my own shadowy reflection in the glass.

"I don't think," Terry said behind me, "I don't think that was wise, old chum. I don't think that was wise at all." He didn't sound angry, or menacing, or anything much, really, except maybe wistful—yes, that's the word: wistful.

Then he spoke again and his voice had changed. "Ah," he said, "it's you. What's that you've got there?"

I turned from the window. Terry was still sitting on the piano stool with his back to me. Beyond him, Clare's brother, Everett, was standing in the open doorway, that floppy lock of hair hanging down across his forehead. He didn't look in much better shape than when I'd seen him last, but at least he was conscious. He wore pajamas and a silk dressing gown with dragons embroidered on it. He had on penny loafers—they looked odd with the pajamas— and he had a pistol in his hand. It was a dainty little thing, some kind of a Colt, I thought. I could see it had a pearl handle. It didn't look serious at all, but all guns, even the daintiest of them, can knock a hole in the toughest heart.

He looked at me as I stepped forward, out of the shadow of the drapes, and his eyes grew uncertain. I was what he hadn't expected.

"Hello, Everett," I said. "Did we wake you? Your mother was here just now." He stared at me. He looked younger than he was because his face was weak. And, I suppose, because his mother spoiled and cosseted him and protected him from the big bad world. At least, that's what she thought she was doing.

"Who are you?" he said. His eyes were sunken, ringed with dark purple shadows.

"Name's Marlowe," I said. "We met before, on a couple of occasions. The first time you were awake, and we talked on the lawn—you remember? You thought maybe I was the new chauffeur. The second time, you didn't know I was there."

"What are you talking about?"

"You asked me who I was," I said, "and I was explaining."

I made myself smile. I was playing for time. Everett Edwards the Third might have been a milksop, as Wilber Canning would have said, but he was also a heroin addict, and he had a gun in his hand.

"Oh, yes," he said, in a tone of disgust. "I remember now: you're the fellow who was looking for Clare that day. Some kind of a detective, aren't you?" He giggled suddenly. "A detective! That's rich. I have a gun, and you're a detective. That's really rich."

He turned his attention to Terry. "You," he said, not giggling now, "why are you here?"

Terry considered. "Well, I'm sort of a friend of the family, Rett. You know me." I could still only see Terry's back, and the back of his head, but he seemed pretty calm. I was glad. Everyone was going to have to be very, very calm for the next few minutes.

Terry went on: "Remember the good times we had, down in Acapulco? Remember the day I taught you to water-ski? That was a good day, wasn't it? And then we all had dinner at that place on the beach, Pedro's, it's called. It's still there. I often go, and when I do I think of you, and the fine times we had."

"You bastard," Everett said quietly. "You were the one who got me started. You were the one who gave me that stuff in the first place." His hand was quivering and the gun in it was quivering too. That wasn't a good thing. A quivering gun can easily go off; I've seen it happen. Everett was close to tears, but they would be tears of rage. *"You were the one."*

"Oh, don't be so melodramatic, Rett," Terry said with a little laugh. "You were a very nervous boy in those days, and I thought an occasional pinch of happy powder would do you good. I'm sorry if I was wrong."

"How dare you come here, to this house," Everett said, and his hand shook even more and the gun barrel yawed in a way that made me clench my teeth.

"Listen," I said, "listen, Rett, why don't you give me the gun?"

The young man stared at me for a moment, then let out a high-pitched squeal of laughter. "Is that how detectives talk," he said, "is it really? I thought that only happened in the movies." He put on a mock-serious face and deepened his voice so that it sounded something like mine: *"Why don't you give me the gun, Everett, before someone gets hurt."* He threw his eyes to the ceiling. "Don't you get it, you stupid man? That's the whole point—someone *is* going to get hurt. Someone is going to get hurt very badly. Isn't that so, *Terry*? Isn't that so, my old playmate from Acapulco days?"

That was when Terry made his mistake. In situations like that, someone always does; someone always makes the wrong, the stupid move, and all hell follows. He suddenly propelled himself off the piano stool and lunged forward, like a swimmer making a shallow dive into an oncoming wave, landed on his stomach, and snatched up the glass ashtray that was on the floor there, beside the chair where I had been sitting. He meant to fling it at Everett, a lethal discus. He didn't realize that when you're lying on your front like that, you can't get much force into a throw. Besides, Everett was too quick for him, and Terry was still drawing back his arm when Everett took a step forward, the gun held out at arm's length, and pointed it at Terry's head and pulled the trigger.

The slug caught Terry in the forehead, just below the hairline. He stayed as he was for a moment, lying flat-out with the ashtray in one hand and the other braced beside him on the floor as he tried to get himself up. But he wasn't going to get up, not ever again. There were two holes in his head, the one in his forehead and another, bigger one at the back, at the base of his skull. There was a lot of blood coming out of this second hole, and some sticky-looking gray stuff, too. His head dropped and his face slammed onto the carpet.

Everett looked like he was going to fire again, but I reached him before he could get off a second shot. I didn't have much trouble taking the gun away from him. In fact, he as good as handed it to me. He had gone as limp as a girl, and he stood there, his lower lip trembling, staring down at Terry where he lay bleeding on the floor. One of Terry's feet, the right one, twitched a few times and then went still. I noticed, as I've had occasion to notice before, how much like fried bacon gunpowder smells.

Behind Everett the door opened again, and this time Clare came in. She stopped in the doorway and looked at the scene before her with an expression of horror and disbelief. Then she strode forward and pushed her brother aside and fell to her knees. She lifted Terry's head and cradled it in her lap. She said nothing. She didn't even weep. She really had loved him; I saw that clearly now. How could I not?

She looked up at me, at the gun in my hand. "Did you—?"

I shook my head.

She turned to her brother. "Was it you?" He would not look at her. "I'll never forgive you," she said to him, in a calm, almost formal-sounding voice. "I'll never forgive you, and I hope you die.

I hope you give yourself an overdose, very soon, and go into a coma and never come out of it. I always hated you, and now I know why. I knew someday you'd ruin my life."

Everett still didn't look at her, didn't reply, didn't say a word. After all, there wasn't much to say.

Behind us, Richard Cavendish got to his feet and shambled forward. Seeing Terry, and the bright blood soaking into the front of his wife's blue gown, he stopped. Nothing happened for a few seconds; then Cavendish suddenly laughed. "Well, well," he said. "Man down, eh?" And he laughed again. I figured he thought he was having a dream, that none of what he was seeing was real. He advanced again and, stepping over Terry's body, put out a hand and patted Clare on the head and then reeled on through the doorway, humming to himself, and was gone.

At last, Clare began to cry. I thought of going to her, but what would I have done? It was too late for me to do anything.

$$\equiv\; 25 \;\equiv$$

I didn't call Bernie. I reckoned he'd had enough of me for a while, and I'd sure had enough of him—I didn't want him shouting down the line at me again, and calling me names, and telling me to do things to myself that the greatest contortionist in the world couldn't have managed. So I phoned Joe Green instead, good old Joe, who'd drink a beer with you and share a joke and yap about the ball game, and whose underpants got all balled up in his crotch when the weather was hot.

Joe was on duty, as always, and twenty minutes after he got my call he arrived at Langrishe Lodge with a couple of squad cars yowling in his wake. By then Everett Edwards was curled up like a hedgehog on the sofa his drunken brother-in-law had earlier vacated. He was weeping bitter tears, not of remorse, it seemed. but some kind of frustration, though why he should feel frustrated I couldn't say. Maybe he thought Terry had died too quickly, with not enough pain. Or maybe he was disappointed by the banality of what had happened; maybe he'd wanted some grand scene with swordplay and speeches and corpses strewn all over the place, like something that other Marlowe, the one who saw Christ's blood streaming in the what's-it, might have written for him.

Joe stood in the middle of the room and looked around with a worried scowl. He was out of his depth here. He was used to pounding up tenement stairs and kicking in doors and backing punks in sweat-stained undershirts up against walls and jamming the barrel of his .38 Special into their mouths to make them stop yelling. That was Joe's world. What he had here looked like a parlor game among the country club set that had gone spectacularly wrong.

He hunkered down and squinted at the bullet holes in Terry's skull, looked across at Everett Edwards cowering on the sofa, then at me. "Jesus Christ, Phil," he said in an undertone, "what the hell is all this?"

I held out my hands and shrugged. Where to begin?

Joe got to his feet with a grunt and turned to Clare Cavendish. Clare, with her stricken face and her bloodstained hands hanging by her sides and the front of her blue gown soaked and glistening with gore, was a figure from an older type of play, one written long ago, by an ancient Greek. Joe began by calling her Mrs. Langrishe, which was my cue to step in and correct him. "Cavendish is the name, Joe," I said. "Mrs. Clare Cavendish."

Clare seemed to register nothing, just stood there like a statue. She was in shock. Her brother, on the sofa, let fall a juicy sob. Joe looked at me again, shaking his head. He was lost.

In the end he handed Clare over to one of the patrolmen, a big Irish lump with carroty hair and freckles, who gave her a Barry Fitzgerald smile and said she wasn't to worry at all, at all. He had found a blanket somewhere, and he draped it over her shoulders and led her solicitously from the room. She went without the least resistance, gliding to the door in her bloodied dress, graceful as ever, straight-backed, expressionless, showing us all her lovely profile.

They clamped the cuffs on Everett and led him away, too, in his pj's and his loafers. He looked at no one. His eyes were red from weeping and there were smears of snot on his cheeks. I wondered if he realized what was waiting for him in the coming weeks and months, not to mention in the years afterward that he was going to have to spend up at San Quentin, unless his mother bought a lawyer tough and clever enough to get him out through some legal loophole that no one had thought to plug. It wouldn't be the first time the son of a rich family got away with murder.

Next thing, when her son and her daughter were gone, who should come wandering in again but Ma Langrishe, in her hairnet and her mask of white mud. She looked at the body on the floor, which someone had thrown a blanket over, but seemed not to know what it was. She looked at me, and then at Joe. She couldn't understand any of it. She was just a sad, old woman, confused and lost.

When it was all over and the squad cars had left, Joe and I stood outside on the gravel beside his car and had a smoke together.

"Christ, Phil," Joe said, "you ever think of going into some other line of work?"

"All the time," I said. "All the time."

"You know you're going to have to come downtown and file a statement."

"Yeah," I said, "I know. But listen, Joe, do me a favor. Let me go home now and sleep, and I'll come in first thing tomorrow."

"I dunno, Phil," he said, rubbing his chin in his worried way.

"First thing, Joe—I give you my word."

"Oh, go on, then."

"You're a pal."

"I'm a pushover, is what I am."

"No, Joe," I said, dropping my cigarette on the gravel and grinding it in with my heel, "I'm the pushover."

I went home and had a shower and fell into bed and slept for whatever there was left of the night. At seven my alarm sounded. I got myself up somehow and drank a cup of scalding coffee and drove down to the station, as I'd promised Joe I would, and gave my statement to the desk man on duty.

I didn't say much, just enough to keep Joe happy and to satisfy the court when the case of *State of California vs. Everett Edwards III* came around. I'd be called as a witness, of course, but I didn't mind that. What I did mind was the prospect of testifying in the witness box and seeing Clare Cavendish sitting there in the front row of the court, gazing at her brother, known now as the accused, the one who had murdered her lover. No, that was a prospect I didn't relish. I recalled her mother, that day at the Ritz-Beverly, saying how people could get damaged in this affair. I had thought she meant that I might hurt her daughter, but that wasn't what she was talking about. It was me she meant; I was the one who was going to end up with the scars, and somehow she'd known it then. I should have listened to her.

When I came out of the station the Olds was standing in the sun, the heat humming off the hood. That steering wheel was going to be awful hot.

You think I'm going to say that later that day I went over to Victor's and drank a gimlet in memory of my dead friend. But I didn't. The Terry I knew had died a long time before Everett Edwards put a bullet through his brain. I wouldn't ever have said it to him, but Terry Lennox had been my idea of a gentleman. Yes, despite the drinking and the women and the people he hung around with, like Mendy Menendez, despite the fact that when it came down to it he cared for no one but himself, Terry was, in some unlikely way, a man of honor.

That was the Terry I had known, or thought I knew, anyway.

What happened to him, what was it that stopped him from being decent and upright and loyal? He used to blame the war, used to tap himself on the chest and say how since he'd come back from the fighting there was nothing alive left inside him. I didn't buy that; it had too much of a doomed-romantic ring to it. Maybe life down there in sunny Mexico, with the waterskiing and the cocktails on the waterfront and having to be Mendy Menendez's legman and fixer, had destroyed something in him, so that the style, the fine high polish, remained, while the metal underneath was all eaten away by acid and rust and canker. The Terry I knew would never have hooked a kid like Everett Edwards on heroin. He'd never have tied himself to a hood like Mendy Menendez. Above all, he'd never have gotten the woman who loved him to seduce another man for his own convenience.

That last bit of treachery I've decided to cancel. I'm going to believe Clare Cavendish fell into my bed of her own choice—I think of her that night, with Terry still behind the curtains, lowering her voice and putting a finger to her lips to stop me saying how we had been in bed together. And even if it wasn't me she wanted, even if she slept with me only to get me involved in the search for Nico Peterson, I'm going to believe it was all her own work, and that Terry didn't put her up to it. Some things you have to force yourself to believe. What was it she'd said? Make a Pascalian wager. Well, that's what I've done. I'm still not too sure what Pascal was betting on, but I'm thinking it must have been something pretty significant.

Just now I opened my desk drawer and searched around until I found an old airlines timetable and started looking up flights to Paris. There's no chance of my going there, but it's a nice thing to dream about. Except I keep remembering that wedding band on the bottom of the swimming pool at the Cahuilla Club and wondering if maybe it was some kind of warning.

I did make one symbolic gesture, when I took the lamp with

the painted roses on it from the table beside my bed and carried it out to the backyard and dropped it in the garbage can, then went inside again and filled a pipe. That was, for me, the last of Clare Cavendish. She'd walked into my life and made me love her—well, maybe she didn't make me, but she knew what she was doing, all the same—and now she was gone.

I can't say I didn't, don't, miss her. Her kind of beauty doesn't slip through your fingers without leaving them singed. I know I'm better off without her. It's what I keep telling myself. I know it, and someday I'll believe it, too.

She was playing the piano for Terry that night when I arrived at the house. I guess it's not vulgar to play for someone when you love him.

She never did pay me, for what she hired me to do.

AUTHOR'S NOTE

In all the Marlowe novels his creator played fast and loose with the topography of Southern California, and I have allowed myself the same license. Yet there were many details that had to be accurate and of which I was unsure. I therefore depended heavily on advice from a quintet of informants who know the area intimately. These are Candice Bergen, Brian Siberell, Robert Bookman, and my agents Ed Victor and Geoffrey Sanford. For their expertise, generosity, patience, and good humor I wish to express my deepest gratitude. I am especially appreciative of the care, thought, and inventiveness that Candice Bergen devoted to the text, and of the numerous pitfalls she steered me past. And I am sorry that the peacock made only a fleeting appearance.

Others to whom I owe warm thanks are: María Fasce Ferri, Rodrigo Fresan, Graham C. Greene and the Estate of Raymond Chandler, Dr. Gregory Page, Maria Rejt, Fiona Ruane, John Sterling, and my manuscript editor nonpareil, Bonnie Thompson.

Finally, warm thanks to my brother, Vincent Banville, who introduced me to Marlowe, and whose own crime novels showed me how it could be done.